T0279361

# THE DAMNATIONS

## M.R. JAMES SHORT STORIES

Including an Introduction &
Short Story by Ramsey Campbell

## FLAME TREE PUBLISHING

6 Melbray Mews, Fulham,
London SW6 3NS, United Kingdom
www.flametreepublishing.com

First published and copyright © 2024
Flame Tree Publishing Ltd
Intro text copyright © 2024 Ramsey Campbell
Bonus short story 'Someone to Blame' © 2022 Ramsey Campbell, originally
published in *Classic Monsters Unleashed*, edited by James Aquilone, 2022.

**Publisher's Note:**

This is a work of fiction. Names, characters, places, and incidents are a product
of the authors' imaginations. Locales and public names are sometimes used for
atmospheric purposes. Any resemblance to actual people, living or dead, or to
businesses, companies, events, institutions, or locales is completely coincidental.
Due to the historical nature of the classic text, we're aware that there may be
some language used which has the potential to cause offence to the modern
reader. However, wishing overall to preserve the integrity of the text, rather
than imposing contemporary sensibilities, we have left it unaltered.

The cover is created by Flame Tree Studio, featuring a detail of:
Henry Fuseli, *The Nightmare*, 1790–91.

Special Hardback ISBN: 978-1-78758-940-7
ebook ISBN: 978-1-78758-941-4

A copy of the CIP data for this book is available from
the British Library and the Library of Congress.

Printed in China

# THE
# DAMNATIONS

## M.R. JAMES
## SHORT STORIES

Including an Introduction &
Short Story by Ramsey Campbell

A SPECIAL
RAMSEY
CAMPBELL
EDITION

FLAME TREE
PUBLISHING

# CONTENTS

# CONTENTS

# INTRODUCTION

## by Ramsey Campbell

Montague Rhodes James (1862–1936) was among the greatest masters of supernatural dread in English fiction. Recently readers have tried to claim him for cosy horror, a currently fashionable and likely short-lived term. True, the academic locales of his tales, or their antiquarian backgrounds, feel reassuringly comfortable, but it's a world where the most familiar setting or object can be invaded by presences so uncanny as to border on the surreal – a bag with arms, a mouth under a pillow. He refined the ghost story and distilled pure terror in a sentence or a phrase, lending it a new compressed intensity. Alas, though Lovecraft admired his work, the regard wasn't reciprocated.

James wrote tales to read aloud at Christmas, which some take to mean his prose can be reformatted on the page without harm. Since presumably he saw proofs of his collections, I contend he endorsed how the contents were set out. For me the paragraphing – the way the uncanny often lies low in the body of a paragraph – is essential to his timing. Our book presents the texts as originally collected.

'Canon Alberic's Scrapbook' sets out his method: the accumulating hints of unease in background and dialogue, the way historical detail confers verisimilitude, the creatures that 'act in ways not inconsistent with the rules of folklore' (his words, situating him within folk horror). 'Must there be horror? …I think so,' he writes elsewhere, along with 'a modicum of blood' – but 'not less necessary… is reticence.' 'Lost Hearts' exemplifies these, as do 'Count Magnus' and 'The Treasure of Abbot Thomas'. Both of the latter demonstrate how capacious James's definition of the ghostly was, embracing the demonic and the still less human, which may itself embrace the unhappy victim.

'A School Story' uses conversational narration and dialogue to convey a sense of mounting terror. 'The Rose Garden' embeds fright in chat too, and expresses the author's modernist impatience with irrelevant chatter ('etc', etc). The circumstantial banality of the eventual apparition is a nightmarishly inspired device. By contrast, 'The Tractate Middoth' confronts us with an especially grisly spectre and his scuttling entourage. When James's dead return, they tend to do so in a monstrously transformed or horribly augmented shape. Their merest relic can summon whatever they've become, as the ghastly remnant in 'The Diary of Mr. Poynter' goes to show.

James's historical and architectural guide *Suffolk and Norfolk* includes glimpses of the macabre, and 'The Stalls of Barchester Cathedral' makes these academic elements both the background and the medium through which the uncanny manifests itself, impelled by an underlying paganism. 'An Episode of Cathedral History' modulates a report of a restoration into an account of a haunting conveyed almost wholly indirectly, a difficult feat to render effective. The obliqueness with which he often suggests motivations, not least those of his horrors, reaches an extreme in 'Two Doctors' – a deliberate enigma or an unfinished but published work, given the precedent of such as Schubert, or both? Let me merely say it repays pondering. In 'The Haunted Dolls' House' he sets himself the task of drawing dread from the innocent titular toy. As for 'After Dark in the Playing Fields', it epitomises the sly humour his stories often feature.

"I once asked him about his favourite among his stories, and he more or less felt undecided about or between 'A View from a Hill' and 'Count Magnus'..." August Derleth told me back in 1962. 'A View from a Hill' enshrines an enviably original notion, inventively developed. 'A Warning to the Curious' may be his most powerfully sustained tale of (as Lovecraft styled it) dread suspense. 'Wailing Well' was composed to be read to boy scouts, James's equivalent of a campfire tale, but most of his final tales were written for publication, not for reading aloud. One such is 'Rats', which contains his longest paragraph, surely verifying his structural preference (and indeed an alarming image lurks at its heart). 'The Malice of Inanimate Objects' dilates on the titular subject, demonstrating how closely allied horror and dark humour can be. 'I will not put dots or stars, for I dislike them' – but his restraint provides a potent alternative. 'A Vignette' was his last completed tale; some take it to be autobiographical, but it needn't be in order to produce an authentic chill.

His influence remains crucial to the field, less in simple emulations (though there are effective examples) but in work that subsumes his style of uncanny terror. Fritz Leiber's seminal 'Smoke Ghost' applied it to forties Chicago and evolved the urban supernatural, while L.T.C. Rolt imbued British industrial landscapes with it. Reggie Oliver has inherited James's elegance, though not by imitation. Novels – *The Green Man* (Kingsley Amis), *No One Gets Out Alive* (Adam L.G. Nevill) have developed his achievement. His example remains vital, and I hope some of my novels and short stories are the better for it. Herein I've dared to resurrect Count Magnus and his inhuman companion. May they remain between the pages of our book.

*Ramsey Campbell*
*Wallasey, Merseyside*
*13 March 2024*

# AFTER DARK IN THE PLAYING FIELDS

The hour was late and the night was fair. I had halted not far from Sheeps' Bridge and was thinking about the stillness, only broken by the sound of the weir, when a loud tremulous hoot just above me made me jump. It is always annoying to be startled, but I have a kindness for owls. This one was evidently very near: I looked about for it. There it was, sitting plumply on a branch about twelve feet up. I pointed my stick at it and said, "Was that you?" "Drop it," said the owl. "I know it ain't only a stick, but I don't like it. Yes, of course it was me: who do you suppose it would be if it warn't?"

We will take as read the sentences about my surprise. I lowered the stick. "Well," said the owl, "what about it? If you will come out here of a Midsummer evening like what this is, what do you expect?" "I beg your pardon," I said, "I should have remembered. May I say that I think myself very lucky to have met you tonight? I hope you have time for a little talk?" "Well," said the owl ungraciously, "I don't know as it matters so particular tonight. I've had me supper as it happens, and if you ain't too long over it – ah-h-h!" Suddenly it broke into a loud scream, flapped its wings furiously, bent forward and clutched its perch tightly, continuing to scream. Plainly something was pulling hard at it from behind. The strain relaxed abruptly, the owl nearly fell over, and then whipped round, ruffling up all over, and made a vicious dab at something unseen by me. "Oh, I *am* sorry," said a small clear voice in a solicitous tone. "I made sure it was loose. I do hope I didn't hurt you." "Didn't 'urt me?" said the owl bitterly. "Of course you 'urt me, and well you know it, you young infidel. That feather was no more loose than

– oh, if I could git at you! Now I shouldn't wonder but what you've throwed me all out of balance. Why can't you let a person set quiet for two minutes at a time without you must come creepin' up and – well, you've done it this time, anyway. I shall go straight to 'eadquarters and" – (finding it was now addressing the empty air) – "why, where have you got to now? Oh, it is too bad, that it is!"

"Dear me!" I said, "I'm afraid this isn't the first time you've been annoyed in this way. May I ask exactly what happened?"

"Yes, you may ask," said the owl, still looking narrowly about as it spoke, "but it 'ud take me till the latter end of next week to tell you. Fancy coming and pulling out anyone's tail feather! 'Urt me something crool, it did. And what for, I should like to know? Answer me that! Where's the *reason* of it?"

All that occurred to me was to murmur, "The clamorous owl that nightly hoots and wonders at our quaint spirits." I hardly thought the point would be taken, but the owl said sharply: "What's that? Yes, you needn't to repeat it. I 'eard. And I'll tell you what's at the bottom of it, and you mark my words." It bent towards me and whispered, with many nods of its round head: "Pride! stand-offishness! that's what it is! *Come not near our fairy queen*" (this in a tone of bitter contempt). "Oh, dear no! we ain't good enough for the likes of them. Us that's been noted time out of mind for the best singers in the Fields: now, ain't that so?"

"Well," I said, doubtfully enough, "*I* like to hear you very much: but, you know, some people think a lot of the thrushes and nightingales and so on; you must have heard of that, haven't you? And then, perhaps – of course I don't know – perhaps your style of singing isn't exactly what they think suitable to accompany their dancing, eh?"

"I should kindly 'ope not," said the owl, drawing itself up. "Our family's never give in to dancing, nor never won't neither. Why, what ever are you thinkin' of!" it went on with rising temper. "A pretty thing it would be for me to set there hiccuppin' at them" – it stopped and looked cautiously all round it and up and down and then continued in a louder voice – "them little ladies and gentlemen. If it ain't sootable for them, I'm very sure it ain't sootable for me. And" (temper rising again) "if they expect me never to say a word just because they're dancin' and carryin' on with their foolishness, they're very much mistook, and so I tell 'em."

From what had passed before I was afraid this was an imprudent line to take, and I was right. Hardly had the owl given its last emphatic nod when four small slim forms dropped from a bough above, and in a twinkling some sort of grass rope was thrown round the body of the unhappy bird, and it was borne off through the air, loudly protesting, in the direction of Fellows' Pond. Splashes and gurgles and shrieks of unfeeling laughter were heard as I hurried up. Something darted away over my head, and as I stood peering over the bank of the pond, which was all in commotion, a very angry and dishevelled owl scrambled heavily up the bank, and stopping near my feet shook itself and flapped and hissed for several minutes without saying anything I should care to repeat.

Glaring at me, it eventually said – and the grim suppressed rage in its voice was such that I hastily drew back a step or two – "'Ear that? Said they was very sorry, but they'd mistook me for a duck. Oh, if it ain't enough to make anyone go reg'lar distracted in their mind and tear everythink to flinders for miles round." So carried away was it by passion, that it began the process at once by rooting up a large beakful of grass, which alas! got into its throat; and the choking that resulted made me really afraid that it would break a vessel. But the paroxysm was mastered, and the owl sat up, winking and breathless but intact.

Some expression of sympathy seemed to be required; yet I was chary of offering it, for in its present state of mind I felt that the bird might interpret the best-meant phrase as a fresh insult. So we stood looking at each other without speech for a very awkward minute, and then came a diversion. First the thin voice of the pavilion clock, then the deeper sound from the Castle quadrangle, then Lupton's Tower, drowning the Curfew Tower by its nearness.

"What's that?" said the owl, suddenly and hoarsely. "Midnight, I should think," said I, and had recourse to my watch. "Midnight?" cried the owl, evidently much startled, "and me too wet to fly a yard! Here, you pick me up and put me in the tree; don't, I'll climb up your leg, and you won't ask me to do that twice. Quick now!" I obeyed. "Which tree do you want?" "Why, my tree, to be sure! Over there!"

It nodded towards the Wall. "All right. Bad-calx tree do you mean?" I said, beginning to run in that direction. "'Ow should I know what silly names you call it? The one what 'as like a door in it. Go faster! They'll be coming in another minute." "Who? What's the matter?" I asked as I ran, clutching the wet creature, and much afraid of stumbling and coming over with it in the long grass. "*You'll* see fast enough," said this selfish bird. "You just let me git on the tree, *I* shall be all right."

And I suppose it was, for it scrabbled very quickly up the trunk with its wings spread and disappeared in a hollow without a word of thanks. I looked round, not very comfortably. The Curfew Tower was still playing St. David's tune and the little chime that follows, for the third and last time, but the other bells had finished what they had to say, and now there was silence, and again the 'restless changing weir' was the only thing that broke – no, that emphasised it.

Why had the owl been so anxious to get into hiding? That of course was what now exercised me. Whatever and whoever was coming, I was sure that this was no time for me to cross the open field: I should do best to dissemble my presence by staying on the darker side of the tree. And that is what I did.

★   ★   ★

All this took place some years ago, before summertime came in. I do sometimes go into the Playing Fields at night still, but I come in before true midnight. And I find I do not like a crowd after dark – for example at the Fourth of June fireworks. You see – no, you do not, but I see – such curious faces: and the people to whom they belong flit about so oddly, often at your elbow when you least expect it, and looking close into your face, as if they were searching for someone – who may be thankful, I think, if they do not find him. "Where do they come from?" Why, some, I think, out of the water, and some out of the ground. They look like that. But I am sure it is best to take no notice of them, and not to touch them.

Yes, I certainly prefer the daylight population of the Playing Fields to that which comes there after dark.

# CANON ALBERIC'S
# SCRAP-BOOK

St. Bertrand de Comminges is a decayed town on the spurs of the Pyrenees, not very far from Toulouse, and still nearer to Bagnères-de-Luchon. It was the site of a bishopric until the Revolution, and has a cathedral which is visited by a certain number of tourists. In the spring of 1883 an Englishman arrived at this old-world place – I can hardly dignify it with the name of city, for there are not a thousand inhabitants. He was a Cambridge man, who had come specially from Toulouse to see St. Bertrand's Church, and had left two friends, who were less keen archaeologists than himself, in their hotel at Toulouse, under promise to join him on the following morning. Half an hour at the church would satisfy them, and all three could then pursue their journey in the direction of Auch. But our Englishman had come early on the day in question, and proposed to himself to fill a notebook and to use several dozens of plates in the process of describing and photographing every corner of the wonderful church that dominates the little hill of Comminges. In order to carry out this design satisfactorily, it was necessary to monopolise the verger of the church for the day. The verger or sacristan (I prefer the latter appellation, inaccurate as it may be) was accordingly sent for by the somewhat brusque lady who keeps the inn of the Chapeau Rouge; and when he came, the Englishman found him an unexpectedly interesting object of study. It was not in the personal appearance of the little, dry, wizened old man that the interest lay, for he was precisely like dozens of other church-guardians in France, but in a curious furtive or rather hunted and oppressed air which he had. He was perpetually half glancing behind him; the muscles of his back and shoulders seemed to be hunched in a continual nervous contraction, as if he were expecting every moment to find himself in the clutch of an enemy. The Englishman hardly knew whether to put him down as a man haunted by a fixed delusion, or as one oppressed by a guilty conscience, or as an unbearably henpecked husband. The probabilities, when reckoned up, certainly pointed to the last idea; but, still, the impression conveyed was that of a more formidable persecutor even than a termagant wife.

However, the Englishman (let us call him Dennistoun) was soon too deep in his notebook and too busy with his camera to give more than an occasional glance to the sacristan. Whenever he did look at him, he found him at no great distance, either huddling himself back against the wall or crouching in one of the gorgeous stalls. Dennistoun became rather fidgety after a time. Mingled suspicions that he was keeping the old man from his déjeuner, that he was regarded as likely to make away with St. Bertrand's ivory crozier, or with the dusty stuffed crocodile that hangs over the font, began to torment him.

"Won't you go home?" he said at last; "I'm quite well able to finish my notes alone; you can lock me in if you like. I shall want at least two hours more here, and it must be cold for you, isn't it?"

"Good heavens!" said the little man, whom the suggestion seemed to throw into a state of unaccountable terror, "such a thing cannot be thought of for a moment. Leave monsieur alone in the church? No, no; two hours, three hours, all will be the same to me. I have breakfasted, I am not at all cold, with many thanks to monsieur."

"Very well, my little man," quoth Dennistoun to himself: "you have been warned, and you must take the consequences."

Before the expiration of the two hours, the stalls, the enormous dilapidated organ, the choir-screen of Bishop John de Mauléon, the remnants of glass and tapestry, and the objects in the treasure-chamber had been well and truly examined; the sacristan still keeping at Dennistoun's heels, and every now and then whipping round as if he had been stung, when one or other of the strange noises that trouble a large empty building fell on his ear. Curious noises they were, sometimes.

"Once," Dennistoun said to me, "I could have sworn I heard a thin metallic voice laughing high up in the tower. I darted an inquiring glance at my sacristan. He was white to the lips. 'It is he – that is – it is no one; the door is locked,' was all he said, and we looked at each other for a full minute."

Another little incident puzzled Dennistoun a good deal. He was examining a large dark picture that hangs behind the altar, one of a series illustrating the miracles of St. Bertrand. The composition of the picture is well-nigh indecipherable, but there is a Latin legend below, which runs thus:

> Qualiter S. Bertrandus liberavit hominem
> quem diabolus diu volebat strangulare.
> (How St. Bertrand delivered a man whom
> the Devil long sought to strangle.)

Dennistoun was turning to the sacristan with a smile and a jocular remark of some sort on his lips, but he was confounded to see the old man on his knees, gazing at the picture with the eye of a suppliant in agony, his hands tightly clasped, and a rain of tears on his cheeks. Dennistoun naturally pretended to have noticed nothing, but the question would not go away from him, "Why should a daub of this kind affect anyone so strongly?" He seemed to himself to be getting some sort of clue to the reason of the strange look that had been puzzling him all the day: the man must be a monomaniac; but what was his monomania?

It was nearly five o'clock; the short day was drawing in, and the church began to fill with shadows, while the curious noises – the muffled footfalls and distant talking voices that had been perceptible all day – seemed, no doubt because of the fading light and the consequently quickened sense of hearing, to become more frequent and insistent.

The sacristan began for the first time to show signs of hurry and impatience. He heaved a sigh of relief when camera and notebook were finally packed up and stowed away, and hurriedly beckoned Dennistoun to the western door of the church, under the tower. It was time to ring the

Angelus. A few pulls at the reluctant rope, and the great bell Bertrande, high in the tower, began to speak, and swung her voice up among the pines and down to the valleys, loud with mountain-streams, calling the dwellers on those lonely hills to remember and repeat the salutation of the angel to her whom he called Blessed among women. With that a profound quiet seemed to fall for the first time that day upon the little town, and Dennistoun and the sacristan went out of the church.

On the doorstep they fell into conversation.

"Monsieur seemed to interest himself in the old choir-books in the sacristy."

"Undoubtedly. I was going to ask you if there were a library in the town."

"No, monsieur; perhaps there used to be one belonging to the Chapter, but it is now such a small place—" Here came a strange pause of irresolution, as it seemed; then, with a sort of plunge, he went on: "But if monsieur is *amateur des vieux livres*, I have at home something that might interest him. It is not a hundred yards."

At once all Dennistoun's cherished dreams of finding priceless manuscripts in untrodden corners of France flashed up, to die down again the next moment. It was probably a stupid missal of Plantin's printing, about 1580. Where was the likelihood that a place so near Toulouse would not have been ransacked long ago by collectors? However, it would be foolish not to go; he would reproach himself forever after if he refused. So they set off. On the way the curious irresolution and sudden determination of the sacristan recurred to Dennistoun, and he wondered in a shamefaced way whether he was being decoyed into some purlieu to be made away with as a supposed rich Englishman. He contrived, therefore, to begin talking with his guide, and to drag in, in a rather clumsy fashion, the fact that he expected two friends to join him early the next morning. To his surprise, the announcement seemed to relieve the sacristan at once of some of the anxiety that oppressed him.

"That is well," he said quite brightly – "that is very well. Monsieur will travel in company with his friends: they will be always near him. It is a good thing to travel thus in company – sometimes."

The last word appeared to be added as an afterthought and to bring with it a relapse into gloom for the poor little man.

They were soon at the house, which was one rather larger than its neighbours, stone-built, with a shield carved over the door, the shield of Alberic de Mauléon, a collateral descendant, Dennistoun tells me, of Bishop John de Mauléon. This Alberic was a Canon of Comminges from 1680 to 1701. The upper windows of the mansion were boarded up, and the whole place bore, as does the rest of Comminges, the aspect of decaying age.

Arrived on his doorstep, the sacristan paused a moment.

"Perhaps," he said, "perhaps, after all, monsieur has not the time?"

"Not at all – lots of time – nothing to do till tomorrow. Let us see what it is you have got."

The door was opened at this point, and a face looked out, a face far younger than the sacristan's, but bearing something of the same distressing look: only here it seemed to be the mark, not so much of fear for personal safety as of acute anxiety on behalf of another. Plainly the owner of the face was the sacristan's daughter; and, but for the expression I have described, she was a handsome girl enough. She brightened up considerably on seeing her father accompanied by an able-bodied stranger. A few remarks passed between father and daughter of which Dennistoun only caught these words, said by the sacristan: "He was laughing in the church," words which were answered only by a look of terror from the girl.

But in another minute they were in the sitting room of the house, a small, high chamber with a stone floor, full of moving shadows cast by a wood-fire that flickered on a great hearth. Something of the character of an oratory was imparted to it by a tall crucifix, which reached almost to the ceiling on one side; the figure was painted of the natural colours, the cross was black. Under this stood a chest of some age and solidity, and when a lamp had been brought, and chairs set, the sacristan went to this chest, and produced therefrom, with growing excitement and nervousness, as Dennistoun thought, a large book, wrapped in a white cloth, on which cloth a cross was rudely embroidered in red thread.

Even before the wrapping had been removed, Dennistoun began to be interested by the size and shape of the volume. "Too large for a missal," he thought, "and not the shape of an antiphoner; perhaps it may be something good, after all." The next moment the book was open, and Dennistoun felt that he had at last lit upon something better than good. Before him lay a large folio, bound, perhaps, late in the seventeenth century, with the arms of Canon Alberic de Mauléon stamped in gold on the sides. There may have been a hundred and fifty leaves of paper in the book, and on almost every one of them was fastened a leaf from an illuminated manuscript. Such a collection Dennistoun had hardly dreamed of in his wildest moments. Here were ten leaves from a copy of Genesis, illustrated with pictures, which could not be later than A.D. 700. Further on was a complete set of pictures from a Psalter, of English execution, of the very finest kind that the thirteenth century could produce; and, perhaps best of all, there were twenty leaves of uncial writing in Latin, which, as a few words seen here and there told him at once, must belong to some very early unknown patristic treatise. Could it possibly be a fragment of the copy of Papias 'On the Words of Our Lord', which was known to have existed as late as the twelfth century at Nimes?[1] In any case, his mind was made up; that book must return to Cambridge with him, even if he had to draw the whole of his balance from the bank and stay at St. Bertrand till the money came. He glanced up at the sacristan to see if his face yielded any hint that the book was for sale. The sacristan was pale, and his lips were working.

"If monsieur will turn on to the end," he said.

So monsieur turned on, meeting new treasures at every rise of a leaf; and at the end of the book he came upon two sheets of paper, of much more recent date than anything he had seen yet, which puzzled him considerably. They must be contemporary, he decided, with the unprincipled Canon Alberic, who had doubtless plundered the Chapter library of St. Bertrand to form this priceless scrap-book. On the first of

---

1    We now know that these leaves did contain a considerable fragment of that work, if not of that actual copy of it.

the paper sheets was a plan, carefully drawn and instantly recognisable by a person who knew the ground, of the south aisle and cloisters of St. Bertrand's. There were curious signs looking like planetary symbols, and a few Hebrew words in the corners; and in the north-west angle of the cloister was a cross drawn in gold paint. Below the plan were some lines of writing in Latin, which ran thus:

*Responsa 12(mi) Dec. 1694. Interrogatum est: Inveniamne?*
*Responsum est: Invenies. Fiamne dives? Fies. Vivamne invidendus?*
*Vives. Moriame in lecto meo? Ita.*
*(Answers of the 12th of December, 1694. It was asked: Shall I find it?*
*Answer: Thou shalt. Shall I become rich? Thou wilt. Shall I live an*
*object of envy? Thou wilt. Shall I die in my bed? Thou wilt.)*

"A good specimen of the treasure-hunter's record – quite reminds one of Mr. Minor-Canon Quatremain in Old St. Paul's," was Dennistoun's comment, and he turned the leaf.

What he then saw impressed him, as he has often told me, more than he could have conceived any drawing or picture capable of impressing him. And, though the drawing he saw is no longer in existence, there is a photograph of it (which I possess) which fully bears out that statement. The picture in question was a sepia drawing at the end of the seventeenth century, representing, one would say at first sight, a Biblical scene; for the architecture (the picture represented an interior) and the figures had that semi-classical flavour about them which the artists of two hundred years ago thought appropriate to illustrations of the Bible. On the right was a king on his throne, the throne elevated on twelve steps, a canopy overhead, soldiers on either side – evidently King Solomon. He was bending forward with outstretched sceptre, in attitude of command; his face expressed horror and disgust, yet there was in it also the mark of imperious command and confident power. The left half of the picture was the strangest, however. The interest plainly centred there.

On the pavement before the throne were grouped four soldiers, surrounding a crouching figure which must be described in a moment.

A fifth soldier lay dead on the pavement, his neck distorted, and his eyeballs starting from his head. The four surrounding guards were looking at the King. In their faces, the sentiment of horror was intensified; they seemed, in fact, only restrained from flight by their implicit trust in their master. All this terror was plainly excited by the being that crouched in their midst.

I entirely despair of conveying by any words the impression which this figure makes upon anyone who looks at it. I recollect once showing the photograph of the drawing to a lecturer on morphology – a person of, I was going to say, abnormally sane and unimaginative habits of mind. He absolutely refused to be alone for the rest of that evening, and he told me afterwards that for many nights he had not dared to put out his light before going to sleep. However, the main traits of the figure I can at least indicate.

At first you saw only a mass of coarse, matted black hair; presently it was seen that this covered a body of fearful thinness, almost a skeleton, but with the muscles standing out like wires. The hands were of a dusky pallor, covered, like the body, with long, coarse hairs, and hideously taloned. The eyes, touched in with a burning yellow, had intensely black pupils, and were fixed upon the throned King with a look of beast-like hate. Imagine one of the awful bird-catching spiders of South America translated into human form, and endowed with intelligence just less than human, and you will have some faint conception of the terror inspired by the appalling effigy. One remark is universally made by those to whom I have shown the picture: "It was drawn from the life."

As soon as the first shock of his irresistible fright had subsided, Dennistoun stole a look at his hosts. The sacristan's hands were pressed upon his eyes; his daughter, looking up at the cross on the wall, was telling her beads feverishly.

At last the question was asked: "Is this book for sale?"

There was the same hesitation, the same plunge of determination that he had noticed before, and then came the welcome answer: "If monsieur pleases."

"How much do you ask for it?"

"I will take two hundred and fifty francs."

This was confounding. Even a collector's conscience is sometimes stirred, and Dennistoun's conscience was tenderer than a collector's.

"My good man!" he said again and again, "your book is worth far more than two hundred and fifty francs. I assure you – far more."

But the answer did not vary: "I will take two hundred and fifty francs – not more."

There was really no possibility of refusing such a chance. The money was paid, the receipt signed, a glass of wine drunk over the transaction, and then the sacristan seemed to become a new man. He stood upright, he ceased to throw those suspicious glances behind him, he actually laughed or tried to laugh. Dennistoun rose to go.

"I shall have the honour of accompanying monsieur to his hotel?" said the sacristan.

"Oh, no, thanks! It isn't a hundred yards. I know the way perfectly, and there is a moon."

The offer was pressed three or four times and refused as often.

"Then, monsieur will summon me if – if he finds occasion; he will keep the middle of the road, the sides are so rough."

"Certainly, certainly," said Dennistoun, who was impatient to examine his prize by himself; and he stepped out into the passage with his book under his arm.

Here he was met by the daughter; she, it appeared, was anxious to do a little business on her own account; perhaps, like Gehazi, to 'take somewhat' from the foreigner whom her father had spared.

"A silver crucifix and chain for the neck; monsieur would perhaps be good enough to accept it?"

Well, really, Dennistoun hadn't much use for these things. What did mademoiselle want for it?

"Nothing – nothing in the world. Monsieur is more than welcome to it."

The tone in which this and much more was said was unmistakably genuine, so that Dennistoun was reduced to profuse thanks, and submitted to have the chain put round his neck. It really seemed as if he had rendered the father and daughter some service which they hardly knew how to repay. As he set off with his book they stood at the door looking after him, and they were still looking when he waved them a last goodnight from the steps of the Chapeau Rouge.

Dinner was over, and Dennistoun was in his bedroom, shut up alone with his acquisition. The landlady had manifested a particular interest in him since he had told her that he had paid a visit to the sacristan and bought an old book from him. He thought, too, that he had heard a hurried dialogue between her and the said sacristan in the passage outside the *salle à manger*; some words to the effect that "Pierre and Bertrand would be sleeping in the house" had closed the conversation.

All this time a growing feeling of discomfort had been creeping over him – nervous reaction, perhaps, after the delight of his discovery. Whatever it was, it resulted in a conviction that there was someone behind him, and that he was far more comfortable with his back to the wall. All this, of course, weighed light in the balance as against the obvious value of the collection he had acquired. And now, as I said, he was alone in his bedroom, taking stock of Canon Alberic's treasures, in which every moment revealed something more charming.

"Bless Canon Alberic!" said Dennistoun, who had an inveterate habit of talking to himself. "I wonder where he is now? Dear me! I wish that landlady would learn to laugh in a more cheering manner; it makes one feel as if there was someone dead in the house. Half a pipe more, did you say? I think perhaps you are right. I wonder what that crucifix is that the young woman insisted on giving me? Last century, I suppose. Yes, probably. It is rather a nuisance of a thing to have round one's neck – just too heavy. Most likely her father has been wearing it for years. I think I might give it a clean up before I put it away."

He had taken the crucifix off, and laid it on the table, when his attention was caught by an object lying on the red cloth just by his left elbow. Two or three ideas of what it might be flitted through his brain with their own incalculable quickness.

A penwiper? No, no such thing in the house. A rat? No, too black. A large spider? I trust to goodness not – no. Good God! A hand like the hand in that picture!

In another infinitesimal flash he had taken it in. Pale, dusky skin, covering nothing but bones and tendons of appalling strength; coarse black hairs, longer than ever grew on a human hand; nails rising from the ends of the fingers and curving sharply down and forward, grey, horny, and wrinkled.

He flew out of his chair with deadly, inconceivable terror clutching at his heart. The shape, whose left hand rested on the table, was rising to a standing posture behind his seat, its right hand crooked above his scalp. There was black and tattered drapery about it; the coarse hair covered it as in the drawing. The lower jaw was thin – what can I call it? – shallow, like a beast's; teeth showed behind the black lips; there was no nose; the eyes, of a fiery yellow, against which the pupils showed black and intense, and the exulting hate and thirst to destroy life which shone there, were the most horrifying features in the whole vision. There was intelligence of a kind in them – intelligence beyond that of a beast, below that of a man.

The feelings which this horror stirred in Dennistoun were the intensest physical fear and the most profound mental loathing. What did he do? What could he do? He has never been quite certain what words he said, but he knows that he spoke, that he grasped blindly at the silver crucifix, that he was conscious of a movement towards him on the part of the demon, and that he screamed with the voice of an animal in hideous pain.

Pierre and Bertrand, the two sturdy little serving-men, who rushed in, saw nothing, but felt themselves thrust aside by something that passed out between them, and found Dennistoun in a swoon. They sat up with him that night, and his two friends were at St. Bertrand by nine o'clock next morning. He himself, though still shaken and nervous, was almost himself by that time, and his story found credence with them, though not until they had seen the drawing and talked with the sacristan.

Almost at dawn the little man had come to the inn on some pretence, and had listened with the deepest interest to the story retailed by the landlady. He showed no surprise.

"It is he – it is he! I have seen him myself," was his only comment; and to all questionings but one reply was vouchsafed: "*Deux fois je l'ai vu: mille fois je l'ai senti.*" He would tell them nothing of the provenance of the book, nor any details of his experiences. "I shall soon sleep, and my rest will be sweet. Why should you trouble me?" he said.[2]

We shall never know what he or Canon Alberic de Mauléon suffered. At the back of that fateful drawing were some lines of writing which may be supposed to throw light on the situation:

*Contradictio Salomonis cum demonio nocturno.*
*Albericus de Mauléone delineavit.*
*V. Deus in adiutorium. Ps. Qui habitat.*
*Sancte Bertrande, demoniorum effugator, intercede pro me miserrimo.*
*Primum uidi nocte 12(mi) Dec. 1694:*
*uidebo mox ultimum. Peccaui et passus*
*sum, plura adhuc passurus.*
*Dec. 29, 1701.*[3]

I have never quite understood what was Dennistoun's view of the events I have narrated. He quoted to me once a text from Ecclesiasticus: "Some spirits there be that are created for vengeance, and in their fury lay on sore strokes." On another occasion he said: "Isaiah was a very sensible man; doesn't he say something about night monsters living in the ruins of Babylon? These things are rather beyond us at present."

Another confidence of his impressed me rather, and I sympathised with it. We had been, last year, to Comminges, to see Canon Alberic's tomb. It is a great marble erection with an effigy of the Canon in a large

---

2    He died that summer; his daughter married, and settled at St. Papoul. She never understood the circumstances of her father's 'obsession'.

3    *I.E.*, The Dispute of Solomon with a demon of the night. Drawn by Alberic de Mauléon. *Versicle.* O Lord, make haste to help me. *Psalm.* Whoso dwelleth xci.

Saint Bertrand, who puttest devils to flight, pray for me most unhappy. I saw it first on the night of Dec. 12, 1694: soon I shall see it for the last time. I have sinned and suffered, and have more to suffer yet.

Dec. 29, 1701.

The 'Gallia Christiana' gives the date of the Canon's death as December 31, 1701, 'in bed, of a sudden seizure'. Details of this kind are not common in the great work of the Sammarthani.

wig and soutane, and an elaborate eulogy of his learning below. I saw Dennistoun talking for some time with the Vicar of St. Bertrand's, and as we drove away he said to me: "I hope it isn't wrong: you know I am a Presbyterian – but I – I believe there will be 'saying of Mass and singing of dirges' for Alberic de Mauléon's rest." Then he added, with a touch of the Northern British in his tone, "I had no notion they came so dear."

\* \* \*

The book is in the Wentworth Collection at Cambridge. The drawing was photographed and then burnt by Dennistoun on the day when he left Comminges on the occasion of his first visit.

# COUNT MAGNUS

By what means the papers out of which I have made a connected story came into my hands is the last point which the reader will learn from these pages. But it is necessary to prefix to my extracts from them a statement of the form in which I possess them.

They consist, then, partly of a series of collections for a book of travels, such a volume as was a common product of the forties and fifties. Horace Marryat's *Journal of a Residence in Jutland and the Danish Isles* is a fair specimen of the class to which I allude. These books usually treated of some unknown district on the Continent. They were illustrated with woodcuts or steel plates. They gave details of hotel accommodation and of means of communication, such as we now expect to find in any well-regulated guide-book, and they dealt largely in reported conversations with intelligent foreigners, racy innkeepers, and garrulous peasants. In a word, they were chatty.

Begun with the idea of furnishing material for such a book, my papers as they progressed assumed the character of a record of one single personal experience, and this record was continued up to the very eve, almost, of its termination.

The writer was a Mr. Wraxall. For my knowledge of him I have to depend entirely on the evidence his writings afford, and from these I deduce that he was a man past middle age, possessed of some private means, and very much alone in the world. He had, it seems, no settled abode in England, but was a denizen of hotels and boarding-houses. It is probable that he entertained the idea of settling down at some future time which never came; and I think it also likely that the Pantechnicon fire in the early seventies must have destroyed a great deal that would have thrown light on his antecedents, for he refers once or twice to property of his that was warehoused at that establishment.

It is further apparent that Mr. Wraxall had published a book, and that it treated of a holiday he had once taken in Brittany. More than this I cannot say about his work, because a diligent search in bibliographical works has convinced me that it must have appeared either anonymously or under a pseudonym.

As to his character, it is not difficult to form some superficial opinion. He must have been an intelligent and cultivated man. It seems that he was near being a Fellow of his college at Oxford – Brasenose, as I judge from the Calendar. His besetting fault was pretty clearly that of over-inquisitiveness, possibly a good fault in a traveller, certainly a fault for which this traveller paid dearly enough in the end.

On what proved to be his last expedition, he was plotting another book. Scandinavia, a region not widely known to Englishmen forty years ago, had struck him as an interesting field. He must have alighted on some old books of Swedish history or memoirs, and the idea had struck him that there was room for a book descriptive of travel in Sweden, interspersed with episodes from the history of some of the great Swedish families. He procured letters of introduction, therefore, to some persons of quality in Sweden, and set out thither in the early summer of 1863.

Of his travels in the North there is no need to speak, nor of his residence of some weeks in Stockholm. I need only mention that some *savant* resident there put him on the track of an important collection of family papers belonging to the proprietors of an ancient manor-house in Vestergothland, and obtained for him permission to examine them.

The manor-house, or *herrgård*, in question is to be called Råbäck (pronounced something like Roebeck), though that is not its name. It is one of the best buildings of its kind in all the country, and the picture of it in Dahlenberg's *Suecia antiqua et moderna*, engraved in 1694, shows it very much as the tourist may see it today. It was built soon after 1600, and is, roughly speaking, very much like an English house of that period in respect of material – red-brick with stone facings – and style. The man who built it was a scion of the great house of De la Gardie, and his descendants possess it still. De la Gardie is the name by which I will designate them when mention of them becomes necessary.

They received Mr. Wraxall with great kindness and courtesy, and pressed him to stay in the house as long as his researches lasted. But, preferring to be independent, and mistrusting his powers of conversing in Swedish, he settled himself at the village inn, which turned out quite sufficiently comfortable, at any rate during the summer months. This arrangement would entail a short walk daily to and from the manor-house of something under a mile. The house itself stood in a park, and was protected – we should say grown up – with large old timber. Near it you found the walled garden, and then entered a close wood fringing one of the small lakes with which the whole country is pitted. Then came the wall of the demesne, and you climbed a steep knoll – a knob of rock lightly covered with soil – and on the top of this stood the church, fenced in with tall dark trees. It was a curious building to English eyes. The nave and aisles were low, and filled with pews and galleries. In the western gallery stood the handsome old organ, gaily painted, and with silver pipes. The ceiling was flat, and had been adorned by a seventeenth-century artist with a strange and hideous 'Last Judgement', full of lurid flames, falling cities, burning ships, crying souls, and brown and smiling demons. Handsome brass coronae hung from the roof; the pulpit was like a doll's-house covered with little painted wooden cherubs and saints; a stand with three hour-glasses was hinged to the preacher's desk. Such sights as these may be seen in many a church in Sweden now, but what distinguished this one was an addition to the original building. At the eastern end of the north aisle the builder of the manor-house had erected a mausoleum for himself and his family. It was a largish eight-sided building, lighted by a series of oval windows, and it had a domed roof, topped by a kind of pumpkin-shaped object rising into a spire, a form in which Swedish architects greatly delighted. The roof was of copper externally, and was painted black, while the walls, in common with those of the church, were staringly white. To this mausoleum there was no access from the church. It had a portal and steps of its own on the northern side.

Past the churchyard the path to the village goes, and not more than three or four minutes bring you to the inn door.

On the first day of his stay at Råbäck Mr. Wraxall found the church door open, and made these notes of the interior which I have epitomised. Into the mausoleum, however, he could not make his way. He could by looking through the keyhole just descry that there were fine marble effigies and sarcophagi of copper, and a wealth of armorial ornament, which made him very anxious to spend some time in investigation.

The papers he had come to examine at the manor-house proved to be of just the kind he wanted for his book. There were family correspondence, journals, and account-books of the earliest owners of the estate, very carefully kept and clearly written, full of amusing and picturesque detail. The first De la Gardie appeared in them as a strong and capable man. Shortly after the building of the mansion there had been a period of distress in the district, and the peasants had risen and attacked several châteaux and done some damage. The owner of Råbäck took a leading part in suppressing trouble, and there was reference to executions of ring-leaders and severe punishments inflicted with no sparing hand.

The portrait of this Magnus de la Gardie was one of the best in the house, and Mr. Wraxall studied it with no little interest after his day's work. He gives no detailed description of it, but I gather that the face impressed him rather by its power than by its beauty or goodness; in fact, he writes that Count Magnus was an almost phenomenally ugly man.

On this day Mr. Wraxall took his supper with the family, and walked back in the late but still bright evening.

"I must remember," he writes, "to ask the sexton if he can let me into the mausoleum at the church. He evidently has access to it himself, for I saw him tonight standing on the steps, and, as I thought, locking or unlocking the door."

I find that early on the following day Mr. Wraxall had some conversation with his landlord. His setting it down at such length as he does surprised me at first; but I soon realised that the papers I was reading were, at least in their beginning, the materials for the book he was meditating, and that it was to have been one of those quasi-journalistic productions which admit of the introduction of an admixture of conversational matter.

His object, he says, was to find out whether any traditions of Count Magnus de la Gardie lingered on in the scenes of that gentleman's activity, and whether the popular estimate of him were favourable or not. He found that the Count was decidedly not a favourite. If his tenants came late to their work on the days which they owed to him as Lord of the Manor, they were set on the wooden horse, or flogged and branded in the manor-house yard. One or two cases there were of men who had occupied lands which encroached on the lord's domain, and whose houses had been mysteriously burnt on a winter's night, with the whole family inside. But what seemed to dwell on the innkeeper's mind most – for he returned to the subject more than once – was that the Count had been on the Black Pilgrimage, and had brought something or someone back with him.

You will naturally inquire, as Mr. Wraxall did, what the Black Pilgrimage may have been. But your curiosity on the point must remain unsatisfied for the time being, just as his did. The landlord was evidently unwilling to give a full answer, or indeed any answer, on the point, and, being called out for a moment, trotted out with obvious alacrity, only putting his head in at the door a few minutes afterwards to say that he was called away to Skara, and should not be back till evening.

So Mr. Wraxall had to go unsatisfied to his day's work at the manor-house. The papers on which he was just then engaged soon put his thoughts into another channel, for he had to occupy himself with glancing over the correspondence between Sophia Albertina in Stockholm and her married cousin Ulrica Leonora at Råbäck in the years 1705–10. The letters were of exceptional interest from the light they threw upon the culture of that period in Sweden, as anyone can testify who has read the full edition of them in the publications of the Swedish Historical Manuscripts Commission.

In the afternoon he had done with these, and after returning the boxes in which they were kept to their places on the shelf, he proceeded, very naturally, to take down some of the volumes nearest to them, in order to determine which of them had best be his principal subject of investigation next day. The shelf he had hit upon was occupied mostly by a collection of account-books in the writing of the first Count Magnus. But one among them was not an account-book, but a book of alchemical and other tracts in another sixteenth-century hand. Not being very familiar with alchemical literature, Mr. Wraxall spends much space which he might have spared in setting out the names and beginnings of the various treatises: The book of the Phoenix, book of the Thirty Words, book of the Toad, book of Miriam, Turba philosophorum, and so forth; and then he announces with a good deal of circumstance his delight at finding, on a leaf originally left blank near the middle of the book, some writing of Count Magnus himself headed '*Liber nigrae peregrinationis*'. It is true that only a few lines were written, but there was quite enough to show that the landlord had that morning been referring to a belief at least as old as the time of Count Magnus, and probably shared by him. This is the English of what was written:

'If any man desires to obtain a long life, if he would obtain a faithful messenger and see the blood of his enemies, it is necessary that he should first go into the city of Chorazin, and there salute the prince...' Here there was an erasure of one word, not very thoroughly done, so that Mr. Wraxall felt pretty sure that he was right in reading it as *aëris* ('of the air'). But there was no more of the text copied, only a line in Latin: *Quaere reliqua hujus materiei inter secretiora* (see the rest of this matter among the more private things).

It could not be denied that this threw a rather lurid light upon the tastes and beliefs of the Count; but to Mr. Wraxall, separated from him by nearly three centuries, the thought that he might have added to his general forcefulness alchemy, and to alchemy something like magic, only made him a more picturesque figure, and when, after a rather prolonged contemplation of his picture in the hall, Mr. Wraxall set out on his homeward way, his mind was full of the thought of Count Magnus. He had no eyes for his surroundings, no perception of the evening scents of the woods or the evening light on the lake; and when all of a sudden he pulled up short, he was astonished to find himself already at the gate of the churchyard, and within a few minutes of his dinner. His eyes fell on the mausoleum.

"Ah," he said, "Count Magnus, there you are. I should dearly like to see you."

"Like many solitary men," he writes, "I have a habit of talking to myself aloud; and, unlike some of the Greek and Latin particles, I do not expect an answer. Certainly, and perhaps fortunately in this case, there was neither voice nor any that regarded: only the woman who, I suppose, was cleaning up the church, dropped some metallic object on the floor, whose clang startled me. Count Magnus, I think, sleeps sound enough."

That same evening the landlord of the inn, who had heard Mr. Wraxall say that he wished to see the clerk or deacon (as he would be called in Sweden) of the parish, introduced him to that official in the inn parlour. A visit to the De la Gardie tomb-house was soon arranged for the next day, and a little general conversation ensued.

Mr. Wraxall, remembering that one function of Scandinavian deacons is to teach candidates for Confirmation, thought he would refresh his own memory on a Biblical point.

"Can you tell me," he said, "anything about Chorazin?"

The deacon seemed startled, but readily reminded him how that village had once been denounced.

"To be sure," said Mr. Wraxall; "it is, I suppose, quite a ruin now?"

"So I expect," replied the deacon. "I have heard some of our old priests say that Antichrist is to be born there; and there are tales—"

"Ah! what tales are those?" Mr. Wraxall put in.

"Tales, I was going to say, which I have forgotten," said the deacon; and soon after that he said good night.

The landlord was now alone, and at Mr. Wraxall's mercy; and that inquirer was not inclined to spare him.

"Herr Nielsen," he said, "I have found out something about the Black Pilgrimage. You may as well tell me what you know. What did the Count bring back with him?"

Swedes are habitually slow, perhaps, in answering, or perhaps the landlord was an exception. I am not sure; but Mr. Wraxall notes that the landlord spent at least one minute in looking at him before he said anything at all. Then he came close up to his guest, and with a good deal of effort he spoke:

"Mr. Wraxall, I can tell you this one little tale, and no more – not any more. You must not ask anything when I have done. In my grandfather's time – that is, ninety-two years ago – there were two men who said: 'The Count is dead; we do not care for him. We will go tonight and have a free hunt in his wood' – the long wood on the hill that you have seen behind Råbäck. Well, those that heard them say this, they said: 'No, do not go; we are sure you will meet with persons walking who should not be walking. They should be resting, not walking.' These men laughed. There were no forestmen to keep the wood, because no one wished to live there. The family were not here at the house. These men could do what they wished.

"Very well, they go to the wood that night. My grandfather was sitting here in this room. It was the summer, and a light night. With the window open, he could see out to the wood, and hear.

"So he sat there, and two or three men with him, and they listened. At first they hear nothing at all; then they hear someone – you know how far away it is – they hear someone scream, just as if the most inside part of his soul was twisted out of him. All of them in the room caught hold of each other, and they sat so for three-quarters of an hour. Then they hear someone else, only about three hundred ells off. They hear him laugh out loud: it was not one of those two men that laughed, and, indeed, they have all of them said that it was not any man at all. After that they hear a great door shut.

"Then, when it was just light with the sun, they all went to the priest. They said to him:

"'Father, put on your gown and your ruff, and come to bury these men, Anders Bjornsen and Hans Thorbjorn.'

"You understand that they were sure these men were dead. So they went to the wood – my grandfather never forgot this. He said they were all like so many dead men themselves. The priest, too, he was in a white fear. He said when they came to him:

"'I heard one cry in the night, and I heard one laugh afterwards. If I cannot forget that, I shall not be able to sleep again.'

"So they went to the wood, and they found these men on the edge of the wood. Hans Thorbjorn was standing with his back against a tree, and all the time he was pushing with his hands – pushing something away from him which was not there. So he was not dead. And they led him away, and took him to the house at Nykjoping, and he died before the winter; but he went on pushing with his hands. Also Anders Bjornsen was there; but he was dead. And I tell you this about Anders Bjornsen, that he was once a beautiful man, but now his face was not there, because the flesh of it was sucked away off the bones. You understand that? My grandfather did not forget that. And they laid him on the bier which they brought, and they put a cloth over his head, and the priest walked before; and they began to sing the psalm for the dead as well as they could. So, as they were singing the end of the first verse, one fell down, who was carrying the head of the bier, and the others looked back, and they saw that the cloth had fallen off, and the eyes of Anders Bjornsen were looking up, because there was nothing to close over them. And this they could not bear. Therefore the priest laid the cloth upon him, and sent for a spade, and they buried him in that place."

The next day Mr. Wraxall records that the deacon called for him soon after his breakfast, and took him to the church and mausoleum. He noticed that the key of the latter was hung on a nail just by the pulpit, and it occurred to him that, as the church door seemed to be left unlocked as a rule, it would not be difficult for him to pay a second and more private visit to the monuments if there proved to be more of interest among them than could be digested at first. The building, when he entered it, he found not unimposing. The monuments, mostly large erections of the seventeenth and eighteenth centuries, were dignified if luxuriant, and the epitaphs and heraldry were copious. The central space of the domed room was occupied by three copper sarcophagi, covered with finely-engraved ornament. Two of them had, as is commonly the case in Denmark and Sweden, a large metal crucifix on the lid. The third, that of Count Magnus, as it appeared, had, instead of that, a full-length effigy engraved upon it, and round the edge were several bands of similar ornament representing various scenes. One was a battle, with cannon belching out smoke, and walled towns, and troops of pikemen. Another showed an execution. In a third, among trees, was a man running at full speed, with flying hair and outstretched hands. After him followed a strange form; it would be hard to say whether the artist had intended it for a man, and was unable to give the requisite similitude, or whether it was intentionally made as monstrous as it looked. In view of the skill with which the rest of the drawing was done, Mr. Wraxall felt inclined to adopt the latter idea. The figure was unduly short, and was for the most part muffled in a hooded garment which swept the ground. The only part of the form which projected from that shelter was not shaped like any hand or arm. Mr. Wraxall compares it to the tentacle of a devil-fish, and continues: "On seeing this, I said to myself, 'This, then, which is evidently an allegorical representation of some kind – a fiend pursuing a hunted soul – may be the origin of the story of Count Magnus and his mysterious companion. Let us see how the huntsman is pictured: doubtless it will be a demon blowing his horn.'" But, as it turned out, there was no such sensational figure, only the semblance of a cloaked man on a hillock, who stood leaning on a stick, and watching the hunt with an interest which the engraver had tried to express in his attitude.

Mr. Wraxall noted the finely-worked and massive steel padlocks – three in number – which secured the sarcophagus. One of them, he saw, was detached, and lay on the pavement. And then, unwilling to delay the deacon longer or to waste his own working-time, he made his way onward to the manor-house.

"It is curious," he notes, "how, on retracing a familiar path, one's thoughts engross one to the absolute exclusion of surrounding objects. Tonight, for the second time, I had entirely failed to notice where I was going (I had planned a private visit to the tomb-house to copy the epitaphs), when I suddenly, as it were, awoke to consciousness, and found myself (as before) turning in at the churchyard gate, and, I believe, singing or chanting some such words as, 'Are you awake, Count Magnus? Are you asleep, Count Magnus?' and then something more which I have failed to recollect. It seemed to me that I must have been behaving in this nonsensical way for some time."

He found the key of the mausoleum where he had expected to find it, and copied the greater part of what he wanted; in fact, he stayed until the light began to fail him.

"I must have been wrong," he writes, "in saying that one of the padlocks of my Count's sarcophagus was unfastened; I see tonight that two are loose. I picked both up, and laid them carefully on the window-ledge, after trying unsuccessfully to close them. The remaining one is still firm, and, though I take it to be a spring lock, I cannot guess how it is opened. Had I succeeded in undoing it, I am almost afraid I should have taken the liberty of opening the sarcophagus. It is strange, the interest I feel in the personality of this, I fear, somewhat ferocious and grim old noble."

The day following was, as it turned out, the last of Mr. Wraxall's stay at Råbäck. He received letters connected with certain investments which made it desirable that he should return to England; his work among the papers was practically done, and travelling was slow. He decided, therefore, to make his farewells, put some finishing touches to his notes, and be off.

These finishing touches and farewells, as it turned out, took more time than he had expected. The hospitable family insisted on his staying to dine with them – they dined at three – and it was verging on half past six before he was outside the iron gates of Råbäck. He dwelt on every step of his walk by the lake, determined to saturate himself, now that he trod it for the last time, in the sentiment of the place and hour. And when he reached the summit of the churchyard knoll, he lingered for many minutes, gazing at the limitless prospect of woods near and distant, all dark beneath a sky of liquid green. When at last he turned to go, the thought struck him that surely he must bid farewell to Count Magnus as well as the rest of the De la Gardies. The church was but twenty yards away, and he knew where the key of the mausoleum hung. It was not long before he was standing over the great copper coffin, and, as usual, talking to himself aloud: "You may have been a bit of a rascal in your time, Magnus," he was saying, "but for all that I should like to see you, or, rather—"

"Just at that instant," he says, "I felt a blow on my foot. Hastily enough I drew it back, and something fell on the pavement with a clash. It was the third, the last of the three padlocks which had fastened the sarcophagus. I stooped to pick it up, and – Heaven is my witness that I am writing only the bare truth – before I had raised myself there was a sound of metal hinges creaking, and I distinctly saw the lid shifting upwards. I may have behaved like a coward, but I could not for my life stay for one moment. I was outside that dreadful building in less time than I can write – almost as quickly as I could have said – the words; and what frightens me yet more, I could not turn the key in the lock. As I sit here in my room noting these facts, I ask myself (it was not twenty minutes ago) whether that noise of creaking metal continued, and I cannot tell whether it did or not. I only know that there was something more than I have written that alarmed me, but whether it was sound or sight I am not able to remember. What is this that I have done?"

★   ★   ★

Poor Mr. Wraxall! He set out on his journey to England on the next day, as he had planned, and he reached England in safety; and yet, as I gather from his changed hand and inconsequent jottings, a broken man. One of the several small note-books that have come to me with his papers gives, not a key to, but a kind of inkling of, his experiences. Much of his journey was made by canal-boat, and I find not less than six painful attempts to enumerate and describe his fellow-passengers. The entries are of this kind:

24. *Pastor of village in Skane. Usual black coat and soft black hat.*
25. *Commercial traveller from Stockholm going to Trollhättan.*
    *Black cloak, brown hat.*
26. *Man in long black cloak, broad-leafed hat, very old-fashioned.*

This entry is lined out, and a note added: "Perhaps identical with No. 13. Have not yet seen his face." On referring to No. 13, I find that he is a Roman priest in a cassock.

The net result of the reckoning is always the same. Twenty-eight people appear in the enumeration, one being always a man in a long black cloak and broad hat, and another a 'short figure in dark cloak and hood'. On the other hand, it is always noted that only twenty-six passengers appear at meals, and that the man in the cloak is perhaps absent, and the short figure is certainly absent.

On reaching England, it appears that Mr. Wraxall landed at Harwich, and that he resolved at once to put himself out of the reach of some person or persons whom he never specifies, but whom he had evidently come to regard as his pursuers. Accordingly he took a vehicle – it was a closed fly – not trusting the railway and drove across country to the village of Belchamp St. Paul. It was about nine o'clock on a moonlight August night when he neared the place. He was sitting forward, and looking out of the window at the fields and thickets – there was little else to be seen – racing past him. Suddenly he came to a cross-road. At the corner two figures were standing motionless; both were in dark cloaks; the taller one wore a hat, the shorter a hood. He had no time to see their faces, nor did they make any motion that he could discern. Yet the horse shied violently and broke into a gallop, and Mr. Wraxall sank back into his seat in something like desperation. He had seen them before.

Arrived at Belchamp St. Paul, he was fortunate enough to find a decent furnished lodging, and for the next twenty-four hours he lived, comparatively speaking, in peace. His last notes were written on this day. They are too disjointed and ejaculatory to be given here in full, but the substance of them is clear enough. He is expecting a visit from his pursuers – how or when he knows not – and his constant cry is "What has he done?" and "Is there no hope?" Doctors, he knows, would call him mad, policemen would laugh at him. The parson is away. What can he do but lock his door and cry to God?

People still remember last year at Belchamp St. Paul how a strange gentleman came one evening in August years back; and how the next morning but one he was found dead, and there was an inquest; and the jury that viewed the body fainted, seven of 'em did, and none of 'em wouldn't speak to what they see, and the verdict was visitation of God; and how the people as kep' the 'ouse moved out that same week, and went away from that part. But they do not, I think, know that any glimmer of light has ever been thrown, or could be thrown, on the mystery. It so happened that last year the little house came into my hands as part of a legacy. It had stood empty since 1863, and there seemed no prospect of letting it; so I had it pulled down, and the papers of which I have given you an abstract were found in a forgotten cupboard under the window in the best bedroom.

# THE DIARY OF
# MR. POYNTER

The sale-room of an old and famous firm of book auctioneers in London is, of course, a great meeting-place for collectors, librarians, dealers: not only when an auction is in progress, but perhaps even more notably when books that are coming on for sale are upon view. It was in such a sale-room that the remarkable series of events began which were detailed to me not many months ago by the person whom they principally affected, namely, Mr. James Denton, M.A., F.S.A., etc., etc., some time of Trinity Hall, now, or lately, of Rendcomb Manor in the county of Warwick.

He, on a certain spring day not many years since, was in London for a few days upon business connected principally with the furnishing of the house which he had just finished building at Rendcomb. It may be a disappointment to you to learn that Rendcomb Manor was new; that I cannot help. There had, no doubt, been an old house; but it was not remarkable for beauty or interest. Even had it been, neither beauty nor interest would have enabled it to resist the disastrous fire which about a couple of years before the date of my story had razed it to the ground. I am glad to say that all that was most valuable in it had been saved, and that it was fully insured. So that it was with a comparatively light heart that Mr. Denton was able to face the task of building a new and considerably more convenient dwelling for himself and his aunt who constituted his whole *ménage*.

Being in London, with time on his hands, and not far from the sale-room at which I have obscurely hinted, Mr. Denton thought that he would spend an hour there upon the chance of finding, among that portion of the famous Thomas collection of MSS., which he knew to be then on view, something bearing upon the history or topography of his part of Warwickshire.

He turned in accordingly, purchased a catalogue and ascended to the sale-room, where, as usual, the books were disposed in cases and some laid out upon the long tables. At the shelves, or sitting about at the tables, were figures, many of whom were familiar to him. He exchanged nods and greetings with several, and then settled down to examine his catalogue and note likely items. He had made good progress through about two hundred of the five hundred lots – every now and then rising to take a volume from the shelf and give it a cursory glance – when a hand was laid on his shoulder, and he looked up. His interrupter was one of those intelligent men with a pointed beard and a flannel shirt, of whom the last quarter of the nineteenth century was, it seems to me, very prolific.

It is no part of my plan to repeat the whole conversation which ensued between the two. I must content myself with stating that it largely referred to common acquaintances, e.g., to the nephew of Mr. Denton's friend who had recently married and settled in Chelsea, to the sister-in-law of Mr. Denton's friend who had been seriously indisposed, but was now better, and to a piece of china which Mr. Denton's friend had purchased some months before at a price much below its true value. From which you will rightly infer that the conversation was rather in the nature of a monologue. In due time, however, the friend bethought himself that Mr. Denton was there for a purpose, and said he, "What are you looking out for in particular? I don't think there's much in this lot." "Why, I thought there might be some Warwickshire collections, but I don't see anything under Warwick in the catalogue." "No, apparently not," said the friend. "All the same, I believe I noticed something like a Warwickshire diary. What was the name again? Drayton? Potter? Painter – either a P or a D, I feel sure." He turned over the leaves quickly. "Yes, here it is. Poynter. Lot 486. That might interest you. There are the books, I think: out on the table. Someone has been looking at them. Well, I must be getting on. Goodbye, you'll look us up, won't you?

Couldn't you come this afternoon? we've got a little music about four. Well, then, when you're next in town." He went off. Mr. Denton looked at his watch and found to his confusion that he could spare no more than a moment before retrieving his luggage and going for the train. The moment was just enough to show him that there were four largish volumes of the diary – that it concerned the years about 1710, and that there seemed to be a good many insertions in it of various kinds. It seemed quite worth while to leave a commission of five and twenty pounds for it, and this he was able to do, for his usual agent entered the room as he was on the point of leaving it.

That evening he rejoined his aunt at their temporary abode, which was a small dower-house not many hundred yards from the Manor. On the following morning the two resumed a discussion that had now lasted for some weeks as to the equipment of the new house. Mr. Denton laid before his relative a statement of the results of his visit to town – particulars of carpets, of chairs, of wardrobes, and of bedroom china. "Yes, dear," said his aunt, "but I don't see any chintzes here. Did you go to—?" Mr. Denton stamped on the floor (where else, indeed, could he have stamped?). "Oh dear, oh dear," he said, "the one thing I missed. I *am* sorry. The fact is I was on my way there and I happened to be passing Robins's." His aunt threw up her hands. "Robins's! Then the next thing will be another parcel of horrible old books at some outrageous price. I do think, James, when I am taking all this trouble for you, you might contrive to remember the one or two things which I specially begged you to see after. It's not as if I was asking it for myself. I don't know whether you think I get any pleasure out of it, but if so I can assure you it's very much the reverse. The thought and worry and trouble I have over it you have no idea of, and *you* have simply to go to the shops and order the things." Mr. Denton interposed a moan of penitence. "Oh, aunt—" "Yes, that's all very well, dear, and I don't want to speak sharply, but you *must* know how very annoying it is: particularly as it delays the whole of our business for I can't tell how long: here is Wednesday – the Simpsons come tomorrow, and you can't leave them. Then on Saturday we have friends, as you know, coming for tennis. Yes, indeed, you spoke of asking them yourself, but, of course, I had to write the notes, and it is ridiculous, James, to look like that. We must occasionally be civil to our neighbours: you wouldn't like to have it said we were perfect bears. What was I saying? Well, anyhow it comes to this, that it must be Thursday in next week at least, before you can go to town again, and until we have decided upon the chintzes it is impossible to settle upon one single other thing."

Mr. Denton ventured to suggest that as the paint and wallpapers had been dealt with, this was too severe a view: but this his aunt was not prepared to admit at the moment. Nor, indeed, was there any proposition he could have advanced which she would have found herself able to accept. However, as the day went on, she receded a little from this position: examined with lessening disfavour the samples and price lists submitted by her nephew, and even in some cases gave a qualified approval to his choice.

As for him, he was naturally somewhat dashed by the consciousness of duty unfulfilled, but more so by the prospect of a lawn-tennis party, which, though an inevitable evil in August, he had thought there was no occasion to fear in May. But he was to some extent cheered by the arrival on the Friday morning of an intimation that he had secured at the price of £12 10s. the four volumes of Poynter's manuscript diary, and still more by the arrival on the next morning of the diary itself.

The necessity of taking Mr. and Mrs. Simpson for a drive in the car on Saturday morning and of attending to his neighbours and guests that afternoon prevented him from doing more than open the parcel until the party had retired to bed on the Saturday night. It was then that he made certain of the fact, which he had before only suspected, that he had indeed acquired the diary of Mr. William Poynter, Squire of Acrington (about four miles from his own parish) – that same Poynter who was for a time a member of the circle of Oxford antiquaries, the centre of which was Thomas Hearne, and with whom Hearne seems ultimately to have quarrelled – a not uncommon episode in the career of that excellent man. As is the case with Hearne's own collections, the diary of Poynter contained a good many notes from printed books, descriptions of coins and other antiquities that had been brought to his notice, and drafts of letters on these subjects, besides the chronicle of everyday events. The description in the sale-catalogue had given Mr. Denton no idea of the amount of interest which seemed to lie in the book, and he sat up reading in the first of the four volumes until a reprehensibly late hour.

On the Sunday morning, after church, his aunt came into the study and was diverted from what she had been going to say to him by the sight of the four brown leather quartos on the table. "What are these?" she said suspiciously. "New, aren't they? Oh! Are these the things that made you forget my chintzes? I thought so. Disgusting. What did you give for them, I should like to know? Over Ten Pounds? James, it is really sinful. Well, if you have money to throw away on this kind of thing, there *can* be no reason why you should not subscribe – and subscribe handsomely – to my anti-Vivisection League. There is not, indeed, James, and I shall be very seriously annoyed if—. Who did you say wrote them? Old Mr. Poynter, of Acrington? Well, of course, there is some interest in getting together old papers about this neighbourhood. But Ten Pounds!" She picked up one of the volumes – not that which her nephew had been reading – and opened it at random, dashing it to the floor the next instant with a cry of disgust as a earwig fell from between the pages. Mr. Denton picked it up with a smothered expletive and said, "Poor book! I think you're rather hard on Mr. Poynter." "Was I, my dear? I beg his pardon, but you know I cannot abide those horrid creatures. Let me see if I've done any mischief." "No, I think all's well: but look here what you've opened him on." "Dear me, yes, to be sure! how very interesting. Do unpin it, James, and let me look at it."

It was a piece of patterned stuff about the size of the quarto page, to which it was fastened by an old-fashioned pin. James detached it and handed it to his aunt, carefully replacing the pin in the paper.

Now, I do not know exactly what the fabric was; but it had a design printed upon it, which completely fascinated Miss Denton. She went into raptures over it, held it against the wall, made James do the same, that she might retire to contemplate it from a distance: then pored over it at close quarters, and ended her examination by expressing in the warmest terms her appreciation of the taste of the ancient Mr. Poynter who had had the happy idea of preserving this sample in his diary. "It is a most charming pattern," she said, "and remarkable too. Look, James, how delightfully the lines ripple. It reminds one of hair, very much, doesn't it. And then these knots of ribbon at intervals. They give just the relief of colour that is wanted. I wonder—" "I was going to say," said James with deference, "I wonder if it would cost much to have it copied for our curtains." "Copied? how could you have it copied, James?" "Well, I don't know the details, but I suppose that is a printed pattern, and that you could have a block cut from it in wood or metal." "Now, really, that is a capital idea, James. I am almost inclined to be glad that you were so – that you forgot the chintzes on Monday. At any rate, I'll promise to forgive and forget if you get this *lovely* old thing copied. No one will have anything in the least like it, and mind, James, we won't allow it to be sold. Now I *must* go, and I've totally forgotten what it was I came in to say: never mind, it'll keep."

After his aunt had gone James Denton devoted a few minutes to examining the pattern more closely than he had yet had a chance of doing. He was puzzled to think why it should have struck Miss Denton so forcibly. It seemed to him not specially remarkable or pretty. No doubt it was suitable enough for a curtain pattern: it ran in vertical bands, and there was some indication that these were intended to converge at the top. She was right, too, in thinking that these main bands resembled rippling – almost curling – tresses of hair. Well, the main thing was to find out by means of trade directories, or otherwise, what firm would undertake the reproduction of an old pattern of this kind. Not to delay the reader over this portion of the story, a list of likely names was made out, and Mr. Denton fixed a day for calling on them, or some of them, with his sample.

The first two visits which he paid were unsuccessful: but there is luck in odd numbers. The firm in Bermondsey which was third on his list was accustomed to handling this line. The evidence they were able to produce justified their being entrusted with the job. "Our Mr. Cattell" took a fervent personal interest in it. "It's 'eartrending, isn't it, sir," he said, "to picture the quantity of reelly lovely medeevial stuff of this kind that lays well-nigh unnoticed in many of our residential country 'ouses: much of it in peril, I take it, of being cast aside as so much rubbish. What is it Shakespeare says – unconsidered trifles. Ah, I often say he 'as a word for us all, sir. I say Shakespeare, but I'm well aware all don't 'old with me there – I 'ad something of an upset the other day when a gentleman came in – a titled man, too, he was, and I think he told me he'd wrote on the topic, and I 'appened to cite out something about 'Ercules and the painted cloth. Dear me, you never see such a pother. But as to this, what you've kindly confided to us, it's a piece of work we shall take a reel enthusiasm in achieving it out to the very best of our ability. What man 'as done, as I was observing only a few weeks back to another esteemed client, man can do, and in three to four weeks' time, all being well, we shall 'ope to lay before you evidence to that effect, sir. Take the address, Mr. 'Iggins, if you please."

Such was the general drift of Mr. Cattell's observations on the occasion of his first interview with Mr. Denton. About a month later, being advised that some samples were ready for his inspection, Mr. Denton met him again, and had, it seems, reason to be satisfied with the faithfulness of the reproduction of the design. It had been finished off at the top in accordance with the indication I mentioned, so that the vertical bands joined. But something still needed to be done in the way of matching the colour of the original. Mr. Cattell had suggestions of a technical kind to offer, with which I need not trouble you. He had also views as to the general desirability of the pattern which were vaguely adverse. "You say you don't wish this to be supplied excepting to personal friends equipped with a authorisation from yourself, sir. It shall be done. I quite understand your wish to keep it exclusive: lends a catchit, does it not, to the suite? What's every man's, it's been said, is no man's."

"Do you think it would be popular if it were generally obtainable?" asked Mr. Denton.

"I 'ardly think it, sir," said Cattell, pensively clasping his beard. "I 'ardly think it. Not popular: it wasn't popular with the man that cut the block, was it, Mr. 'Iggins?"

"Did he find it a difficult job?"

"He'd no call to do so, sir; but the fact is that the artistic temperament – and our men are artists, sir, every man of them – true artists as much as many that the world styles by that term – it's apt to take some strange 'ardly accountable likes or dislikes, and here was an example. The twice or thrice that I went to inspect his progress: language I could understand, for that's 'abitual to him, but reel distaste for what I should call a dainty enough thing, I did not, nor am I now able to fathom. It seemed," said Mr. Cattell, looking narrowly upon Mr. Denton, "as if the man scented something almost Hevil in the design."

"Indeed? did he tell you so? I can't say I see anything sinister in it myself."

"Neether can I, sir. In fact I said as much. 'Come, Gatwick,' I said, 'what's to do here? What's the reason of your prejudice – for I can call it no more than that?' But, no! no explanation was forthcoming. And I was merely reduced, as I am now, to a shrug of the shoulders, and a *cui bono*. However, here it is," and with that the technical side of the question came to the front again.

The matching of the colours for the background, the hem, and the knots of ribbon was by far the longest part of the business, and necessitated many sendings to and fro of the original pattern and of new samples. During part of August and September, too, the Dentons were away from the Manor. So that it was not until October was well in that a sufficient quantity of the stuff had been manufactured to furnish curtains for the three or four bedrooms which were to be fitted up with it.

On the feast of Simon and Jude the aunt and nephew returned from a short visit to find all completed, and their satisfaction at the general effect was great. The new curtains, in particular, agreed to admiration with their surroundings. When Mr. Denton was dressing for dinner, and took stock of his room, in which there was a large amount of the chintz displayed, he congratulated himself over and over again on the luck which had first made him forget his aunt's commission and had then put into his hands this extremely effective means of remedying his mistake. The pattern was, as he said at dinner, so restful and yet so far from being dull. And Miss Denton – who, by the way, had none of the stuff in her own room – was much disposed to agree with him.

At breakfast next morning he was induced to qualify his satisfaction to some extent – but very slightly. "There is one thing I rather regret," he said, "that we allowed them to join up the vertical bands of the pattern at the top. I think it would have been better to leave that alone."

"Oh?" said his aunt interrogatively.

"Yes: as I was reading in bed last night they kept catching my eye rather. That is, I found myself looking across at them every now and then. There was an effect as if someone kept peeping out between the curtains in one place or another, where there was no edge, and I think that was due to the joining up of the bands at the top. The only other thing that troubled me was the wind."

"Why, I thought it was a perfectly still night."

"Perhaps it was only on my side of the house, but there was enough to sway my curtains and rustle them more than I wanted."

That night a bachelor friend of James Denton's came to stay, and was lodged in a room on the same floor as his host, but at the end of a long passage, halfway down which was a red baize door, put there to cut off the draught and intercept noise.

The party of three had separated. Miss Denton a good first, the two men at about eleven. James Denton, not yet inclined for bed, sat him down in an arm-chair and read for a time. Then he dozed, and then he woke, and bethought himself that his brown spaniel, which ordinarily slept in his room, had not come upstairs with him. Then he thought he was mistaken: for happening to move his hand which hung down over the arm of the chair within a few inches of the floor, he felt on the back of it just the slightest touch of a surface of hair, and stretching it out in that direction he stroked and patted a rounded something. But the feel of it, and still more the fact that instead of a responsive movement, absolute stillness greeted his touch, made him look over the arm. What he had been touching rose to meet him. It was in the attitude of one that had crept along the floor on its belly, and it was, so far as could be collected, a human figure. But of the face which was now rising to within a few inches of his own no feature was discernible, only hair. Shapeless as it was, there was about it so horrible an air of menace that as he bounded from his chair and rushed from the room he heard himself moaning with fear: and doubtless he did right to fly. As he dashed into the baize door that cut the passage in two, and – forgetting that it opened towards him – beat against it with all the force in him, he felt a soft ineffectual tearing at his back which, all the same, seemed to be growing in power, as if the hand, or whatever worse than a hand was there, were becoming more material as the pursuer's rage was more concentrated. Then he remembered the trick of the door – he got it open – he shut it behind him – he gained his friend's room, and that is all we need know.

It seems curious that, during all the time that had elapsed since the purchase of Poynter's diary, James Denton should not have sought an explanation of the presence of the pattern that had been pinned into it. Well, he had read the diary through without finding it mentioned, and had concluded that there was nothing to be said. But, on leaving Rendcomb Manor (he did not know whether for good), as he naturally insisted upon doing on the day after experiencing the horror I have tried to put into words, he took the diary with him. And at his seaside lodgings he examined more narrowly the portion whence the pattern had been taken. What he remembered having suspected about it turned out to be correct. Two or three leaves were pasted together, but written upon, as was patent when they were held up to the light. They yielded easily to steaming, for the paste had lost much of its strength, and they contained something relevant to the pattern.

The entry was made in 1707.

*Old Mr. Casbury, of Acrington, told me this day much of young Sir Everard Charlett, whom he remember'd Commoner of University College, and thought was of the same Family as Dr. Arthur Charlett, now master of ye Coll. This Charlett was a personable young gent., but a loose atheistical companion, and a great Lifter, as they then call'd the hard drinkers, and for what I know do so now. He was noted, and subject to severall censures at different times for his extravagancies: and if the full history of his debaucheries had bin known, no doubt would have been expell'd ye Coll., supposing that no interest had been imploy'd on his behalf, of which Mr. Casbury had some suspicion. He was a very beautiful person, and constantly wore his own Hair, which was very abundant, from which, and his loose way of living, the cant name for him was Absalom, and he was accustom'd to say that indeed he believ'd he had shortened old David's days, meaning his father, Sir Job Charlett, an old worthy cavalier.*

*Note that Mr. Casbury said that he remembers not the year of Sir Everard Charlett's death, but it was 1692 or 3. He died suddenly in October.* [Several lines describing his unpleasant habits and reputed delinquencies are omitted.] *Having seen him in such topping spirits the night before, Mr. Casbury was amaz'd when he learn'd the death. He was found in the town ditch, the hair as was said pluck'd clean off his head. Most bells in Oxford rung out for him, being a nobleman, and he was buried next night in St. Peter's in the East. But two years after, being to be moved to his country estate by his successor, it was said the coffin, breaking by mischance, proved quite full of Hair: which sounds fabulous, but yet I believe precedents are upon record, as in Dr. Plot's* History of Staffordshire.

*His chambers being afterwards stripp'd, Mr. Casbury came by part of the hangings of it, which 'twas said this Charlett had design'd expressly for a memoriall of his Hair, giving the Fellow that drew it a lock to work by, and the piece which I have fasten'd in here was parcel of the same, which Mr. Casbury gave to me. He said he believ'd there was a subtlety in the drawing, but had never discover'd it himself, nor much liked to pore upon it.*

★   ★   ★

The money spent upon the curtains might as well have been thrown into the fire, as they were. Mr. Cattell's comment upon what he heard of the story took the form of a quotation from Shakespeare. You may guess it without difficulty. It began with the words 'There are more things'.

# AN EPISODE OF
# CATHEDRAL HISTORY

There was once a learned gentleman who was deputed to examine and report upon the archives of the Cathedral of Southminster. The examination of these records demanded a very considerable expenditure of time: hence it became advisable for him to engage lodgings in the city: for though the Cathedral body were profuse in their offers of hospitality, Mr. Lake felt that he would prefer to be master of his day. This was recognised as reasonable. The Dean eventually wrote advising Mr. Lake, if he were not already suited, to communicate with Mr. Worby, the principal Verger, who occupied a house convenient to the church and was prepared to take in a quiet lodger for three or four weeks. Such an arrangement was precisely what Mr. Lake desired. Terms were easily agreed upon, and early in December, like another Mr. Datchery (as he remarked to himself), the investigator found himself in the occupation of a very comfortable room in an ancient and 'cathedraly' house.

One so familiar with the customs of Cathedral churches, and treated with such obvious consideration by the Dean and Chapter of this Cathedral in particular, could not fail to command the respect of the Head Verger. Mr. Worby even acquiesced in certain modifications of statements he had been accustomed to offer for years to parties of visitors. Mr. Lake, on his part, found the Verger a very cheery companion, and took advantage of any occasion that presented itself for enjoying his conversation when the day's work was over.

One evening, about nine o'clock, Mr. Worby knocked at his lodger's door. "I've occasion," he said, "to go across to the Cathedral, Mr. Lake, and I think I made you a promise when I did so next I would give you the opportunity to see what it looks like at night time. It is quite fine and dry outside, if you care to come."

"To be sure I will; very much obliged to you, Mr. Worby, for thinking of it, but let me get my coat."

"Here it is, sir, and I've another lantern here that you'll find advisable for the steps, as there's no moon."

"Anyone might think we were Jasper and Durdles, over again, mightn't they," said Lake, as they crossed the close, for he had ascertained that the Verger had read *Edwin Drood*.

"Well, so they might," said Mr. Worby, with a short laugh, "though I don't know whether we ought to take it as a compliment. Odd ways, I often think, they had at that Cathedral, don't it seem so to you, sir? Full choral matins at seven o'clock in the morning all the year round. Wouldn't suit our boys' voices nowadays, and I think there's one or two of the men would be applying for a rise if the Chapter was to bring it in – particular the alltoes."

They were now at the south-west door. As Mr. Worby was unlocking it, Lake said, "Did you ever find anybody locked in here by accident?"

"Twice I did. One was a drunk sailor; however he got in I don't know. I s'pose he went to sleep in the service, but by the time I got to him he was praying fit to bring the roof in. Lor'! what a noise that man did make! said it was the first time he'd been inside a church for ten years, and blest if ever he'd try it again. The other was an old sheep: them boys it was, up to their games. That was the last time they tried it on, though. There, sir, now you see what we look like; our late Dean used now and again to bring parties in, but he preferred a moonlight night, and there was a piece of verse he'd coat to 'em, relating to a Scotch cathedral, I understand; but I don't know; I almost think the effect's better when it's all dark-like. Seems to add to the size and heighth. Now if you won't mind stopping somewhere in the nave while I go up into the choir where my business lays, you'll see what I mean."

Accordingly Lake waited, leaning against a pillar, and watched the light wavering along the length of the church, and up the steps into the choir, until it was intercepted by some screen or other furniture, which only allowed the reflection to be seen on the piers and roof. Not many minutes had passed before Worby reappeared at the door of the choir and by waving his lantern signalled to Lake to rejoin him.

"I suppose it *is* Worby, and not a substitute," thought Lake to himself, as he walked up the nave. There was, in fact, nothing untoward. Worby showed him the papers which he had come to fetch out of the Dean's stall, and asked him what he thought of the spectacle: Lake agreed that it was well worth seeing. "I suppose," he said, as they walked towards the altar-steps together, "that you're too much used to going about here at night to feel nervous – but you must get a start every now and then, don't you, when a book falls down or a door swings to."

"No, Mr. Lake, I can't say I think much about noises, not nowadays: I'm much more afraid of finding an escape of gas or a burst in the stove pipes than anything else. Still there have been times, years ago. Did you notice that plain altar-tomb there – fifteenth century we say it is, I don't know if you agree to that? Well, if you didn't look at it, just come back and give it a glance, if you'd be so good." It was on the north side of the choir, and rather awkwardly placed: only about three feet from the enclosing stone screen. Quite plain, as the Verger had said, but for some ordinary stone panelling. A metal cross of some size on the northern side (that next to the screen) was the solitary feature of any interest.

Lake agreed that it was not earlier than the Perpendicular period: "but," he said, "unless it's the tomb of some remarkable person, you'll forgive me for saying that I don't think it's particularly noteworthy."

"Well, I can't say as it is the tomb of anybody noted in 'istory," said Worby, who had a dry smile on his face, "for we don't own any record whatsoever of who it was put up to. For all that, if you've half an hour to spare, sir, when we get back to the house, Mr. Lake, I could tell you a tale about that tomb. I won't begin on it now; it strikes cold here, and we don't want to be dawdling about all night."

"Of course I should like to hear it immensely."

"Very well, sir, you shall. Now if I might put a question to you," he went on, as they passed down the choir aisle, "in our little local guide –

and not only there, but in the little book on our Cathedral in the series – you'll find it stated that this portion of the building was erected previous to the twelfth century. Now of course I should be glad enough to take that view, but – mind the step, sir – but, I put it to you – does the lay of the stone 'ere in this portion of the wall (which he tapped with his key) does it to your eye carry the flavour of what you might call Saxon masonry? No, I thought not; no more it does to me: now, if you'll believe me, I've said as much to those men – one's the librarian of our Free Libry here, and the other came down from London on purpose – fifty times, if I have once, but I might just as well have talked to that bit of stonework. But there it is, I suppose everyone's got their opinions."

The discussion of this peculiar trait of human nature occupied Mr. Worby almost up to the moment when he and Lake re-entered the former's house. The condition of the fire in Lake's sitting-room led to a suggestion from Mr. Worby that they should finish the evening in his own parlour. We find them accordingly settled there some short time afterwards.

Mr. Worby made his story a long one, and I will not undertake to tell it wholly in his own words, or in his own order. Lake committed the substance of it to paper immediately after hearing it, together with some few passages of the narrative which had fixed themselves *verbatim* in his mind; I shall probably find it expedient to condense Lake's record to some extent.

Mr. Worby was born, it appeared, about the year 1828. His father before him had been connected with the Cathedral, and likewise his grandfather. One or both had been choristers, and in later life both had done work as mason and carpenter respectively about the fabric. Worby himself, though possessed, as he frankly acknowledged, of an indifferent voice, had been drafted into the choir at about ten years of age.

It was in 1840 that the wave of the Gothic revival smote the Cathedral of Southminster. "There was a lot of lovely stuff went then, sir," said Worby, with a sigh. "My father couldn't hardly believe it when he got his orders to clear out the choir. There was a new dean just come in – Dean Burscough it was – and my father had been 'prenticed to a good firm of joiners in the city, and knew what good work was when he saw it. Crool it was, he used to say: all that beautiful wainscot oak, as good as the day it was put up, and garlands-like of foliage and fruit, and lovely old gilding work on the coats of arms and the organ pipes. All went to the timber yard – every bit except some little pieces worked up in the Lady Chapel, and 'ere in this overmantel. Well – I may be mistook, but I say our choir never looked as well since. Still there was a lot found out about the history of the church, and no doubt but what it did stand in need of repair. There was very few winters passed but what we'd lose a pinnicle." Mr. Lake expressed his concurrence with Worby's views of restoration, but owns to a fear about this point lest the story proper should never be reached. Possibly this was perceptible in his manner.

Worby hastened to reassure him, "Not but what I could carry on about that topic for hours at a time, and do do when I see my opportunity. But Dean Burscough he was very set on the Gothic period, and nothing would serve him but everything must be made agreeable to that. And one morning after service he appointed for my father to meet him in the choir, and he came back after he'd taken off his robes in the vestry, and he'd got a roll of paper with him, and the verger that was then brought in a table, and they begun spreading it out on the table with prayer books to keep it down, and my father helped 'em, and he saw it was a picture of the inside of a choir in a Cathedral; and the Dean – he was a quick spoken gentleman – he says, 'Well, Worby, what do you think of that?' 'Why', says my father, 'I don't think I 'ave the pleasure of knowing that view. Would that be Hereford Cathedral, Mr. Dean?' 'No, Worby,' says the Dean, 'that's Southminster Cathedral as we hope to see it before many years.' 'In-deed, sir,' says my father, and that was all he did say – leastways to the Dean – but he used to tell me he felt really faint in himself when he looked round our choir as I can remember it, all comfortable and furnished-like, and then see this nasty little dry picter, as he called it, drawn out by some London architect. Well, there I am again. But you'll see what I mean if you look at this old view."

Worby reached down a framed print from the wall. "Well, the long and the short of it was that the Dean he handed over to my father a copy of an order of the Chapter that he was to clear out every bit of the choir – make a clean sweep – ready for the new work that was being designed up in town, and he was to put it in hand as soon as ever he could get the breakers together. Now then, sir, if you look at that view, you'll see where the pulpit used to stand: that's what I want you to notice, if you please." It was, indeed, easily seen; an unusually large structure of timber with a domed sounding-board, standing at the east end of the stalls on the north side of the choir, facing the bishop's throne. Worby proceeded to explain that during the alterations, services were held in the nave, the members of the choir being thereby disappointed of an anticipated holiday, and the organist in particular incurring the suspicion of having wilfully damaged the mechanism of the temporary organ that was hired at considerable expense from London.

The work of demolition began with the choir screen and organ loft, and proceeded gradually eastwards, disclosing, as Worby said, many interesting features of older work. While this was going on, the members of the Chapter were, naturally, in and about the choir a great deal, and it soon became apparent to the elder Worby – who could not help overhearing some of their talk – that, on the part of the senior Canons especially, there must have been a good deal of disagreement before the policy now being carried out had been adopted. Some were of opinion that they should catch their deaths of cold in the return-stalls, unprotected by a screen from the draughts in the nave: others objected to being exposed to the view of persons in the choir aisles, especially, they said, during the sermons, when they found it helpful to listen in a posture which was liable to misconstruction. The strongest opposition, however, came from the oldest of the body, who up to the last moment objected to the removal of the pulpit. "You ought not to touch it, Mr. Dean," he said with great emphasis one morning, when the two were standing before it: "you don't know what mischief you may do." "Mischief? it's not a work of any particular merit, Canon." "Don't call me Canon," said the old man with great asperity, "that is, for thirty years I've been known as Dr. Ayloff, and I shall be obliged, Mr. Dean, if you would kindly humour me in that matter. And as to the pulpit (which I've preached from for thirty years, though I don't insist on that) all I'll say is, I *know* you're doing wrong in moving it." "But what sense could there be, my dear Doctor, in leaving it where it is, when we're fitting up the rest of the choir in a totally different *style*? What reason could be given – apart from the look of the thing?" "Reason! reason!" said old Dr. Ayloff; "if you young men – if I may say so without any disrespect, Mr. Dean – if you'd only listen to reason a little, and not be always asking for it, we should get on better. But there, I've said my say." The old gentleman hobbled off, and as it proved, never entered the Cathedral again. The season – it was a hot summer – turned sickly on a sudden. Dr. Ayloff was one of the first to go, with some affection of the muscles of the thorax, which took him painfully at night. And at many services the number of choirmen and boys was very thin.

Meanwhile the pulpit had been done away with. In fact, the sounding-board (part of which still exists as a table in a summer-house in the palace garden) was taken down within an hour or two of Dr. Ayloff's protest. The removal of the base – not effected without considerable trouble – disclosed to view, greatly to the exultation of the restoring party, an altar-tomb – the tomb, of course, to which Worby had attracted Lake's attention that same evening. Much fruitless research was expended in attempts to identify the occupant; from that day to this he has never had a name put to him. The structure had been most carefully boxed in under the pulpit-base, so that such slight ornament as it possessed was not defaced; only on the north side of it there was what looked like an injury; a gap between two of the slabs composing the side. It might be two or three inches across. Palmer, the mason, was directed to fill it up in a week's time, when he came to do some other small jobs near that part of the choir.

The season was undoubtedly a very trying one. Whether the church was built on a site that had once been a marsh, as was suggested, or for whatever reason, the residents in its immediate neighbourhood had, many of them, but little enjoyment of the exquisite sunny days and the calm nights of August and September. To several of the older people – Dr. Ayloff, among others, as we have seen – the summer proved downright fatal, but even among the younger, few escaped either a sojourn in bed for a matter of weeks, or at the least, a brooding sense of oppression, accompanied by hateful nightmares. Gradually there formulated itself a suspicion – which grew into a conviction – that the alterations in the Cathedral had something to say in the matter. The widow of a former old verger, a pensioner of the Chapter of Southminster, was visited by dreams, which she retailed to her friends, of a shape that slipped out of the little door of the south transept as the dark fell in, and flitted – taking a fresh direction every night – about the close, disappearing for a while in house after house, and finally emerging again when the night sky was paling. She could see nothing of it, she said, but that it was a moving form: only she had an impression that when it returned to the church, as it seemed to do in the end of the dream, it turned its head: and then, she could not tell why, but she thought it had red eyes. Worby remembered hearing the old lady tell this dream at a tea-party in the house of the chapter clerk. Its recurrence might, perhaps, he said, be taken as a symptom of approaching illness; at any rate before the end of September the old lady was in her grave.

The interest excited by the restoration of this great church was not confined to its own county. One day that summer an F.S.A., of some celebrity, visited the place. His business was to write an account of the discoveries that had been made, for the Society of Antiquaries, and his wife, who accompanied him, was to make a series of illustrative drawings for his report. In the morning she employed herself in making a general sketch of the choir; in the afternoon she devoted herself to details. She first drew the newly exposed altar-tomb, and when that was finished, she called her husband's attention to a beautiful piece of diaper-ornament on the screen just behind it, which had, like the tomb itself, been completely concealed by the pulpit. Of course, he said, an illustration of that must be made; so she seated herself on the tomb and began a careful drawing which occupied her till dusk.

Her husband had by this time finished his work of measuring and description, and they agreed that it was time to be getting back to their hotel. "You may as well brush my skirt, Frank," said the lady, "it must have got covered with dust, I'm sure." He obeyed dutifully; but, after a moment, he said, "I don't know whether you value this dress particularly, my dear, but I'm inclined to think it's seen its best days. There's a great bit of it gone." "Gone? Where?" said she. "I don't know where it's gone, but it's off at the bottom edge behind here." She pulled it hastily into sight, and was horrified to find a jagged tear extending some way into the substance of the stuff; very much, she said, as if a dog had rent it away. The dress was, in any case, hopelessly spoilt, to her great vexation, and though they looked everywhere, the missing piece could not be found. There were many ways, they concluded, in which the injury might have come about, for the choir was full of old bits of woodwork with nails sticking out of them. Finally, they could only suppose that one of these had caused the mischief, and that the workmen, who had been about all day, had carried off the particular piece with the fragment of dress still attached to it.

It was about this time, Worby thought, that his little dog began to wear an anxious expression when the hour for it to be put into the shed in the back yard approached. (For his mother had ordained that it must not sleep in the house.) One evening, he said, when he was just going to pick it up and carry it out, it looked at him "like a Christian, and waved its 'and, I was going to say – well, you know 'ow they do carry on sometimes, and the end of it was I put it under my coat, and 'uddled it upstairs – and I'm afraid I as good as deceived my poor mother on the subject. After that the dog acted very artful with 'iding itself under the bed for half-an-hour or more before bed-time came, and we worked it so as my mother never found out what we'd done." Of course Worby was glad of its company anyhow, but more particularly when the nuisance that is still remembered in Southminster as 'the crying' set in.

"Night after night," said Worby, "that dog seemed to know it was coming; he'd creep out, he would, and snuggle into the bed and cuddle right up to me shivering, and when the crying come he'd be like a wild thing, shoving his head under my arm, and I was fully near as bad. Six or seven times we'd hear it, not more, and when he'd dror out his 'ed again I'd know it was over for that night. What was it like, sir? Well, I never heard but one thing that seemed to hit it off. I happened to be playing about in the Close, and there was two of the Canons met and said 'Good morning' one to another. 'Sleep well last night?' says one – it was Mr. Henslow that one, and Mr. Lyall was the other – 'Can't say I did,' says Mr. Lyall, 'rather too much of Isaiah 34:14 for me.' '34:14,' says Mr. Henslow, 'what's that?' 'You call yourself a Bible reader!' says Mr. Lyall. (Mr. Henslow, you must know, he was one of what used to be termed Simeon's lot – pretty much what we should call the Evangelical party.) 'You go and look it up.' I wanted to know what he was getting at myself, and so off I ran home and got out my own Bible, and there it was: 'the satyr shall cry to his fellow.' Well, I thought, is that what we've been listening to these past nights? and I tell you it made me look over my shoulder a time or two. Of course I'd asked my father and mother about what it could be before that, but they both said it was most likely cats: but they spoke very short, and I could see they was troubled. My word! that was a noise – 'ungry-like, as if it was calling after someone that wouldn't come. If ever you felt you wanted company, it would be when you was waiting for it to begin again. I believe two or three nights there was men put on to watch in different parts of the Close; but they all used to get together in one corner, the nearest they could to the High Street, and nothing came of it.

"Well, the next thing was this. Me and another of the boys – he's in business in the city now as a grocer, like his father before him – we'd gone up in the Close after morning service was over, and we heard old Palmer the mason bellowing to some of his men. So we went up nearer, because we knew he was a rusty old chap and there might be some fun going. It appears Palmer'd told this man to stop up the chink in that old tomb. Well, there was this man keeping on saying he'd done it the best he could, and there was Palmer carrying on like all possessed about it. 'Call that making a job of it?' he says. 'If you had your rights you'd get the sack for this. What do you suppose I pay you your wages for? What do you suppose I'm going to say to the Dean and Chapter when they come round, as come they may do any time, and see where you've been bungling about covering the 'ole place with mess and plaster and Lord knows what?' 'Well, master, I done the best I could,' says the man; 'I don't know no more than what you do 'ow it come to fall out this way. I tamped it right in the 'ole,' he says, 'and now it's fell out,' he says, 'I never see.'

"'Fell out?' says old Palmer, 'why it's nowhere near the place. Blowed out, you mean,' and he picked up a bit of plaster, and so did I, that was laying up against the screen, three or four feet off, and not dry yet; and old Palmer he looked at it curious-like, and then he turned round on me and he says, 'Now then, you boys, have you been up to some of your games here?' 'No,' I says, 'I haven't, Mr. Palmer; there's none of us been about here till just this minute,' and while I was talking the other boy, Evans, he got looking in through the chink, and I heard him draw in his breath, and he came away sharp and up to us, and says he, 'I believe there's something in there. I saw something shiny.' 'What! I daresay,' says old Palmer; 'Well, I ain't got time to stop about there. You, William, you go off and get some more stuff and make a job of it this time; if not, there'll be trouble in my yard,' he says.

"So the man he went off, and Palmer too, and us boys stopped behind, and I says to Evans, 'Did you really see anything in there?' 'Yes,' he says, 'I did indeed.' So then I says, 'Let's shove something in and stir it up.' And we tried several of the bits of wood that was laying about, but they were all too big. Then Evans he had a sheet of music he'd brought with him, an anthem or a service, I forget which it was now, and he rolled it up small and shoved it in the chink; two or three times he did it, and nothing happened. 'Give it me, boy,' I said, and I had a try. No, nothing happened. Then, I don't know why I thought of it, I'm sure, but I stooped down just opposite the chink and put my two fingers in my mouth and whistled – you know the way – and at that I seemed to think I heard something stirring, and I says to Evans, 'Come away,' I says; 'I don't like this.' 'Oh, rot,' he says, 'Give me that roll,' and he took it and shoved it in. And I don't think ever I see anyone go so pale as he did. 'I say, Worby,' he says, 'it's caught, or else someone's got hold of it.' 'Pull it out or leave it,' I says, 'Come and let's get off.' So he gave a good pull, and it came away. Leastways most of it did, but the end was gone. Torn off it was, and Evans looked at it for a second and then he gave a sort of a croak and let it drop, and we both made off out of there as quick as ever we could. When we got outside Evans says to me, 'Did you see the end of that paper.' 'No,' I says, 'only it was torn.' 'Yes, it was,' he says, 'but it was wet too, and black!' Well, partly because of the fright we had, and partly because that music was wanted in a day or two, and we knew there'd be a set-out about it with the organist, we didn't say nothing to anyone else, and I suppose the workmen they swept up the bit that was left along with the rest of the rubbish. But Evans, if you were to ask him this very day about it, he'd stick to it he saw that paper wet and black at the end where it was torn."

After that the boys gave the choir a wide berth, so that Worby was not sure what was the result of the mason's renewed mending of the tomb. Only he made out from fragments of conversation dropped by the workmen passing through the choir that some difficulty had been met with, and that the governor – Mr. Palmer to wit – had tried his own hand at the job. A little later, he happened to see Mr. Palmer himself knocking at the door of the Deanery and being admitted by the butler. A day or so after that, he gathered from a remark his father let fall at breakfast that something a little out of the common was to be done in the Cathedral after morning service on the morrow. "And I'd just as soon it was today," his father added, "I don't see the use of running risks." "'Father,' I says, 'what are you going to do in the Cathedral tomorrow?' and he turned on me as savage as I ever see him – he was a wonderful good-tempered man as a general thing, my poor father was. 'My lad,' he says, 'I'll trouble you not to go picking up your elders' and betters' talk: it's not manners and it's not straight. What I'm going to do or not going to do in the Cathedral tomorrow is none of your business: and if I catch sight of you hanging about the place tomorrow after your work's done, I'll send you home with a flea in your ear. Now you mind that.' Of course I said I was very sorry and that, and equally of course I went off and laid my plans with Evans. We knew there was a stair up in the corner of the transept which you can get up to the triforium, and in them days the door to it was pretty well always open, and even if it wasn't we knew the key usually laid under a bit of matting hard by. So we made up our minds we'd be putting away music and that, next morning while the rest of the boys was clearing off, and then slip up the stairs and watch from the triforium if there was any signs of work going on.

"Well, that same night I dropped off asleep as sound as a boy does, and all of a sudden the dog woke me up, coming into the bed, and thought I, now we're going to get it sharp, for he seemed more frightened than usual. After about five minutes sure enough came this cry. I can't give you no idea what it was like; and so near too – nearer than I'd heard it yet – and a funny thing, Mr. Lake, you know what a place this Close is for an echo, and particular if you stand this side of it. Well, this crying never made no sign of an echo at all. But, as I said, it was dreadful near this night; and on the top of the start I got with hearing it, I got another fright; for I heard something rustling outside in the passage. Now to be sure I thought I was done; but I noticed the dog seemed to perk up a bit, and next there was someone whispered outside the door, and I very near laughed out loud, for I knew it was my father and mother that had got out of bed with the noise. 'Whatever is it?' says my mother. 'Hush! I don't know,' says my father, excited-like, 'don't disturb the boy. I hope he didn't hear nothing.'

"So, me knowing they were just outside, it made me bolder, and I slipped out of bed across to my little window – giving on the Close – but the dog he bored right down to the bottom of the bed – and I looked out. First go off I couldn't see anything. Then right down in the shadow under a buttress I made out what I shall always say was two spots of red – a dull red it was – nothing like a lamp or a fire, but just so as you could pick 'em out of the black shadow. I hadn't but just sighted 'em when it seemed we wasn't the only people that had been disturbed, because I see a window in a house on the left-hand side become lighted up, and the light moving. I just turned my head to make sure of it, and then looked back into the shadow for those two red things, and they were gone, and for all I peered about and stared, there was not a sign more of them. Then come my last fright that night – something come against my bare leg – but that was all right: that was my little dog had come out of bed, and prancing about, making a great to-do, only holding his tongue, and me seeing he was quite in spirits again, I took him back to bed and we slept the night out!

"Next morning I made out to tell my mother I'd had the dog in my room, and I was surprised, after all she'd said about it before, how quiet she took it. 'Did you?' she says. 'Well, by good rights you ought to go without your breakfast for doing such a thing behind my back: but I don't know as there's any great harm done, only another time you ask my permission, do you hear?' A bit after that I said something to my father about having heard the cats again. '*Cats*,' he says, and he looked over at my poor mother, and she coughed and he says, 'Oh! ah! yes, cats. I believe I heard 'em myself.'

"That was a funny morning altogether: nothing seemed to go right. The organist he stopped in bed, and the minor Canon he forgot it was the 19th day and waited for the *Venite*; and after a bit the deputy he set off playing the chant for evensong, which was a minor; and then the Decani boys were laughing so much they couldn't sing, and when it came to the anthem the solo boy he got took with the giggles, and made out his nose was bleeding, and shoved the book at me what hadn't practised the verse and wasn't much of a singer if I had known it. Well, things was rougher, you see, fifty years ago, and I got a nip from the counter-tenor behind me that I remembered.

"So we got through somehow, and neither the men nor the boys weren't by way of waiting to see whether the Canon in residence – Mr. Henslow it was – would come to the vestries and fine 'em, but I don't believe he did: for one thing I fancy he'd read the wrong lesson for the first time in his life, and knew it. Anyhow Evans and me didn't find no difficulty in slipping up the stairs as I told you, and when we got up we laid ourselves down flat on our stomachs where we could just stretch our heads out over the old tomb, and we hadn't but just done so when we heard the verger that was then, first shutting the iron porch-gates and locking the south-west door, and then the transept door, so we knew there was something up, and they meant to keep the public out for a bit.

"Next thing was, the Dean and the Canon come in by their door on the north, and then I see my father, and old Palmer, and a couple of their best men, and Palmer stood a talking for a bit with the Dean in the middle of the choir. He had a coil of rope and the men had crows. All of 'em looked a bit nervous. So there they stood talking, and at last I heard the Dean say, 'Well, I've no time to waste, Palmer. If you think this'll satisfy Southminster people, I'll permit it to be done; but I must say this, that never in the whole course of my life have I heard such arrant nonsense from a practical man as I have from you. Don't you agree with me, Henslow?' As far as I could hear Mr. Henslow said something like 'Oh! well we're told, aren't we, Mr. Dean, not to judge others?' and the Dean he gave a kind of sniff, and walked straight up to the tomb, and took his stand behind it with his back to the screen, and the others they come edging up rather gingerly. Henslow, he stopped on the south side and scratched on his chin, he did. Then the Dean spoke up: 'Palmer,' he says, 'which can you do easiest, get the slab off the top, or shift one of the side slabs?'

"Old Palmer and his men they pottered about a bit looking round the edge of the top slab and sounding the sides on the south and east and west and everywhere but the north. Henslow said something about it being better to have a try at the south side, because there was more light and more room to move about in. Then my father, who'd been watching of them, went round to the north side, and knelt down and felt of the slab by the chink, and he got up and dusted his knees and says to the Dean: 'Beg pardon, Mr. Dean, but I think if Mr. Palmer'll try this here slab he'll find it'll come out easy enough. Seems to me one of the men could prize it out with his crow by means of this chink.' 'Ah! thank you, Worby,' says the Dean; 'that's a good suggestion. Palmer, let one of your men do that, will you?'

"So the man come round, and put his bar in and bore on it, and just that minute when they were all bending over, and we boys got our heads well out over the edge of the triforium, there come a most fearful crash down at the west end of the choir, as if a whole stack of big timber had fallen down a flight of stairs. Well, you can't expect me to tell you everything that happened all in a minute. Of course there was a terrible commotion. I heard the slab fall out, and the crowbar on the floor, and I heard the Dean say 'Good God!'

"When I looked down again I saw the Dean tumbled over on the floor, the men was making off down the choir, Henslow was just going to help the Dean up, Palmer was going to stop the men, as he said afterwards, and my father was sitting on the altar step with his face in his hands. The Dean he was very cross. 'I wish to goodness you'd look where you're coming to, Henslow,' he says. 'Why you should all take to your heels when a stick of wood tumbles down I cannot imagine,' and all Henslow could do, explaining he was right away on the other side of the tomb, would not satisfy him.

"Then Palmer came back and reported there was nothing to account for this noise and nothing seemingly fallen down, and when the Dean finished feeling of himself they gathered round – except my father, he sat where he was – and some one lighted up a bit of candle and they looked into the tomb. 'Nothing there,' says the Dean, 'what did I tell you? Stay! here's something. What's this: a bit of music paper, and a piece of torn stuff – part of a dress it looks like. Both quite modern – no interest whatever. Another time perhaps you'll take the advice of an educated man' – or something like that, and off he went, limping a bit, and out through the north door, only as he went he called back angry to Palmer for leaving the door standing open. Palmer called out 'Very sorry, sir,' but he shrugged his shoulders, and Henslow says, 'I fancy Mr. Dean's mistaken. I closed the door behind me, but he's a little upset.' Then Palmer says, 'Why, where's Worby?' and they saw him sitting on the step and went up to him. He was recovering himself, it seemed, and wiping his forehead, and Palmer helped him up on to his legs, as I was glad to see.

"They were too far off for me to hear what they said, but my father pointed to the north door in the aisle, and Palmer and Henslow both of them looked very surprised and scared. After a bit, my father and Henslow went out of the church, and the others made what haste they could to put the slab back and plaster it in. And about as the clock struck twelve the Cathedral was opened again and us boys made the best of our way home.

"I was in a great taking to know what it was had given my poor father such a turn, and when I got in and found him sitting in his chair taking a glass of spirits, and my mother standing looking anxious at him, I couldn't keep from bursting out and making confession where I'd been. But he didn't seem to take on, not in the way of losing his temper. 'You was there, was you? Well did you see it?' 'I see everything, father,' I said, 'except when the noise came.' 'Did you see what it was knocked the Dean over?' he says, 'that what come out of the monument? You didn't? Well, that's a mercy.' 'Why, what was it, father?' I said. 'Come, you must have seen it,' he says. '*Didn't* you see? A thing like a man, all over hair, and two great eyes to it?'

"Well, that was all I could get out of him that time, and later on he seemed as if he was ashamed of being so frightened, and he used to put me off when I asked him about it. But years after, when I was got to be a grown man, we had more talk now and again on the matter, and he always said the same thing. 'Black it was,' he'd say, 'and a mass of hair, and two legs, and the light caught on its eyes.'

"Well, that's the tale of that tomb, Mr. Lake; it's one we don't tell to our visitors, and I should be obliged to you not to make any use of it till I'm out of the way. I doubt Mr. Evans'll feel the same as I do, if you ask him."

This proved to be the case. But over twenty years have passed by, and the grass is growing over both Worby and Evans; so Mr. Lake felt no difficulty about communicating his notes – taken in 1890 – to me. He accompanied them with a sketch of the tomb and a copy of the short inscription on the metal cross which was affixed at the expense of Dr. Lyall to the centre of the northern side. It was from the Vulgate of Isaiah xxxiv., and consisted merely of the three words:

**IBI CUBAVIT LAMIA.**

# THE HAUNTED DOLLS' HOUSE

I suppose you get stuff of that kind** through your hands pretty often?"
said Mr. Dillet, as he pointed with his stick to an object which shall
be described when the time comes: and when he said it, he lied in
his throat, and knew that he lied. Not once in twenty years – perhaps
not once in a lifetime – could Mr. Chittenden, skilled as he was in
ferreting out the forgotten treasures of half a dozen counties, expect to
handle such a specimen. It was collectors' palaver, and Mr. Chittenden
recognised it as such.

"Stuff of that kind, Mr. Dillet! It's a museum piece, that is."

"Well, I suppose there are museums that'll take anything."

"I've seen one, not as good as that, years back," said Mr. Chittenden
thoughtfully. "But that's not likely to come into the market: and I'm
told they 'ave some fine ones of the period over the water. No: I'm only
telling you the truth, Mr. Dillet, when I was to say that if you was to
place an unlimited order with me for the very best that could be got –
and you know I 'ave facilities for getting to know of such things, and a
reputation to maintain – well, all I can say is, I should lead you straight
up to that one and say, 'I can't do no better for you than that, sir.'"

"Hear, hear!" said Mr. Dillet, applauding ironically with the end
of his stick on the floor of the shop. "How much are you sticking the
innocent American buyer for it, eh?"

"Oh, I shan't be over hard on the buyer, American or otherwise.
You see, it stands this way, Mr. Dillet – if I knew just a bit more about
the pedigree—"

"Or just a bit less," Mr. Dillet put in.

"Ha, ha! You will have your joke, sir. No, but as I was saying, if I
knew just a little more than what I do about the piece – though anyone

can see for themselves it's a genuine thing, every last corner of it, and there's not been one of my men allowed to so much as touch it since it came into the shop – there'd be another figure in the price I'm asking."

"And what's that: five and twenty?"

"Multiply that by three and you've got it, sir. Seventy-five's my price."

"And fifty's mine," said Mr. Dillet. The point of agreement was, of course, somewhere between the two, it does not matter exactly where – I think sixty guineas. But half an hour later the object was being packed, and within an hour Mr. Dillet had called for it in his car and driven away. Mr. Chittenden, holding the cheque in his hand, saw him off from the door with smiles, and returned, still smiling, into the parlour where his wife was making the tea. He stopped at the door.

"It's gone," he said. "Thank God for that!" said Mrs. Chittenden, putting down the teapot. "Mr. Dillet, was it?"

"Yes, it was."

"Well, I'd sooner it was him than another."

"Oh, I don't know; he ain't a bad feller, my dear."

"Maybe not, but in my opinion he'd be none the worse for a bit of a shake up."

"Well, if that's your opinion, it's my opinion he's put himself into the way of getting one. Anyhow, we shan't have no more of it, and that's something to be thankful for." And so Mr. and Mrs. Chittenden sat down to tea.

And what of Mr. Dillet and his new acquisition? What it was, the title of this story will have told you. What it was like, I shall have to indicate as well as I can.

There was only just enough room for it in the car, and Mr. Dillet had to sit with the driver: he had also to go slow, for though the rooms of the Dolls' House had all been stuffed carefully with soft cottonwool, jolting was to be avoided, in view of the immense number of small objects which thronged them; and the ten-mile drive was an anxious time for him, in spite of all the precautions he insisted upon. At last his front door was reached, and Collins, the butler, came out.

"Look here, Collins, you must help me with this thing – it's a delicate job. We must get it out upright, see? It's full of little things that mustn't be displaced more than we can help. Let's see, where shall we have it? (After a pause for consideration.) Really, I think I shall have to put it in my own room, to begin with at any rate. On the big table – that's it."

It was conveyed – with much talking – to Mr. Dillet's spacious room on the first floor, looking out on the drive. The sheeting was unwound from it, and the front thrown open, and for the next hour or two Mr. Dillet was fully occupied in extracting the padding and setting in order the contents of the rooms.

When this thoroughly congenial task was finished, I must say that it would have been difficult to find a more perfect and attractive specimen of a Dolls' House in Strawberry Hill Gothic than that which now stood on Mr. Dillet's large kneehole table, lighted up by the evening sun which came slanting through three tall slash-windows.

It was quite six feet long, including the Chapel or Oratory which flanked the front on the left as you faced it, and the stable on the right. The main block of the house was, as I have said, in the Gothic manner: that is to say, the windows had pointed arches and were surmounted by what are called ogival hoods, with crockets and finials such as we see on the canopies of tombs built into church walls. At the angles were absurd turrets covered with arched panels. The Chapel had pinnacles and buttresses, and a bell in the turret and coloured glass in the windows. When the front of the house was open you saw four large rooms, bedroom, dining-room, drawing-room and kitchen, each with its appropriate furniture in a very complete state.

The stable on the right was in two storeys, with its proper complement of horses, coaches and grooms, and with its clock and Gothic cupola for the clock bell.

Pages, of course, might be written on the outfit of the mansion – how many frying-pans, how many gilt chairs, what pictures, carpets, chandeliers, four-posters, table linen, glass, crockery and plate it possessed; but all this must be left to the imagination. I will only say that the base or plinth on which the house stood (for it was fitted with one of some depth which allowed of a flight of steps to the front door and a terrace, partly balustraded) contained a shallow drawer or drawers in which were neatly stored sets of embroidered curtains, changes of raiment for the inmates, and, in short, all the materials for an infinite series of variations and refittings of the most absorbing and delightful kind.

"Quintessence of Horace Walpole, that's what it is: he must have had something to do with the making of it." Such was Mr. Dillet's murmured reflection as he knelt before it in a reverent ecstasy. "Simply wonderful! This is my day and no mistake. Five hundred pounds coming in this morning for that cabinet which I never cared about, and now this tumbling into my hands for a tenth, at the very most, of what it would fetch in town. Well, well! It almost makes one afraid something'll happen to counter it. Let's have a look at the population, anyhow."

Accordingly, he set them before him in a row. Again, here is an opportunity, which some would snatch at, of making an inventory of costume: I am incapable of it.

There were a gentleman and lady, in blue satin and brocade respectively. There were two children, a boy and a girl. There was a cook, a nurse, a footman, and there were the stable servants, two postilions, a coachman, two grooms.

"Anyone else? Yes, possibly."

The curtains of the four-poster in the bedroom were closely drawn round all four sides of it, and he put his finger in between them and felt in the bed. He drew the finger back hastily, for it almost seemed to him as if something had – not stirred, perhaps, but yielded – in an odd live way as he pressed it. Then he put back the curtains, which ran on rods in the proper manner, and extracted from the bed a white-haired old gentleman in a long linen night-dress and cap, and laid him down by the rest. The tale was complete.

Dinner-time was now near, so Mr. Dillet spent but five minutes in putting the lady and children into the drawing-room, the gentleman into the dining-room, the servants into the kitchen and stables, and the old man back into his bed. He retired into his dressing-room next door, and we see and hear no more of him until something like eleven o'clock at night.

His whim was to sleep surrounded by some of the gems of his collection. The big room in which we have seen him contained his bed: bath, wardrobe, and all the appliances of dressing were in a commodious room adjoining: but his four-poster, which itself was a valued treasure, stood in the large room where he sometimes wrote, and often sat, and even received visitors. Tonight he repaired to it in a highly complacent frame of mind.

There was no striking clock within earshot – none on the staircase, none in the stable, none in the distant church tower. Yet it is indubitable that Mr. Dillet was started out of a very pleasant slumber by a bell tolling One.

He was so much startled that he did not merely lie breathless with wide-open eyes, but actually sat up in his bed.

He never asked himself, till the morning hours, how it was that, though there was no light at all in the room, the Dolls' House on the kneehole table stood out with complete clearness. But it was so. The effect was that of a bright harvest moon shining full on the front of a big white stone mansion – a quarter of a mile away it might be, and yet every detail was photographically sharp. There were trees about it, too – trees rising behind the chapel and the house. He seemed to be conscious of the scent of a cool still September night. He thought he could hear an occasional stamp and clink from the stables, as of horses stirring. And with another shock he realised that, above the house, he was looking, not at the wall of his room with its pictures, but into the profound blue of a night sky.

There were lights, more than one, in the windows, and he quickly saw that this was no four-roomed house with a movable front, but one of many rooms and staircases – a real house, but seen as if through the wrong end of a telescope.

"You mean to show me something," he muttered to himself, and he gazed earnestly on the lighted windows. They would in real life have been shuttered or curtained, no doubt, he thought; but, as it was, there was nothing to intercept his view of what was being transacted inside the rooms.

Two rooms were lighted – one on the ground floor to the right of the door, one upstairs, on the left – the first brightly enough, the other rather dimly. The lower room was the dining-room: a table was laid, but the meal was over, and only wine and glasses were left on the table. The man of the blue satin and the woman of the brocade were alone in the room, and they were talking very earnestly, seated close together at the table, their elbows on it: every now and again stopping to listen, as it seemed. Once he rose, came to the window and opened it and put his head out and his hand to his ear. There was a lighted taper in a silver candlestick on a sideboard. When the man left the window he seemed to leave the room also; and the lady, taper in hand, remained standing and listening. The expression on her face was that of one striving her utmost to keep down a fear that threatened to master her – and succeeding. It was a hateful face, too; broad, flat and sly. Now the man came back and she took some small thing from him and hurried out of the room. He, too, disappeared, but only for a moment or two. The front door slowly opened and he stepped out and stood on the top of the perron, looking this way and that; then turned towards the upper window that was lighted, and shook his fist.

It was time to look at that upper window. Through it was seen a four-post bed: a nurse or other servant in an arm-chair, evidently sound asleep; in the bed an old man lying: awake, and, one would say, anxious, from the way in which he shifted about and moved his fingers, beating tunes on the coverlet. Beyond the bed a door opened. Light was seen on the ceiling, and the lady came in: she set down her candle on a table, came to the fireside and roused the nurse. In her hand she had an old-fashioned wine bottle, ready uncorked. The nurse took it, poured some of the contents into a little silver saucepan, added some spice and sugar from casters on the table, and set it to warm on the fire. Meanwhile the old man in the bed beckoned feebly to the lady, who came to him, smiling, took his wrist as if to feel his pulse, and bit her lip as if in consternation. He looked at her anxiously, and then pointed to the window, and spoke. She nodded, and did as the man below had done; opened the casement and listened – perhaps rather ostentatiously: then drew in her head and shook it, looking at the old man, who seemed to sigh.

By this time the posset on the fire was steaming, and the nurse poured it into a small two-handled silver bowl and brought it to the bedside. The old man seemed disinclined for it and was waving it away, but the lady and the nurse together bent over him and evidently pressed it upon him. He must have yielded, for they supported him into a sitting position, and put it to his lips. He drank most of it, in several draughts, and they laid him down. The lady left the room, smiling goodnight to him, and took the bowl, the bottle and the silver saucepan with her. The nurse returned to the chair, and there was an interval of complete quiet.

Suddenly the old man started up in his bed – and he must have uttered some cry, for the nurse started out of her chair and made but one step of it to the bedside. He was a sad and terrible sight – flushed in the face, almost to blackness, the eyes glaring whitely, both hands clutching at his heart, foam at his lips. For a moment the nurse left him, ran to the door, flung it wide open, and, one supposes, screamed aloud for help, then darted back to the bed and seemed to try feverishly to soothe him – to lay him down – anything. But as the lady, her husband, and several servants, rushed into the room with horrified faces, the old man collapsed under the nurse's hands and lay back, and his features, contorted with agony and rage, relaxed slowly into calm.

A few moments later, lights showed out to the left of the house, and a coach with flambeaux drove up to the door. A white-wigged man in black got nimbly out and ran up the steps, carrying a small leather trunk-shaped box. He was met in the doorway by the man and his wife, she with her handkerchief clutched between her hands, he with a tragic face, but retaining his self-control. They led the new-comer into the dining-room, where he set his box of papers on the table, and, turning to them, listened with a face of consternation at what they had to tell. He nodded his head again and again, threw out his hands slightly, declined, it seemed, offers of refreshment and lodging for the night, and within a few minutes came slowly down the steps, entering the coach and driving off the way he had come. As the man in blue watched him from the top of the steps, a smile not pleasant to see stole slowly over his fat white face. Darkness fell over the whole scene as the lights of the coach disappeared.

But Mr. Dillet remained sitting up in the bed: he had rightly guessed that there would be a sequel. The house front glimmered out again before long. But now there was a difference. The lights were in other windows, one at the top of the house, the other illuminating the range of coloured windows of the chapel. How he saw through these is not quite obvious, but he did. The interior was as carefully furnished as the rest of the establishment, with its minute red cushions on the desks, its Gothic stall-canopies, and its western gallery and pinnacled organ with gold pipes. On the centre of the black and white pavement was a bier: four tall candles burned at the corners. On the bier was a coffin covered with a pall of black velvet.

As he looked the folds of the pall stirred. It seemed to rise at one end: it slid downwards: it fell away, exposing the black coffin with its silver handles and name-plate. One of the tall candlesticks swayed and toppled over. Ask no more, but turn, as Mr. Dillet hastily did, and look in at the lighted window at the top of the house, where a boy and girl lay in two truckle-beds, and a four-poster for the nurse rose above them. The nurse was not visible for the moment; but the father and mother were there, dressed now in mourning, but with very little sign of mourning in their demeanour. Indeed, they were laughing and talking with a good deal of animation, sometimes to each other, and sometimes throwing a remark to one or other of the children, and again laughing at the answers. Then the father was seen to go on tiptoe out of the room, taking with him as he went a white garment that hung on a peg near the door. He shut the door after him. A minute or two later it was slowly opened again, and a muffled head poked round it. A bent form of sinister shape stepped across to the truckle-beds, and suddenly stopped, threw up its arms and revealed, of course, the father, laughing. The children were in agonies of terror, the boy with the bedclothes over his head, the girl throwing herself out of bed into her mother's arms. Attempts at consolation followed – the parents took the children on their laps, patted them, picked up the white gown and showed there was no harm in it, and so forth; and at last putting the children back into bed, left the room with encouraging waves of the hand. As they left it, the nurse came in, and soon the light died down.

Still Mr. Dillet watched immovable.

A new sort of light – not of lamp or candle – a pale ugly light, began to dawn around the door-case at the back of the room. The door was opening again. The seer does not like to dwell upon what he saw entering the room: he says it might be described as a frog – the size of a man – but it had scanty white hair about its head. It was busy about the truckle-beds, but not for long. The sound of cries – faint, as if coming out of a vast distance – but, even so, infinitely appalling, reached the ear.

There were signs of a hideous commotion all over the house: lights moved along and up, and doors opened and shut, and running figures passed within the windows. The clock in the stable turret tolled one, and darkness fell again.

It was only dispelled once more, to show the house front. At the bottom of the steps dark figures were drawn up in two lines, holding flaming torches. More dark figures came down the steps, bearing, first one, then another small coffin. And the lines of torch-bearers with the coffins between them moved silently onward to the left.

The hours of night passed on – never so slowly, Mr. Dillet thought. Gradually he sank down from sitting to lying in his bed – but he did not close an eye: and early next morning he sent for the doctor.

The doctor found him in a disquieting state of nerves, and recommended sea-air. To a quiet place on the East Coast he accordingly repaired by easy stages in his car.

One of the first people he met on the sea front was Mr. Chittenden, who, it appeared, had likewise been advised to take his wife away for a bit of a change.

Mr. Chittenden looked somewhat askance upon him when they met: and not without cause.

"Well, I don't wonder at you being a bit upset, Mr. Dillet. What? Yes, well, I might say 'orrible upset, to be sure, seeing what me and my poor wife went through ourselves. But I put it to you, Mr. Dillet, one of two things: was I going to scrap a lovely piece like that on the one 'and, or was I going to tell customers: 'I'm selling you a regular picture-palace-dramar in reel life of the olden time, billed to perform regular at one o'clock a.m.?' Why, what would you 'ave said yourself? And next thing you know, two Justices of the Peace in the back parlour, and pore Mr. and Mrs. Chittenden off in a spring cart to the County Asylum and everyone in the street saying, 'Ah, I thought it 'ud come to that. Look at the way the man drank!' – and me next door, or next door but one, to a total abstainer, as you know. Well, there was my position. What? Me 'ave it back in the shop? Well, what do you think? No, but I'll tell you what I will do. You shall have your money back, bar the ten pound I paid for it, and you make what you can."

Later in the day, in what is offensively called the 'smoke-room' of the hotel, a murmured conversation between the two went on for some time.

"How much do you really know about that thing, and where it came from?"

"Honest, Mr. Dillet, I don't know the 'ouse. Of course, it came out of the lumber room of a country 'ouse – that anyone could guess. But I'll go as far as say this, that I believe it's not a hundred miles from this place. Which direction and how far I've no notion. I'm only judging by guess-work. The man as I actually paid the cheque to ain't one of my regular men, and I've lost sight of him; but I 'ave the idea that this part of the country was his beat, and that's every word I can tell you. But now, Mr. Dillet, there's one thing that rather physicks me. That old chap – I suppose you saw him drive up to the door – I thought so: now, would he have been the medical man, do you take it? My wife would have it so, but I stuck to it that was the lawyer, because he had papers with him, and one he took out was folded up."

"I agree," said Mr. Dillet. "Thinking it over, I came to the conclusion that was the old man's will, ready to be signed."

"Just what I thought," said Mr. Chittenden, "and I took it that will would have cut out the young people, eh? Well, well! It's been a lesson to me, I know that. I shan't buy no more dolls' houses, nor waste no more money on the pictures – and as to this business of poisonin' grandpa, well, if I know myself, I never 'ad much of a turn for that. Live and let live: that's bin my motto throughout life, and I ain't found it a bad one."

Filled with these elevated sentiments, Mr. Chittenden retired to his lodgings. Mr. Dillet next day repaired to the local Institute, where he hoped to find some clue to the riddle that absorbed him. He gazed in despair at a long file of the Canterbury and York Society's publications of the Parish Registers of the District. No print resembling the house of his nightmare was among those that hung on the staircase and in the passages. Disconsolate, he found himself at last in a derelict room, staring at a dusty model of a church in a dusty glass case:

> Model of St. Stephen's Church, Coxham. Presented
> by J. Merewether, Esq., of Ilbridge House, 1877.
> The work of his ancestor James Merewether, d. 1786.

There was something in the fashion of it that reminded him dimly of his horror. He retraced his steps to a wall map he had noticed, and made out that Ilbridge House was in Coxham Parish. Coxham was, as it happened, one of the parishes of which he had retained the name when he glanced over the file of printed registers, and it was not long before he found in them the record of the burial of Roger Milford, aged 76, on the 11th of September, 1757, and of Roger and Elizabeth Merewether, aged 9 and 7, on the 19th of the same month. It seemed worthwhile to follow up this clue, frail as it was; and in the afternoon he drove out to Coxham. The east end of the north aisle of the church is a Milford chapel, and on its north wall are tablets to the same persons; Roger, the elder, it seems, was distinguished by all the qualities which adorn 'the Father, the Magistrate and the Man': the memorial was erected by his attached daughter Elizabeth, 'who did not long survive the loss of a parent ever solicitous for her welfare, and of two amiable children'. The last sentence was plainly an addition to the original inscription.

A yet later slab told of James Merewether, husband of Elizabeth, 'who in the dawn of life practised, not without success, those arts which, had he continued their exercise, might in the opinion of the most competent judges have earned for him the name of the British Vitruvius: but who, overwhelmed by the visitation which deprived him of an affectionate partner and a blooming offspring, passed his Prime and Age in a secluded yet elegant Retirement: his grateful Nephew and Heir indulges a pious sorrow by this too brief recital of his excellences.'

The children were more simply commemorated. Both died on the night of the 12th of September.

Mr. Dillet felt sure that in Ilbridge House he had found the scene of his drama. In some old sketchbook, possibly in some old print, he may yet find convincing evidence that he is right. But the Ilbridge House of today is not that which he sought; it is an Elizabethan erection of the forties, in red brick with stone quoins and dressings. A quarter of a mile from it, in a low part of the park, backed by ancient, staghorned, ivy-strangled trees and thick undergrowth, are marks of a terraced platform overgrown with rough grass. A few stone balusters lie here and there, and a heap or two, covered with nettles and ivy, of wrought stones with badly-carved crockets. This, someone told Mr. Dillet, was the site of an older house.

As he drove out of the village, the hall clock struck four, and Mr. Dillet started up and clapped his hands to his ears. It was not the first time he had heard that bell.

Awaiting an offer from the other side of the Atlantic, the dolls' house still reposes, carefully sheeted, in a loft over Mr. Dillet's stables, whither Collins conveyed it on the day when Mr. Dillet started for the sea coast.

# LOST HEARTS

I t was, as far as I can ascertain, in September of the year 1811 that a post-chaise drew up before the door of Aswarby Hall, in the Heart of Lincolnshire. The little boy who jumped out as soon as it had stopped, looked about him with the keenest curiosity during the short interval that elapsed between the ringing of the bell and the opening of the hall door. He saw a tall, square, red-brick house, built in the reign of Anne; a stone-pillared porch had been added in the purest classical style of 1790; the windows of the house were many, tall and narrow, with small panes and thick white woodwork. A pediment, pierced with a round window, crowned the front. There were wings to right and left, connected by curious glazed galleries, supported by colonnades, with the central block. These wings plainly contained the stables and offices of the house. Each was surmounted by an ornamental cupola with a gilded vane.

An evening light shone on the building, making the window-panes glow like so many fires. Away from the Hall in front stretched a flat park studded with oaks and fringed with firs, which stood out against the sky. The clock in the church-tower, buried in trees on the edge of the park, only its golden weather-cock catching the light, was striking six, and the sound came gently beating down the wind. It was altogether a pleasant impression, though tinged with the sort of melancholy appropriate to an evening in early autumn, that was conveyed to the mind of the boy who was standing in the porch waiting for the door to open to him.

The post-chaise had brought him from Warwickshire, where, some six months before, he had been left an orphan. Now, owing to the generous offer of his elderly cousin, Mr. Abney, he had come to live at Aswarby. The offer was unexpected, because all who knew anything of

Mr. Abney looked upon him as a somewhat austere recluse, into whose steady-going household the advent of a small boy would import a new and, it seemed, incongruous element. The truth is that very little was known of Mr. Abney's pursuits or temper. The Professor of Greek at Cambridge had been heard to say that no one knew more of the religious beliefs of the later pagans than did the owner of Aswarby. Certainly his library contained all the then available books bearing on the Mysteries, the Orphic poems, the worship of Mithras, and the Neo-Platonists. In the marble-paved hall stood a fine group of Mithras slaying a bull, which had been imported from the Levant at great expense by the owner. He had contributed a description of it to the *Gentleman's Magazine*, and he had written a remarkable series of articles in the *Critical Museum* on the superstitions of the Romans of the Lower Empire. He was looked upon, in fine, as a man wrapped up in his books, and it was a matter of great surprise among his neighbours that he should even have heard of his cousin, Stephen Elliot, much more that he should have volunteered to make him an inmate of Aswarby Hall.

Whatever may have been expected by his neighbours, it is certain that Mr. Abney – the tall, the thin, the austere – seemed inclined to give his young cousin a kindly reception. The moment the front door was opened he darted out of his study, rubbing his hands with delight.

"How are you, my boy? – how are you? How old are you?" said he – "that is, you are not too much tired, I hope, by your journey to eat your supper?"

"No, thank you, sir," said Master Elliot; "I am pretty well."

"That's a good lad," said Mr. Abney. "And how old are you, my boy?"

It seemed a little odd that he should have asked the question twice in the first two minutes of their acquaintance.

"I'm twelve years old next birthday, sir," said Stephen.

"And when is your birthday, my dear boy? Eleventh of September, eh? That's well – that's very well. Nearly a year hence, isn't it? I like – ha, ha! – I like to get these things down in my book. Sure it's twelve? Certain?"

"Yes, quite sure, Sir."

"Well, Well! Take him to Mrs. Bunch's room, Parkes, and let him have his tea – supper – whatever it is."

"Yes, sir," answered the staid Mr. Parkes: and conducted Stephen to the lower regions.

Mrs. Bunch was the most comfortable and human person whom Stephen had as yet met in Aswarby. She made him completely at home: they were great friends in a quarter of an hour: and great friends they remained. Mrs. Bunch had been born in the neighbourhood some fifty-five years before the date of Stephen's arrival, and her residence at the Hall was of twenty years standing. Consequently, if anyone knew the ins and outs of the house and the district, Mrs. Bunch knew them; and she was by no means disinclined to communicate her information.

Certainly there were plenty of things about the Hall and the Hall gardens which Stephen, who was of an adventurous and enquiring turn, was anxious to have explained to him. Who built the temple at the end of the laurel walk? Who was the old man whose picture hung on the staircase, sitting at a table, with a skull under his hand? These and many similar points were cleared up by the resources of Mrs. Bunch's powerful intellect. There were others, however, of which the explanations furnished were less satisfactory.

One November evening Stephen was sitting by the fire in the housekeeper's room reflecting on his surroundings.

"Is Mr. Abney a good man, and will he go to heaven?" he suddenly asked, with the peculiar confidence which children possess in the ability of their elders to settle these questions, the decision of which is believed to be reserved for other tribunals.

"Good? – bless the child!" said Mrs. Bunch. "Master's as kind a soul as ever I see! Didn't I never tell you of the little boy as he took in out of the street, as you may say, this seven years back? and the little girl, two years after I first come here?"

"No. Do tell me all about them, Mrs. Bunch – now this minute!"

"Well," said Mrs. Bunch, "the little girl I don't seem to recollect so much about. I know master brought her back with him from his walk one day, and give orders to Mrs. Ellis, as was housekeeper then, as she should be took every care with. And the pore child hadn't no one belonging to her – she told me so her own self – and here she lived with us a matter of three weeks it might be; and then, whether she were somethink of a gipsy in her blood or what not, but one morning she out of her bed afore any of us had opened a eye, and neither track nor yet trace of her have I set eyes on since. Master was wonderful put about, and had all the ponds dragged; but it's my belief she was had away by them gypsies, for there was singing round the house for as much as an hour the night she went, and Parkes, he declares he heard them a-calling in the woods all that afternoon. Dear, dear! a hodd child she was, so silent in her ways and all, but I was wonderful taken up with her, so domesticated she was – surprising."

"And what about the little boy?" said Stephen.

"Ah, that poor boy!" sighed Mrs. Bunch. "He were a foreigner – Jevanny he called himself – and he come a-tweakin' his hurdy-gurdy round and about the drive one winter day, and master 'ad him in that minute, and ast all about where he came from, and how old he was, and how he made his way, and where was his relatives, and all as kind as heart could wish. But it went the same way with him. They're a hunruly lot, them foreign nations, I do suppose, and he was off one fine morning just the same as the girl. Why he went and what he done was our question for as much as a year after; for he never took his 'urdy-gurdy, and there it lays on the shelf."

The remainder of the evening was spent by Stephen in miscellaneous cross-examination of Mrs. Bunch and in efforts to extract a tune from the hurdy-gurdy.

That night he had a curious dream. At the end of the passage at the top of the house, in which his bedroom was situated, there was an old disused bathroom. It was kept locked, but the upper half of the door was glazed, and, since the muslin curtains which used to hang there had long been gone, you could look in and see the lead-lined bath affixed to the wall on the right hand, with its head towards the window. On the night of which I am speaking, Stephen Elliot found himself, as he thought, looking through the glazed door. The moon was shining through the window, and he was gazing at a figure which lay in the bath.

His description of what he saw reminds me of what I once beheld myself in the famous vaults of St. Michan's Church in Dublin, which possess the horrid property of preserving corpses from decay for centuries. A figure inexpressibly thin and pathetic, of a dusty leaden colour, enveloped in a shroud-like garment, the thin lips crooked into a faint and dreadful smile, the hands pressed tightly over the region of the heart.

As he looked upon it, a distant, almost inaudible moan seemed to issue from its lips, and the arms began to stir. The terror of the sight forced Stephen backwards, and he awoke to the fact that he was indeed standing on the cold boarded floor of the passage in the full light of the moon. With a courage which I do not think can be common among boys of his age, he went to the door of the bathroom to ascertain if the figure of his dream were really there. It was not, and he went back to bed.

Mrs. Bunch was much impressed next morning by his story, and went so far as to replace the muslin curtain over the glazed door of the bathroom. Mr. Abney, moreover, to whom he confided his experiences at breakfast, was greatly interested, and made notes of the matter in what he called 'his book'.

The spring equinox was approaching, as Mr. Abney frequently reminded his cousin, adding that this had been always considered by the ancients to be a critical time for the young: that Stephen would do well to take care of himself, and shut his bedroom window at night; and that Censorinus had some valuable remarks on the subject. Two incidents that occurred about this time made an impression upon Stephen's mind.

The first was after an unusually uneasy and oppressed night that he had passed – though he could not recall any particular dream that he had had.

The following evening Mrs. Bunch was occupying herself in mending his nightgown.

"Gracious me, Master Stephen!" she broke forth rather irritably, "how do you manage to tear your nightdress all to flinders this way? Look here, sir, what trouble you do give to poor servants that have to darn and mend after you!"

There was indeed a most destructive and apparently wanton series of slits or scorings in the garment, which would undoubtedly require a skilful needle to make good. They were confined to the left side of the chest – long, parallel slits, about six inches in length, some of them not quite piercing the texture of the linen. Stephen could only express his entire ignorance of their origin: he was sure that they were not there the night before.

"But," he said, "Mrs. Bunch, they are just the same as the scratches on the outside of my bedroom door; and I'm sure I never had anything to do with making them."

Mrs. Bunch gazed at him open-mouthed, then snatched up a candle, departed hastily from the room, and was heard making her way upstairs. In a few minutes she came down.

"Well," she said, "Master Stephen, it's a funny thing to me how them marks and scratches can 'a' come there – too high up for any cat or dog to 'ave made 'em, much less a rat; for all the world like a Chinaman's finger-nails, as my uncle in the tea-trade used to tell us of when we was girls together. I wouldn't say nothing to master, not if I was you, Master Stephen, my dear; and just turn the key of your door when you go to your bed."

"I always do, Mrs. Bunch, as soon as I've said my prayers."

"Ah, that's a good child: always say your prayers, and then no one can't hurt you."

Herewith Mrs. Bunch addressed herself to mending the injured nightgown, with intervals of meditation, until bed-time. This was on a Friday night in March, 1812.

On the following evening the usual duet of Stephen and Mrs. Bunch was augmented by the sudden arrival of Mr. Parkes, the butler, who as a rule kept himself rather to himself in the pantry. He did not see that Stephen was there: he was, moreover, flustered, and less slow of speech than was his wont.

"Master may get up his own wine, if he likes, of an evening," was his first remark. "Either I do it in the daytime or not at all, Mrs. Bunch. I don't know what it may be: very like it's the rats, or the wind got into the cellars; but I'm not as young as I was, and I can't go through with it as I have done."

"Well, Mr. Parkes, you know it is a surprising place for the rats, is the Hall."

"I'm not denying that, Mrs. Bunch; and to be sure, many a time I've heard the tale from the men in the shipyards about the rat that could speak. I never laid no confidence in that before; but tonight, if I'd demeaned myself to lay my ear to the door of the further bin, I could pretty much have heard what they was saying."

"Oh, there, Mr. Parkes, I've no patience with your fancies! Rats talking in the wine-cellar indeed!"

"Well, Mrs. Bunch, I've no wish to argue with you: all I say is, if you choose to go to the far bin, and lay your ear to the door, you may prove my words this minute."

"What nonsense you do talk, Mr. Parkes – not fit for children to listen to! Why, you'll be frightening Master Stephen there out of his wits."

"What! Master Stephen?" said Parkes, awaking to the consciousness of the boy's presence. "Master Stephen knows well enough when I'm a-playing a joke with you, Mrs. Bunch."

In fact, Stephen knew much too well to suppose that Mr. Parkes had in the first instance intended a joke. He was interested, not altogether pleasantly, in the situation; but all his questions were unsuccessful in inducing the butler to give any more detailed account of his experiences in the wine-cellar.

★ ★ ★

We have now arrived at March 24, 1812. It was a day of curious experiences for Stephen: a windy, noisy day, which filled the house and the gardens with a restless impression. As Stephen stood by the fence of the grounds, and looked out into the park, he felt as if an endless procession of unseen people were sweeping past him on the wind, borne on restlessly and aimlessly, vainly striving to stop themselves, to catch at something that might arrest their flight and bring them once again into contact with the living world of which they had formed a part. After luncheon that day Mr. Abney said:

"Stephen, my boy, do you think you could manage to come to me tonight as late as eleven o'clock in my study? I shall be busy until that time, and I wish to show you something connected with your future life which it is most important that you should know. You are not to mention this matter to Mrs. Bunch nor to anyone else in the house; and you had better go to your room at the usual time."

Here was a new excitement added to life; Stephen eagerly grasped at the opportunity of sitting up till eleven o'clock. He looked in at the library door on his way upstairs that evening, and saw a brazier, which he had often noticed in the corner of the room, moved out before the fire; an old silver-gilt cup stood on the table, filled with red wine, and some written sheets of paper lay near it. Mr. Abney was sprinkling some incense on the brazier from a round silver box as Stephen passed, but did not seem to notice his step.

The wind had fallen, and there was a still night and a full moon. At about ten o'clock Stephen was standing at the open window of his bedroom, looking out over the country. Still as the night was, the mysterious population of the distant moonlit woods was not yet lulled to rest. From time to time strange cries as of lost and despairing wanderers sounded from across the mere. They might be the notes of owls or water-birds, yet they did not quite resemble either sound. Were not they coming nearer? Now they sounded from the nearer side of the water, and in a few moments they seemed to be floating about among the shrubberies. Then they ceased; but just as Stephen was thinking of shutting the window and resuming his reading of *Robinson Crusoe*, he caught sight of two figures standing on the gravelled terrace that ran along the garden side of the Hall – the figures of a boy and girl, as it seemed; they stood side by side, looking up at the windows. Something in the form of the girl recalled irresistibly his dream of the figure in the bath. The boy inspired him with more acute fear.

Whilst the girl stood still, half smiling, with her hands clasped over her heart, the boy, a thin shape, with black hair and ragged clothing, raised his arms in the air with an appearance of menace and of unappeasable hunger and longing. The moon shone upon his almost transparent hands, and Stephen saw that the nails were fearfully long and that the light shone through them. As he stood with his arms thus raised, he disclosed a terrifying spectacle. On the left side of his chest there opened a black and gaping rent; and there fell upon Stephen's brain, rather than upon his ear, the impression of one of those hungry and desolate cries that he had heard resounding over the woods of Aswarby all that evening. In another moment this dreadful pair had moved swiftly and noiselessly over the dry grass and he saw them no more.

Inexpressibly frightened as he was, he determined to take his candle and go down to Mr. Abney's study, for the hour appointed for their meeting was near at hand. The study or library opened out of the front hall on one side, and Stephen, urged on by his terrors, did not take long in getting there. To effect an entrance was not so easy. The door was not locked, he felt sure, for the key was on the outside of it as usual. His repeated knocks produced no answer. Mr. Abney was engaged: he was speaking. What! why did he try to cry out? and why was the cry choked in his throat? Had, he, too, seen the mysterious children? But now everything was quiet, and the door yielded to Stephen's terrified and frantic pushing.

★   ★   ★

On the table in Mr. Abney's study certain papers were found which explained the situation to Stephen Elliot when he was of an age to understand them. The most important sentences were as follows:

> *It was a belief very strongly and generally held by the ancients – of whose wisdom in these matters I have had such experience as induces me to place*

confidence in their assertions – that by enacting certain processes, which to us moderns have something of a barbaric complexion, a very remarkable enlightenment of the spiritual faculties in man may be attained: that, for example, by absorbing the personalities of a certain number of his fellow-creatures, an individual may gain a complete ascendancy over those orders of spiritual beings which control the elemental forces of our universe.

It is recorded of Simon Magus that he was able to fly in the air, to become invisible, or to assume any form he pleased, by the agency of the soul of a boy whom, to use the libellous phrase employed by the author of the Clementine Recognitions, he had 'murdered'. I find it set down, moreover, with considerable detail in the writings of Hermes Trismegistus, that similar happy results may be produced by the absorption of the hearts of not less than three human beings below the age of twenty-one years. To the testing of the truth of this receipt I have devoted the greater part of the last twenty years, selecting as the corpora vilia of my experiment such persons as could conveniently be removed without occasioning a sensible gap in society. The first step I effected by the removal of one Phoebe Stanley, a girl of gipsy extraction, on March 24, 1792. The second, by the removal of a wandering Italian lad, named Giovanni Paoli, on the night of March 23, 1805. The final 'victim' – to employ a word repugnant in the highest degree to my feelings – must be my cousin, Stephen Elliott. His day must be this March 24, 1812.

The best means of effecting the required absorption is to remove the heart from the living subject, to reduce it to ashes, and to mingle them with about a pint of red wine, preferably port. The remains of the first two subjects, at least, it will be well to conceal: a disused bathroom or wine-cellar will be found convenient for such a purpose. Some annoyance may be experienced from the psychic portion of the subjects, which popular language dignifies with the name of ghosts. But the man of philosophic temperament – to whom alone the experiment is appropriate – will be little prone to attach importance to the feeble efforts of these beings to wreak their vengeance on him. I contemplate with the liveliest satisfaction the enlarged and emancipated existence which the experiment, if successful, will confer on me; not only placing me beyond the reach of human justice (so-called) but eliminating to a great extent the prospect of death itself.

★　　★　　★

Mr. Abney was found in his chair, his head thrown back, his face stamped with an expression of rage, fright and mortal pain. In his left side was a terrible lacerated wound, exposing the heart. There was no blood on his hands, and a long knife that lay on the table was perfectly clean. A savage wild-cat might have inflicted the injuries. The window of the study was open, and it was the opinion of the coroner that Mr. Abney had met his death by the agency of some wild creature. But Stephen Elliot's study of the papers I have quoted led him to a very different conclusion.

# THE MALICE OF INANIMATE OBJECTS

The Malice of Inanimate Objects is a subject upon which an old friend of mine was fond of dilating, and not without justification. In the lives of all of us, short or long, there have been days, dreadful days, on which we have had to acknowledge with gloomy resignation that our world has turned against us. I do not mean the human world of our relations and friends: to enlarge on that is the province of nearly every modern novelist. In their books it is called 'Life' and an odd enough harsh it is as they portray it. No, it is the world of things that do not speak or work or hold congresses and conferences. It includes such beings as the collar stud, the inkstand, the fire, the razor, and, as age increases, the extra step on the staircase which leads you either to expect or not to expect it. By these and such as these (for I have named but the merest fraction of them) the word is passed round, and the day of misery arranged. Is the tale still remembered of how the Cock and Hen went to pay a visit to Squire Korbes? How on the journey they met with and picked up a number of associates, encouraging each with the announcement:

*To Squire Korbes we are going*
*For a visit is owing.*

Thus they secured the company of the Needle, the Egg, the Duck, the Cat, possibly – for memory is a little treacherous here – and finally the Millstone: and when it was discovered that Squire Korbes was for the moment out, they took up positions in his mansion and awaited his return. He did return, wearied no doubt by a day's work among his extensive properties. His nerves were first jarred by the raucous cry of the Cock. He threw himself into his armchair and was lacerated by the Needle. He went to the sink for a refreshing wash and was splashed all over by the Duck. Attempting to dry himself with the towel he broke the Egg upon his face.

He suffered other indignities from the Hen and her accomplices, which I cannot now recollect, and finally, maddened with pain and fear, rushed out by the back door and had his brains dashed out by the Millstone that had perched itself in the appropriate place. 'Truly,' in the concluding words of the story, 'this Squire Korbes must have been either a very wicked or a very unfortunate man.' It is the latter alternative which I incline to accept. There is nothing in the preliminaries to show that any slur rested on his name, or that his visitors had any injury to avenge. And will not this narrative serve as a striking example of that Malice of which I have taken upon me to treat? It is, I know, the fact that Squire Korbes's visitors were not all of them, strictly speaking, inanimate. But are we sure that the perpetrators of this Malice are really inanimate either? There are tales which seem to justify a doubt.

Two men of mature years were seated in a pleasant garden after breakfast. One was reading the day's paper, the other sat with folded arms, plunged in thought, and on his face were a piece of sticking plaster and lines of care. His companion lowered his paper. "What," said he, "is the matter with you? The morning is bright, the birds are singing, I can hear no aeroplanes or motor bikes."

"No," replied Mr. Burton, "it is nice enough, I agree, but I have a bad day before me. I cut myself shaving and spilt my tooth powder."

"Ah," said Mr. Manners, "some people have all the luck," and with this expression of sympathy he reverted to his paper. "Hullo," he exclaimed, after a moment, "here's George Wilkins dead! You won't have any more bother with him, anyhow."

"George Wilkins?" said Mr. Burton, more than a little excitedly, "Why, I didn't even know he was ill."

"No more he was, poor chap. Seems to have thrown up the sponge and put an end to himself. Yes," he went on, "it's some days back: this is the inquest. Seemed very much worried and depressed, they say. What about, I wonder? Could it have been that will you and he were having a row about?"

"Row?" said Mr. Burton angrily, "there was no row: he hadn't a leg to stand on: he couldn't bring a scrap of evidence. No, it may have been half-a-dozen things: but Lord! I never imagined he'd take anything so hard as that."

"I don't know," said Mr. Manners, "he was a man, I thought, who did take things hard: they rankled. Well, I'm sorry, though I never saw much of him. He must have gone through a lot to make him cut his throat. Not the way I should choose, by a long sight. Ugh! Lucky he hadn't a family, anyhow. Look here, what about a walk round before lunch? I've an errand in the village."

Mr. Burton assented rather heavily. He was perhaps reluctant to give the inanimate objects of the district a chance of getting at him. If so, he was right. He just escaped a nasty purl over the scraper at the top of the steps: a thorny branch swept off his hat and scratched his fingers, and as they climbed a grassy slope he fairly leapt into the air with a cry and came down flat on his face. "What in the world?" said his friend coming up. "A great string, of all things! What business – Oh, I see – belongs to that kite" (which lay on the grass a little farther up). "Now if I can find out what little beast has left that kicking about, I'll let him have it – or rather I won't, for he shan't see his kite again. It's rather a good one, too." As they approached, a puff of wind raised the kite and it seemed to sit up on its end and look at them with two large round eyes painted red, and, below them, three large printed red letters, I.C.U. Mr. Manners was amused and scanned the device with care. "Ingenious," he said, "it's a bit off a poster, of course: I see! Full Particulars, the word was." Mr. Burton on the other hand was not amused, but thrust his stick through the kite. Mr. Manners was inclined to regret this. "I dare say it serves him right," he said, "but he'd taken a lot of trouble to make it."

"Who had?" said Mr. Burton sharply. "Oh, I see, you mean the boy."

"Yes, to be sure, who else? But come on down now: I want to leave a message before lunch." As they turned a corner into the main street, a rather muffled and choky voice was heard to say "Look out! I'm coming." They both stopped as if they had been shot.

"Who was that?" said Manners. "Blest if I didn't think I knew" – then, with almost a yell of laughter he pointed with his stick. A cage with a grey parrot in it was hanging in an open window across the way. "I was startled, by George: it gave you a bit of a turn, too, didn't it?" Burton was inaudible. "Well, I shan't be a minute: you can go and make friends with the bird." But when he rejoined Burton, that unfortunate was not, it seemed, in trim for talking with either birds or men; he was some way ahead and going rather quickly. Manners paused for an instant at the parrot window and then hurried on laughing more than ever. "Have a good talk with Polly?" said he, as he came up.

"No, of course not," said Burton, testily. "I didn't bother about the beastly thing."

"Well, you wouldn't have got much out of her if you'd tried," said Manners. "I remembered after a bit; they've had her in the window for years: she's stuffed." Burton seemed about to make a remark, but suppressed it.

Decidedly this was not Burton's day out. He choked at lunch, he broke a pipe, he tripped in the carpet, he dropped his book in the pond in the garden. Later on he had or professed to have a telephone call summoning him back to town next day and cutting short what should have been a week's visit. And so glum was he all the evening that Manners' disappointment in losing an ordinarily cheerful companion was not very sharp.

At breakfast Mr. Burton said little about his night: but he did intimate that he thought of looking in on his doctor. "My hand's so shaky," he said, "I really daren't shave this morning."

"Oh, I'm sorry," said Mr. Manners, "my man could have managed that for you: but they'll put you right in no time."

Farewells were said. By some means and for some reason Mr. Burton contrived to reserve a compartment to himself. (The train was not of the corridor type.) But these precautions avail little against the angry dead.

I will not put dots or stars, for I dislike them, but I will say that apparently someone tried to shave Mr. Burton in the train, and did not succeed overly well. He was however satisfied with what he had done, if we may judge from the fact that on a once white napkin spread on Mr. Burton's chest was an inscription in red letters: GEO. W. FECI.

Do not these facts – if facts they are – bear out my suggestion that there is something not inanimate behind the Malice of Inanimate Objects? Do they not further suggest that when this malice begins to show itself we should be very particular to examine and if possible rectify any obliquities in our recent conduct? And do they not, finally, almost force upon us the conclusion that, like Squire Korbes, Mr. Burton must have been either a very wicked or a singularly unfortunate man?

# RATS

*"And if you was to walk through the bedrooms now, you'd see the ragged,*
*mouldy bed-clothes a-heaving and a-heaving like seas."*
*"And a-heaving and a-heaving with what?" he says.*
*"Why, with the rats under 'em."*

ut was it with the rats? I ask, because in another case it was not.
I cannot put a date to the story, but I was young when I heard it,
and the teller was old. It is an ill-proportioned tale, but that is my
fault, not his.

It happened in Suffolk, near the coast. In a place where the road makes
a sudden dip and then a sudden rise; as you go northward, at the top of
that rise, stands a house on the left of the road. It is a tall red-brick house,
narrow for its height; perhaps it was built about 1770. The top of the front
has a low triangular pediment with a round window in the centre. Behind
it are stables and offices, and such garden as it has is behind them. Scraggy
Scotch firs are near it: an expanse of gorse-covered land stretches away
from it. It commands a view of the distant sea from the upper windows
of the front. A sign on a post stands before the door; or did so stand, for
though it was an inn of repute once, I believe it is so no longer.

To this inn came my acquaintance, Mr. Thomson, when he was
a young man, on a fine spring day, coming from the University of
Cambridge, and desirous of solitude in tolerable quarters and time for
reading. These he found, for the landlord and his wife had been in
service and could make a visitor comfortable, and there was no one else
staying in the inn. He had a large room on the first floor commanding
the road and the view, and if it faced east, why, that could not be helped;
the house was well built and warm.

He spent very tranquil and uneventful days: work all the morning, an afternoon perambulation of the country round, a little conversation with country company or the people of the inn in the evening over the then fashionable drink of brandy and water, a little more reading and writing, and bed; and he would have been content that this should continue for the full month he had at disposal, so well was his work progressing, and so fine was the April of that year – which I have reason to believe was that which Orlando Whistlecraft chronicles in his weather record as the 'Charming Year'.

One of his walks took him along the northern road, which stands high and traverses a wide common, called a heath. On the bright afternoon when he first chose this direction his eye caught a white object some hundreds of yards to the left of the road, and he felt it necessary to make sure what this might be. It was not long before he was standing by it, and found himself looking at a square block of white stone fashioned somewhat like the base of a pillar, with a square hole in the upper surface. Just such another you may see at this day on Thetford Heath. After taking stock of it he contemplated for a few minutes the view, which offered a church tower or two, some red roofs of cottages and windows winking in the sun, and the expanse of sea – also with an occasional wink and gleam upon it – and so pursued his way.

In the desultory evening talk in the bar, he asked why the white stone was there on the common.

"A old-fashioned thing, that is," said the landlord (Mr. Betts), "we was none of us alive when that was put there." "That's right," said another. "It stands pretty high," said Mr. Thomson, "I dare say a sea-mark was on it some time back." "Ah! yes," Mr. Betts agreed, "I 'ave 'eard they could see it from the boats; but whatever there was, it's fell to bits this long time." "Good job too," said a third, "'twarn't a lucky mark, by what the old men used to say; not lucky for the fishin', I mean to say." "Why ever not?" said Thomson. "Well, I never see it myself," was the answer, "but they 'ad some funny ideas, what I mean, peculiar, them old chaps, and I shouldn't wonder but what they made away with it theirselves."

It was impossible to get anything clearer than this: the company, never very voluble, fell silent, and when next someone spoke it was of village affairs and crops. Mr. Betts was the speaker.

Not every day did Thomson consult his health by taking a country walk. One very fine afternoon found him busily writing at three o'clock. Then he stretched himself and rose, and walked out of his room into the passage. Facing him was another room, then the stair-head, then two more rooms, one looking out to the back, the other to the south. At the south end of the passage was a window, to which he went, considering with himself that it was rather a shame to waste such a fine afternoon. However, work was paramount just at the moment; he thought he would just take five minutes off and go back to it, and those five minutes he would employ – the Bettses could not possibly object – to looking at the other rooms in the passage, which he had never seen. Nobody at all, it seemed, was indoors; probably, as it was market day, they were all gone to the town, except perhaps a maid in the bar. Very still the house was, and the sun shone really hot; early flies buzzed in the window-panes. So he explored. The room facing his own was undistinguished except for an old print of Bury St. Edmunds; the two next him on his side of the passage were gay and clean, with one window apiece, whereas his had two. Remained the south-west room, opposite to the last which he had entered. This was locked; but Thomson was in a mood of quite indefensible curiosity, and feeling confident that there could be no damaging secrets in a place so easily got at, he proceeded to fetch the key of his own room, and when that did not answer, to collect the keys of the other three. One of them fitted, and he opened the door. The room had two windows looking south and west, so it was as bright and the sun as hot upon it as could be. Here there was no carpet, but bare boards; no pictures, no washing-stand, only a bed, in the farther corner: an iron bed, with mattress and bolster, covered with a bluish check counterpane. As featureless a room as you can well imagine, and yet there was something that made Thomson close the door very quickly and yet quietly behind him and lean against the window-sill in the passage, actually quivering all over.

It was this, that under the counterpane someone lay, and not only lay, but stirred. That it was some *one* and not some *thing* was certain, because the shape of a head was unmistakable on the bolster; and yet it was all covered, and no one lies with covered head but a dead person; and this was not dead, not truly dead, for it heaved and shivered. If he had seen these things in dusk or by the light of a flickering candle, Thomson could have comforted himself and talked of fancy. On this bright day that was impossible. What was to be done? First, lock the door at all costs. Very gingerly he approached it and bending down listened, holding his breath; perhaps there might be a sound of heavy breathing, and a prosaic explanation. There was absolute silence. But as, with a rather tremulous hand, he put the key into its hole and turned it, it rattled, and on the instant a stumbling padding tread was heard coming towards the door. Thomson fled like a rabbit to his room and locked himself in: futile enough, he knew it was; would doors and locks be any obstacle to what he suspected? but it was all he could think of at the moment, and in fact nothing happened; only there was a time of acute suspense – followed by a misery of doubt as to what to do. The impulse, of course, was to slip away as soon as possible from a house which contained such an inmate. But only the day before he had said he should be staying for at least a week more, and how if he changed plans could he avoid the suspicion of having pried into places where he certainly had no business? Moreover, either the Bettses knew all about the inmate, and yet did not leave the house, or knew nothing, which equally meant that there was nothing to be afraid of, or knew just enough to make them shut up the room, but not enough to weigh on their spirits: in any of these cases it seemed that not much was to be feared, and certainly so far he had had no sort of ugly experience. On the whole the line of least resistance was to stay.

Well, he stayed out his week. Nothing took him past that door, and, often as he would pause in a quiet hour of day or night in the passage and listen, and listen, no sound whatever issued from that direction. You might have thought that Thomson would have made some attempt at ferreting out stories connected with the inn – hardly perhaps from Betts, but from the parson of the parish, or old people in the village; but no, the reticence which commonly falls on people who have had strange experiences, and believe in them, was upon him. Nevertheless, as the end of his stay drew near, his yearning after some kind of explanation grew more and more acute. On his solitary walks he persisted in planning out some way, the least obtrusive, of getting another daylight glimpse into that room, and eventually arrived at this scheme. He would leave by an afternoon train – about four o'clock. When his fly was waiting, and his luggage on it, he would make one last expedition upstairs to look round his own room and see if anything was left unpacked, and then, with that key, which he had contrived to oil (as if that made any difference!), the door should once more be opened, for a moment, and shut.

So it worked out. The bill was paid, the consequent small talk gone through while the fly was loaded: "pleasant part of the country – been very comfortable, thanks to you and Mrs. Betts – hope to come back some time," on one side: on the other, "very glad you've found satisfaction, sir, done our best – always glad to 'ave your good word – very much favoured we've been with the weather, to be sure." Then, "I'll just take a look upstairs in case I've left a book or something out – no, don't trouble, I'll be back in a minute." And as noiselessly as possible he stole to the door and opened it. The shattering of the illusion! He almost laughed aloud. Propped, or you might say sitting, on the edge of the bed was – nothing in the round world but a scarecrow! A scarecrow out of the garden, of course, dumped into the deserted room.... Yes; but here amusement ceased. Have scarecrows bare bony feet? Do their heads loll on to their shoulders? Have they iron collars and links of chain about their necks? Can they get up and move, if never so stiffly, across a floor, with wagging head and arms close at their sides? and shiver?

The slam of the door, the dash to the stair-head, the leap downstairs, were followed by a faint. Awaking, Thomson saw Betts standing over him with the brandy bottle and a very reproachful face. "You shouldn't a done so, sir, really you shouldn't. It ain't a kind way to act by persons as done the best they could for you." Thomson heard words of this kind, but what he said in reply he did not know. Mr. Betts, and perhaps even more Mrs. Betts, found it hard to accept his apologies and his assurances that he would say no word that could damage the good name of the house. However, they *were* accepted. Since the train could not now be caught, it was arranged that Thomson should be driven to the town to sleep there. Before he went the Bettses told him what little they knew. "They says he was landlord 'ere a long time back, and was in with the 'ighwaymen that 'ad their beat about the 'eath. That's how he come by his end: 'ung in chains, they say, up where you see that stone what the gallus stood in. Yes, the fishermen made away with that, I believe, because they see it out at sea and it kep' the fish off, according to their idea. Yes, we 'ad the account from the people that 'ad the 'ouse before we come. 'You keep that room shut up,' they says, 'but don't move the bed out, and you'll find there won't be no trouble.' And no more there 'as been; not once he haven't come out into the 'ouse, though what he may do now there ain't no sayin'. Anyway, you're the first I know on that's seen him since we've been 'ere: I never set eyes on him myself, nor don't want. And ever since we've made the servants' rooms in the stablin', we ain't 'ad no difficulty that way. Only I do 'ope, sir, as you'll keep a close tongue, considerin' 'ow an 'ouse do get talked about": with more to this effect.

The promise of silence was kept for many years. The occasion of my hearing the story at last was this: that when Mr. Thomson came to stay with my father it fell to me to show him to his room, and instead of letting me open the door for him, he stepped forward and threw it open himself, and then for some moments stood in the doorway holding up his candle and looking narrowly into the interior. Then he seemed to recollect himself and said: "I beg your pardon. Very absurd, but I can't help doing that, for a particular reason." What that reason was I heard some days afterwards, and you have heard now.

# THE ROSE GARDEN

M r. and Mrs. Anstruther were at breakfast in the parlour of Westfield Hall, in the county of Essex. They were arranging plans for the day.

"George," said Mrs. Anstruther, "I think you had better take the car to Maldon and see if you can get any of those knitted things I was speaking about which would do for my stall at the bazaar."

"Oh well, if you wish it, Mary, of course I can do that, but I had half arranged to play a round with Geoffrey Williamson this morning. The bazaar isn't till Thursday of next week, is it?"

"What has that to do with it, George? I should have thought you would have guessed that if I can't get the things I want in Maldon I shall have to write to all manner of shops in town: and they are certain to send something quite unsuitable in price or quality the first time. If you have actually made an appointment with Mr. Williamson, you had better keep it, but I must say I think you might have let me know."

"Oh no, no, it wasn't really an appointment. I quite see what you mean. I'll go. And what shall you do yourself?"

"Why, when the work of the house is arranged for, I must see about laying out my new rose garden. By the way, before you start for Maldon I wish you would just take Collins to look at the place I fixed upon. You know it, of course."

"Well, I'm not quite sure that I do, Mary. Is it at the upper end, towards the village?"

"Good gracious no, my dear George; I thought I had made that quite clear. No, it's that small clearing just off the shrubbery path that goes towards the church."

"Oh yes, where we were saying there must have been a summer-house once: the place with the old seat and the posts. But do you think there's enough sun there?"

"My dear George, do allow me *some* common sense, and don't credit me with all your ideas about summer-houses. Yes, there will be plenty of sun when we have got rid of some of those box-bushes. I know what you are going to say, and I have as little wish as you to strip the place bare. All I want Collins to do is to clear away the old seats and the posts and things before I come out in an hour's time. And I hope you will manage to get off fairly soon. After luncheon I think I shall go on with my sketch of the church; and if you please you can go over to the links, or—"

"Ah, a good idea – very good! Yes, you finish that sketch, Mary, and I should be glad of a round."

"I was going to say, you might call on the Bishop; but I suppose it is no use my making *any* suggestion. And now do be getting ready, or half the morning will be gone."

Mr. Anstruther's face, which had shown symptoms of lengthening, shortened itself again, and he hurried from the room, and was soon heard giving orders in the passage. Mrs. Anstruther, a stately dame of some fifty summers, proceeded, after a second consideration of the morning's letters, to her housekeeping.

Within a few minutes Mr. Anstruther had discovered Collins in the greenhouse, and they were on their way to the site of the projected rose garden. I do not know much about the conditions most suitable to these nurseries, but I am inclined to believe that Mrs. Anstruther, though in the habit of describing herself as 'a great gardener', had not been well advised in the selection of a spot for the purpose. It was a small, dank clearing, bounded on one side by a path, and on the other by thick box-bushes, laurels, and other evergreens. The ground was almost bare of grass and dark of aspect. Remains of rustic seats and an old and corrugated oak post somewhere near the middle of the clearing had given rise to Mr. Anstruther's conjecture that a summer-house had once stood there.

Clearly Collins had not been put in possession of his mistress's intentions with regard to this plot of ground: and when he learnt them from Mr. Anstruther he displayed no enthusiasm.

"Of course I could clear them seats away soon enough," he said. "They aren't no ornament to the place, Mr. Anstruther, and rotten too. Look 'ere, sir," – and he broke off a large piece – "rotten right through. Yes, clear them away, to be sure we can do that."

"And the post," said Mr. Anstruther, "that's got to go too."

Collins advanced, and shook the post with both hands: then he rubbed his chin.

"That's firm in the ground, that post is," he said. "That's been there a number of years, Mr. Anstruther. I doubt I shan't get that up not quite so soon as what I can do with them seats."

"But your mistress specially wishes it to be got out of the way in an hour's time," said Mr. Anstruther.

Collins smiled and shook his head slowly. "You'll excuse me, sir, but you feel of it for yourself. No, sir, no one can't do what's impossible to 'em, can they, sir? I could git that post up by after tea-time, sir, but that'll want a lot of digging. What you require, you see, sir, if you'll excuse me naming of it, you want the soil loosening round this post 'ere, and me and the boy we shall take a little time doing of that. But now, these 'ere seats," said Collins, appearing to appropriate this portion of the scheme as due to his own resourcefulness, "why, I can get the barrer round and 'ave them cleared away in, why less than an hour's time from now, if you'll permit of it. Only—"

"Only what, Collins?"

"Well now, it ain't for me to go against orders no more than what it is for you yourself – or anyone else" (this was added somewhat hurriedly), "but if you'll pardon me, sir, this ain't the place I should have picked out for no rose garden myself. Why look at them box and laurestinus, 'ow they reg'lar preclude the light from—"

"Ah yes, but we've got to get rid of some of them, of course."

"Oh, indeed, get rid of them! Yes, to be sure, but – I beg your pardon, Mr. Anstruther—"

"I'm sorry, Collins, but I must be getting on now. I hear the car at the door. Your mistress will explain exactly what she wishes. I'll tell her, then, that you can see your way to clearing away the seats at once, and the post this afternoon. Good morning."

Collins was left rubbing his chin. Mrs. Anstruther received the report with some discontent, but did not insist upon any change of plan.

By four o'clock that afternoon she had dismissed her husband to his golf, had dealt faithfully with Collins and with the other duties of the day, and, having sent a campstool and umbrella to the proper spot, had just settled down to her sketch of the church as seen from the shrubbery, when a maid came hurrying down the path to report that Miss Wilkins had called.

Miss Wilkins was one of the few remaining members of the family from whom the Anstruthers had bought the Westfield estate some few years back. She had been staying in the neighbourhood, and this was probably a farewell visit. "Perhaps you could ask Miss Wilkins to join me here," said Mrs. Anstruther, and soon Miss Wilkins, a person of mature years, approached.

"Yes, I'm leaving the Ashes tomorrow, and I shall be able to tell my brother how tremendously you have improved the place. Of course he can't help regretting the old house just a little – as I do myself – but the garden is really delightful now."

"I am so glad you can say so. But you mustn't think we've finished our improvements. Let me show you where I mean to put a rose garden. It's close by here."

The details of the project were laid before Miss Wilkins at some length; but her thoughts were evidently elsewhere.

"Yes, delightful," she said at last rather absently. "But do you know, Mrs. Anstruther, I'm afraid I was thinking of old times. I'm *very* glad to have seen just this spot again before you altered it. Frank and I had quite a romance about this place."

"Yes?" said Mrs. Anstruther smilingly; "do tell me what it was. Something quaint and charming, I'm sure."

"Not so very charming, but it has always seemed to me curious. Neither of us would ever be here alone when we were children, and I'm not sure that I should care about it now in certain moods. It is one of those things that can hardly be put into words – by me at least – and that sound rather foolish if they are not properly expressed. I can tell you after a fashion what it was that gave us – well, almost a horror of the place when we were alone. It was towards the evening of one very hot autumn day, when Frank had disappeared mysteriously about the grounds, and I was looking for him to fetch him to tea, and going down this path I suddenly saw him, not hiding in the bushes, as I rather expected, but sitting on the bench in the old summer-house – there was a wooden summer-house here, you know – up in the corner, asleep, but with such a dreadful look on his face that I really thought he must be ill or even dead. I rushed at him and shook him, and told him to wake up; and wake up he did, with a scream. I assure you the poor boy seemed almost beside himself with fright. He hurried me away to the house, and was in a terrible state all that night, hardly sleeping. Someone had to sit up with him, as far as I remember. He was better very soon, but for days I couldn't get him to say why he had been in such a condition. It came out at last that he had really been asleep and had had a very odd disjointed sort of dream. He never *saw* much of what was around him, but he *felt* the scenes most vividly. First he made out that he was standing in a large room with a number of people in it, and that someone was opposite to him who was 'very powerful', and he was being asked questions which he felt to be very important, and, whenever he answered them, someone – either the person opposite to him, or someone else in the room – seemed to be, as he said, making something up against him. All the voices sounded to him very distant, but he remembered bits of the things that were said: 'Where were you on the 19th of October?' and 'Is this your handwriting?' and so on. I can see now, of course, that he was dreaming of some trial: but we were never allowed to see the papers, and it was odd that a boy of eight should have such a vivid idea of what went on in a court. All the time he felt, he said, the most intense anxiety and oppression and hopelessness (though I don't suppose he used such words as that to me). Then, after that, there was an interval in which he remembered being dreadfully restless and miserable, and then there came another sort of picture, when he was aware that he had come out of doors on a dark raw morning with a little snow about. It was in a street, or at any rate among houses, and he felt that there were numbers and numbers of people there too, and that he was taken up some creaking wooden steps and stood on a sort of platform, but the only thing he could actually see was a small fire burning somewhere near him. Someone who had been holding his arm left hold of it and went towards this fire, and then he said the fright he was in was worse than at any other part of his dream, and if I had not wakened him up he didn't know what would have become of him. A curious dream for a child to have, wasn't it? Well, so much for that. It must have been later in the year that Frank and I were here, and I was sitting in the arbour just about sunset. I noticed the sun was going down, and told Frank to run in and see if tea was ready while I finished a chapter in the book I was reading. Frank was away longer than I expected, and the light was going so fast that I had to bend over my book to make it out. All at once I became conscious that someone was whispering to me inside the arbour. The only words I could distinguish, or thought I could, were something like 'Pull, pull. I'll push, you pull.'

"I started up in something of a fright. The voice – it was little more than a whisper – sounded so hoarse and angry, and yet as if it came from a long, long way off – just as it had done in Frank's dream. But, though I was startled, I had enough courage to look round and try to make out where the sound came from. And – this sounds very foolish, I know, but still it is the fact – I made sure that it was strongest when I put my ear to an old post which was part of the end of the seat. I was so certain of this that I remember making some marks on the post – as deep as I could with the scissors out of my work-basket. I don't know why. I wonder, by the way, whether that isn't the very post itself.... Well, yes, it might be: there *are* marks and scratches on it – but one can't be sure. Anyhow, it was just like that post you have there. My father got to know that both of us had had a fright in the arbour, and he went down there himself one evening after dinner, and the arbour was pulled down at very short notice. I recollect hearing my father talking about it to an old man who used to do odd jobs in the place, and the old man saying, 'Don't you fear for that, sir: he's fast enough in there without no one don't take and let him out.' But when I asked who it was, I could get no satisfactory answer. Possibly my father or mother might have told me more about it when I grew up, but, as you know, they both died when we were still quite children. I must say it has always seemed very odd to me, and I've often asked the older people in the village whether they knew of anything strange: but either they knew nothing or they wouldn't tell me. Dear, dear, how I have been boring you with my childish remembrances! but indeed that arbour did absorb our thoughts quite remarkably for a time. You can fancy, can't you, the kind of stories that we made up for ourselves. Well, dear Mrs. Anstruther, I must be leaving you now. We shall meet in town this winter, I hope, shan't we?" etc., etc.

The seats and the post were cleared away and uprooted respectively by that evening. Late summer weather is proverbially treacherous, and during dinner-time Mrs. Collins sent up to ask for a little brandy, because her husband had took a nasty chill and she was afraid he would not be able to do much next day.

Mrs. Anstruther's morning reflections were not wholly placid. She was sure some roughs had got into the plantation during the night. "And another thing, George: the moment that Collins is about again, you must tell him to do something about the owls. I never heard anything like them, and I'm positive one came and perched somewhere just outside our window. If it had come in I should have been out of my wits: it must have been a very large bird, from its voice. Didn't you hear it? No, of course not, you were sound asleep as usual. Still, I must say, George, you don't look as if your night had done you much good."

"My dear, I feel as if another of the same would turn me silly. You have no idea of the dreams I had. I couldn't speak of them when I woke up, and if this room wasn't so bright and sunny I shouldn't care to think of them even now."

"Well, really, George, that isn't very common with you, I must say. You must have – no, you only had what I had yesterday – unless you had tea at that wretched club house: did you?"

"No, no; nothing but a cup of tea and some bread and butter. I should really like to know how I came to put my dream together – as I suppose one does put one's dreams together from a lot of little things one has been seeing or reading. Look here, Mary, it was like this – if I shan't be boring you—"

"I *wish* to hear what it was, George. I will tell you when I have had enough."

"All right. I must tell you that it wasn't like other nightmares in one way, because I didn't really *see* anyone who spoke to me or touched me, and yet I was most fearfully impressed with the reality of it all. First I was sitting, no, moving about, in an old-fashioned sort of panelled room. I remember there was a fireplace and a lot of burnt papers in it, and I was in a great state of anxiety about something. There was someone else – a servant, I suppose, because I remember saying to him, 'Horses, as quick as you can,' and then waiting a bit: and next I heard several people coming upstairs and a noise like spurs on a boarded floor, and then the door opened and whatever it was that I was expecting happened."

"Yes, but what was that?"

"You see, I couldn't tell: it was the sort of shock that upsets you in a dream. You either wake up or else everything goes black. That was what happened to me. Then I was in a big dark-walled room, panelled, I think, like the other, and a number of people, and I was evidently—"

"Standing your trial, I suppose, George."

"Goodness! yes, Mary, I was; but did you dream that too? How very odd!"

"No, no; I didn't get enough sleep for that. Go on, George, and I will tell you afterwards."

"Yes; well, I *was* being tried, for my life, I've no doubt, from the state I was in. I had no one speaking for me, and somewhere there was a most fearful fellow – on the bench; I should have said, only that he seemed to be pitching into me most unfairly, and twisting everything I said, and asking most abominable questions."

"What about?"

"Why, dates when I was at particular places, and letters I was supposed to have written, and why I had destroyed some papers; and I recollect his laughing at answers I made in a way that quite daunted me. It doesn't sound much, but I can tell you, Mary, it was really appalling at the time. I am quite certain there was such a man once, and a most horrible villain he must have been. The things he said—"

"Thank you, I have no wish to hear them. I can go to the links any day myself. How did it end?"

"Oh, against me; *he* saw to that. I do wish, Mary, I could give you a notion of the strain that came after that, and seemed to me to last for days: waiting and waiting, and sometimes writing things I knew to be enormously important to me, and waiting for answers and none coming, and after that I came out—"

"Ah!"

"What makes you say that? Do you know what sort of thing I saw?"

"Was it a dark cold day, and snow in the streets, and a fire burning somewhere near you?"

"By George, it was! You *have* had the same nightmare! Really not? Well, it is the oddest thing! Yes; I've no doubt it was an execution for high treason. I know I was laid on straw and jolted along most wretchedly, and then had to go up some steps, and someone was holding my arm, and I remember seeing a bit of a ladder and hearing a sound of a lot of people. I really don't think I could bear now to go into a crowd of people and hear the noise they make talking. However, mercifully, I didn't get to the real business. The dream passed off with a sort of thunder inside my head. But, Mary—"

"I know what you are going to ask. I suppose this is an instance of a kind of thought-reading. Miss Wilkins called yesterday and told me of a dream her brother had as a child when they lived here, and something did no doubt make me think of that when I was awake last night listening to those horrible owls and those men talking and laughing in the shrubbery (by the way, I wish you would see if they have done any damage, and speak to the police about it); and so, I suppose, from my brain it must have got into yours while you were asleep. Curious, no doubt, and I am sorry it gave you such a bad night. You had better be as much in the fresh air as you can today."

"Oh, it's all right now; but I think I *will* go over to the Lodge and see if I can get a game with any of them. And you?"

"I have enough to do for this morning; and this afternoon, if I am not interrupted, there is my drawing."

"To be sure – I want to see that finished very much."

No damage was discoverable in the shrubbery. Mr. Anstruther surveyed with faint interest the site of the rose garden, where the uprooted post still lay, and the hole it had occupied remained unfilled. Collins, upon inquiry made, proved to be better, but quite unable to come to his work. He expressed, by the mouth of his wife, a hope that he hadn't done nothing wrong clearing away them things. Mrs. Collins added that there was a lot of talking people in Westfield, and the hold ones was the worst: seemed to think everything of them having been in the parish longer than what other people had. But as to what they said no more could then be ascertained than that it had quite upset Collins, and was a lot of nonsense.

★   ★   ★

Recruited by lunch and a brief period of slumber, Mrs. Anstruther settled herself comfortably upon her sketching chair in the path leading through the shrubbery to the side-gate of the churchyard. Trees and buildings were among her favourite subjects, and here she had good studies of both. She worked hard, and the drawing was becoming a really pleasant thing to look upon by the time that the wooded hills to the west had shut off the sun. Still she would have persevered, but the light changed rapidly, and it became obvious that the last touches must be added on the morrow. She rose and turned towards the house, pausing for a time to take delight in the limpid green western sky. Then she passed on between the dark box-bushes, and, at a point just before the path debouched on the lawn, she stopped once again and considered the quiet evening landscape, and made a mental note that that must be the tower of one of the Roothing churches that one caught on the sky-line. Then a bird (perhaps) rustled in the box-bush on her left, and she turned and started at seeing what at first she took to be a Fifth of November mask peeping out among the branches. She looked closer.

It was not a mask. It was a face – large, smooth, and pink. She remembers the minute drops of perspiration which were starting from its forehead: she remembers how the jaws were clean-shaven and the eyes shut. She remembers also, and with an accuracy which makes the thought intolerable to her, how the mouth was open and a single tooth appeared below the upper lip. As she looked the face receded into the darkness of the bush. The shelter of the house was gained and the door shut before she collapsed.

Mr. and Mrs. Anstruther had been for a week or more recruiting at Brighton before they received a circular from the Essex Archaeological Society, and a query as to whether they possessed certain historical portraits which it was desired to include in the forthcoming work on Essex Portraits, to be published under the Society's auspices. There was an accompanying letter from the Secretary which contained the following passage: 'We are specially anxious to know whether you possess the original of the engraving of which I enclose a photograph. It represents Sir—, Lord Chief Justice under Charles II, who, as you doubtless know, retired after his disgrace to Westfield, and is supposed to have died there of remorse. It may interest you to hear that a curious entry has recently been found in the registers, not of Westfield but of Priors Roothing, to the effect that the parish was so much troubled after his death that the rector of Westfield summoned the parsons of all the Roothings to come and lay him; which they did. The entry ends by saying: 'The stake is in a field adjoining to the churchyard of Westfield, on the west side.' Perhaps you can let us know if any tradition to this effect is current in your parish.'

The incidents which the 'enclosed photograph' recalled were productive of a severe shock to Mrs. Anstruther. It was decided that she must spend the winter abroad.

Mr. Anstruther, when he went down to Westfield to make the necessary arrangements, not unnaturally told this story to the rector (an old gentleman), who showed little surprise.

"Really I had managed to piece out for myself very much what must have happened, partly from old people's talk and partly from what I saw in your grounds. Of course we have suffered to some extent also. Yes, it was bad at first: like owls, as you say, and men talking sometimes. One night it was in this garden, and at other times about several of the cottages. But lately there has been very little: I think it will die out. There is nothing in our registers except the entry of the burial, and what I for a long time took to be the family motto: but last time I looked at it I noticed that it was added in a later hand and had the initials of one of our rectors quite late in the seventeenth century, A.C. – Augustine Crompton. Here it is, you see – *quieta non movere*. I suppose – Well, it is rather hard to say exactly what I do suppose."

# A SCHOOL STORY

Two men in a smoking-room were talking of their private-school days. "At *our* school," said A., "we had a ghost's footmark on the staircase. What was it like? Oh, very unconvincing. Just the shape of a shoe, with a square toe, if I remember right. The staircase was a stone one. I never heard any story about the thing. That seems odd, when you come to think of it. Why didn't somebody invent one, I wonder?"

"You never can tell with little boys. They have a mythology of their own. There's a subject for you, by the way – 'The Folklore of Private Schools'."

"Yes; the crop is rather scanty, though. I imagine, if you were to investigate the cycle of ghost stories, for instance, which the boys at private schools tell each other, they would all turn out to be highly-compressed versions of stories out of books."

"Nowadays the *Strand* and *Pearson's*, and so on, would be extensively drawn upon."

"No doubt: they weren't born or thought of in *my* time. Let's see. I wonder if I can remember the staple ones that I was told. First, there was the house with a room in which a series of people insisted on passing a night; and each of them in the morning was found kneeling in a corner, and had just time to say, 'I've seen it,' and died."

"Wasn't that the house in Berkeley Square?"

"I dare say it was. Then there was the man who heard a noise in the passage at night, opened his door, and saw someone crawling towards him on all fours with his eye hanging out on his cheek. There was besides, let me think – Yes! the room where a man was found dead in bed with a horseshoe mark on his forehead, and the floor under the bed was covered with marks of horseshoes also; I don't know why. Also there was the lady who, on locking her bedroom door in a strange house, heard a thin voice among the bed-curtains say, 'Now we're shut in for the night.' None of those had any explanation or sequel. I wonder if they go on still, those stories."

"Oh, likely enough – with additions from the magazines, as I said. You never heard, did you, of a real ghost at a private school? I thought not; nobody has that ever I came across."

"From the way in which you said that, I gather that *you* have."

"I really don't know; but this is what was in my mind. It happened at my private school thirty odd years ago, and I haven't any explanation of it.

"The school I mean was near London. It was established in a large and fairly old house – a great white building with very fine grounds about it; there were large cedars in the garden, as there are in so many of the older gardens in the Thames valley, and ancient elms in the three or four fields which we used for our games. I think probably it was quite an attractive place, but boys seldom allow that their schools possess any tolerable features.

"I came to the school in a September, soon after the year 1870; and among the boys who arrived on the same day was one whom I took to: a Highland boy, whom I will call McLeod. I needn't spend time in describing him: the main thing is that I got to know him very well. He was not an exceptional boy in any way – not particularly good at books or games – but he suited me.

"The school was a large one: there must have been from 120 to 130 boys there as a rule, and so a considerable staff of masters was required, and there were rather frequent changes among them.

"One term – perhaps it was my third or fourth – a new master made his appearance. His name was Sampson. He was a tallish, stoutish, pale, black-bearded man. I think we liked him: he had travelled a good deal, and had stories which amused us on our school walks, so that there was some competition among us to get within earshot of him. I remember too – dear me, I have hardly thought of it since then! – that he had a charm on his watch-chain that attracted my attention one day, and he let me examine it. It was, I now suppose, a gold Byzantine coin; there was an effigy of some absurd emperor on one side; the other side had been worn practically smooth, and he had had cut on it – rather barbarously – his own initials, G.W.S., and a date, 24 July, 1865. Yes, I can see it now: he told me he had picked it up in Constantinople: it was about the size of a florin, perhaps rather smaller.

"Well, the first odd thing that happened was this. Sampson was doing Latin grammar with us. One of his favourite methods – perhaps it is rather a good one – was to make us construct sentences out of our own heads to illustrate the rules he was trying to make us learn. Of course that is a thing which gives a silly boy a chance of being impertinent: there are lots of school stories in which that happens – or anyhow there might be. But Sampson was too good a disciplinarian for us to think of trying that on with him. Now, on this occasion he was telling us how to express *remembering* in Latin: and he ordered us each to make a sentence bringing in the verb *memini*, 'I remember'. Well, most of us made up some ordinary sentence such as 'I remember my father', or 'He remembers his book', or something equally uninteresting: and I dare say a good many put down *memino librum meum*, and so forth: but the boy I mentioned – McLeod – was evidently thinking of something more elaborate than that. The rest of us wanted to have our sentences passed, and get on to something else, so some kicked him under the desk, and I, who was next to him, poked him and whispered to him to look sharp. But he didn't seem to attend. I looked at his paper and saw he had put down nothing at all. So I jogged him again harder than before and upbraided him sharply for keeping us all waiting. That did have some effect. He started and seemed to wake up, and then very quickly he scribbled about a couple of lines on his paper, and showed it up with the rest. As it was the last, or nearly the last, to come in, and as Sampson had a good deal to say to the boys who had written *meminiscimus patri meo* and the rest of it, it turned out that the clock struck twelve before he had got to McLeod, and McLeod had to wait afterwards to have his sentence corrected. There was nothing much going on outside when I got out, so I waited for him to come. He came very slowly when he did arrive, and I guessed there had been some sort of trouble. 'Well,' I said, 'what did you get?' 'Oh, I don't know,' said McLeod, 'nothing much: but I think Sampson's rather sick with me.' 'Why, did you show him up some rot?' 'No fear,' he said. 'It was all right as far as I could see: it was like this: *Memento* – that's right enough for remember, and it takes a genitive, – *memento putei inter quatuor taxos.*' 'What silly rot!' I said. 'What made you shove that down? What does it mean?' 'That's the funny part,' said McLeod. 'I'm not quite sure what it does mean. All I know is, it just came into my head and I corked it down. I know what I *think* it means, because just before I wrote it down I had a sort of picture of it in my head: I believe it means 'Remember the well among the four' – what are those dark sort of trees that have red berries on them?' 'Mountain ashes, I s'pose you mean.' 'I never heard of them,' said McLeod; 'no, *I'll* tell you – yews.' 'Well, and what did Sampson say?' 'Why, he was jolly odd about it. When he read it he got up and went to the mantelpiece and stopped quite a long time without saying anything, with his back to me. And then he said, without turning round, and rather quiet, 'What do you suppose that means?' I told him what I thought; only I couldn't remember the name of the silly tree: and then he wanted to know why I put it down, and I had to say something or other. And after that he left off talking about it, and asked me how long I'd been here, and where my people lived, and things like that: and then I came away: but he wasn't looking a bit well.'"

"I don't remember any more that was said by either of us about this. Next day McLeod took to his bed with a chill or something of the kind, and it was a week or more before he was in school again. And as much as a month went by without anything happening that was noticeable. Whether or not Mr. Sampson was really startled, as

McLeod had thought, he didn't show it. I am pretty sure, of course, now, that there was something very curious in his past history, but I'm not going to pretend that we boys were sharp enough to guess any such thing.

"There was one other incident of the same kind as the last which I told you. Several times since that day we had had to make up examples in school to illustrate different rules, but there had never been any row except when we did them wrong. At last there came a day when we were going through those dismal things which people call Conditional Sentences, and we were told to make a conditional sentence, expressing a future consequence. We did it, right or wrong, and showed up our bits of paper, and Sampson began looking through them. All at once he got up, made some odd sort of noise in his throat, and rushed out by a door that was just by his desk. We sat there for a minute or two, and then – I suppose it was incorrect – but we went up, I and one or two others, to look at the papers on his desk. Of course I thought someone must have put down some nonsense or other, and Sampson had gone off to report him. All the same, I noticed that he hadn't taken any of the papers with him when he ran out. Well, the top paper on the desk was written in red ink – which no one used – and it wasn't in anyone's hand who was in the class. They all looked at it – McLeod and all – and took their dying oaths that it wasn't theirs. Then I thought of counting the bits of paper. And of this I made quite certain: that there were seventeen bits of paper on the desk, and sixteen boys in the form. Well, I bagged the extra paper, and kept it, and I believe I have it now. And now you will want to know what was written on it. It was simple enough, and harmless enough, I should have said.

"'*Si tu non veneris ad me, ego veniam ad te,*' which means, I suppose, 'If you don't come to me, I'll come to you.'"

"Could you show me the paper?' interrupted the listener.

"Yes, I could: but there's another odd thing about it. That same afternoon I took it out of my locker – I know for certain it was the same bit, for I made a finger-mark on it – and no single trace of writing of any kind was there on it. I kept it, as I said, and since that time I have tried various experiments to see whether sympathetic ink had been used, but absolutely without result.

"So much for that. After about half an hour Sampson looked in again: said he had felt very unwell, and told us we might go. He came rather gingerly to his desk and gave just one look at the uppermost paper: and I suppose he thought he must have been dreaming: anyhow, he asked no questions.

"That day was a half-holiday, and next day Sampson was in school again, much as usual. That night the third and last incident in my story happened.

"We – McLeod and I – slept in a dormitory at right angles to the main building. Sampson slept in the main building on the first floor. There was a very bright full moon. At an hour which I can't tell exactly, but some time between one and two, I was woken up by somebody shaking me. It was McLeod; and a nice state of mind he seemed to be in. 'Come,' he said, – 'come! there's a burglar getting in through Sampson's window.' As soon as I could speak, I said, 'Well, why not call out and wake everybody up?' 'No, no,' he said, 'I'm not sure who it is: don't make a row: come and look.' Naturally I came and looked, and naturally there was no one there. I was cross enough, and should have called McLeod plenty of names: only – I couldn't tell why – it seemed to me that there *was* something wrong – something that made me very glad I wasn't alone to face it. We were still at the window looking out, and as soon as I could, I asked him what he had heard or seen. 'I didn't *hear* anything at all,' he said, 'but about five minutes before I woke you, I found myself looking out of this window here, and there was a man sitting or kneeling on Sampson's window-sill, and looking in, and I thought he was beckoning.' 'What sort of man?' McLeod wriggled. 'I don't know,' he said, 'but I can tell you one thing – he was beastly thin: and he looked as if he was wet all over: and,' he said, looking round and whispering as if he hardly liked to hear himself, 'I'm not at all sure that he was alive.'

"We went on talking in whispers some time longer, and eventually crept back to bed. No one else in the room woke or stirred the whole time. I believe we did sleep a bit afterwards, but we were very cheap next day.

"And next day Mr. Sampson was gone: not to be found: and I believe no trace of him has ever come to light since. In thinking it over, one of the oddest things about it all has seemed to me to be the fact that neither McLeod nor I ever mentioned what we had seen to any third person whatever. Of course no questions were asked on the subject, and if they had been, I am inclined to believe that we could not have made any answer: we seemed unable to speak about it.

"That is my story," said the narrator. "The only approach to a ghost story connected with a school that I know, but still, I think, an approach to such a thing."

★   ★   ★

The sequel to this may perhaps be reckoned highly conventional; but a sequel there is, and so it must be produced. There had been more than one listener to the story, and, in the latter part of that same year, or of the next, one such listener was staying at a country house in Ireland.

One evening his host was turning over a drawer full of odds and ends in the smoking-room. Suddenly he put his hand upon a little box. "Now," he said, "you know about old things; tell me what that is." My friend opened the little box, and found in it a thin gold chain with an object attached to it. He glanced at the object and then took off his spectacles to examine it more narrowly. "What's the history of this?" he asked. "Odd enough," was the answer. "You know the yew thicket in the shrubbery: well, a year or two back we were cleaning out the old well that used to be in the clearing here, and what do you suppose we found?"

"Is it possible that you found a body?" said the visitor, with an odd feeling of nervousness.

"We did that: but what's more, in every sense of the word, we found two."

"Good Heavens! Two? Was there anything to show how they got there? Was this thing found with them?"

"It was. Amongst the rags of the clothes that were on one of the bodies. A bad business, whatever the story of it may have been. One body had the arms tight round the other. They must have been there thirty years or more – long enough before we came to this place. You may judge we filled the well up fast enough. Do you make anything of what's cut on that gold coin you have there?"

"I think I can," said my friend, holding it to the light (but he read it without much difficulty); "it seems to be G.W.S., 24 July, 1865."

# THE STALLS OF BARCHESTER CATHEDRAL

This matter began, as far as I am concerned, with the reading of a notice in the obituary section of the *Gentleman's Magazine* for an early year in the nineteenth century:

*On February 26th, at his residence in the Cathedral Close of Barchester, the Venerable John Benwell Haynes, D.D., aged 57, Archdeacon of Sowerbridge and Rector of Pickhill and Candley. He was of —— College, Cambridge, and where, by talent and assiduity, he commanded the esteem of his seniors; when, at the usual time, he took his first degree, his name stood high in the list of wranglers. These academical honours procured for him within a short time a Fellowship of his College. In the year 1783 he received Holy Orders, and was shortly afterwards presented to the perpetual Curacy of Ranxton-sub-Ashe by his friend and patron the late truly venerable Bishop of Lichfield.... His speedy preferments, first to a Prebend, and subsequently to the dignity of Precentor in the Cathedral of Barchester, form an eloquent testimony to the respect in which he was held and to his eminent qualifications. He succeeded to the Archdeaconry upon the sudden decease of Archdeacon Pulteney in 1810. His sermons, ever conformable to the principles of the religion and Church which he adorned, displayed in no ordinary degree, without the least trace of enthusiasm, the refinement of the scholar united with the graces of the Christian. Free from sectarian violence, and informed by the spirit of the truest charity, they will long dwell in the memories of his hearers. [Here a further omission.] The productions of his pen include an able defence of Episcopacy, which, though often perused by the author of this tribute to his memory, afford but one additional instance of the want of liberality and enterprise which is a too common characteristic of the publishers of our generation. His published works are, indeed, confined to a spirited and elegant version of the* Argonautica *of Valerius Flaccus, a volume of* Discourses upon the Several Events in the Life of Joshua, *delivered in his Cathedral, and a number of the charges which he pronounced at various visitations to the clergy of his Archdeaconry. These are distinguished by etc., etc. The urbanity and hospitality of the subject of these lines will not readily be forgotten by those who enjoyed his acquaintance. His interest in the venerable and awful pile under whose hoary vault he was so punctual an attendant, and particularly in the musical portion of its rites, might be termed filial, and formed a strong and delightful contrast to the polite indifference displayed by too many of our Cathedral dignitaries at the present time.*

The final paragraph, after informing us that Dr. Haynes died a bachelor, says:

*It might have been augured that an existence so placid and benevolent would have been terminated in a ripe old age by a dissolution equally gradual and calm. But how unsearchable are the workings of Providence! The peaceful and retired seclusion amid which the honoured evening of Dr. Haynes' life was mellowing to its close was destined to be disturbed, nay, shattered, by a tragedy as appalling as it was unexpected. The morning of the 26th of February—*

But perhaps I shall do better to keep back the remainder of the narrative until I have told the circumstances which led up to it. These, as far as they are now accessible, I have derived from another source.

I had read the obituary notice which I have been quoting, quite by chance, along with a great many others of the same period. It had excited some little speculation in my mind, but, beyond thinking that, if I ever had an opportunity of examining the local records of the period indicated, I would try to remember Dr. Haynes, I made no effort to pursue his case.

Quite lately I was cataloguing the manuscripts in the library of the college to which he belonged. I had reached the end of the numbered volumes on the shelves, and I proceeded to ask the librarian whether there were any more books which he thought I ought to include in my description. "I don't think there are," he said, "but we had better come and look at the manuscript class and make sure. Have you time to do that now?" I had time. We went to the library, checked off the manuscripts, and, at the end of our survey, arrived at a shelf of which I had seen nothing. Its contents consisted for the most part of sermons, bundles of fragmentary papers, college exercises, *Cyrus*, an epic poem in several cantos, the product of a country clergyman's leisure, mathematical tracts by a deceased professor, and other similar material of a kind with which I am only too familiar. I took brief notes of these. Lastly, there was a tin box, which was pulled out and dusted. Its label, much faded, was thus inscribed: 'Papers of the Ven. Archdeacon Haynes. Bequeathed in 1834 by his sister, Miss Letitia Haynes.'

I knew at once that the name was one which I had somewhere encountered, and could very soon locate it. "That must be the Archdeacon Haynes who came to a very odd end at Barchester. I've read his obituary in the *Gentleman's Magazine*. May I take the box home? Do you know if there is anything interesting in it?"

The librarian was very willing that I should take the box and examine it at leisure. "I never looked inside it myself," he said, "but I've always been meaning to. I am pretty sure that is the box which our old Master once said ought never to have been accepted by the college. He said that to Martin years ago; and he said also that as long as he had control over the library it should never be opened. Martin told me about it, and said that he wanted terribly to know what was in it; but the Master was librarian, and always kept the box in the lodge, so there was no getting at it in his time, and when he died it was taken away by mistake by his heirs, and only returned a few years ago. I can't think why I haven't opened it; but, as I have to go away from Cambridge this afternoon, you had better have first go at it. I think I can trust you not to publish anything undesirable in our catalogue."

I took the box home and examined its contents, and thereafter consulted the librarian as to what should be done about publication, and, since I have his leave to make a story out of it, provided I disguise the identity of the people concerned, I will try what can be done.

The materials are, of course, mainly journals and letters. How much I shall quote and how much epitomise must be determined by considerations of space. The proper understanding of the situation has necessitated a little – not very arduous – research, which has been greatly facilitated by the excellent illustrations and text of the Barchester volume in Bell's *Cathedral Series*.

When you enter the choir of Barchester Cathedral now, you pass through a screen of metal and coloured marbles, designed by Sir Gilbert Scott, and find yourself in what I must call a very bare and odiously furnished place. The stalls are modern, without canopies. The places of the dignitaries and the names of the prebends have fortunately been allowed to survive, and are inscribed on small brass plates affixed to the stalls. The organ is in the triforium, and what is seen of the case is Gothic. The reredos and its surroundings are like every other.

Careful engravings of a hundred years ago show a very different state of things. The organ is on a massive classical screen. The stalls are also classical and very massive. There is a baldacchino of wood over the altar, with urns upon its corners. Farther east is a solid altar screen, classical in design, of wood, with a pediment, in which is a triangle surrounded by rays, enclosing certain Hebrew letters in gold. Cherubs contemplate these. There is a pulpit with a great sounding-board at the eastern end of the stalls on the north side, and there is a black and white marble pavement. Two ladies and a gentleman are admiring the general effect. From other sources I gather that the archdeacon's stall then, as now, was next to the bishop's throne at the south-eastern end of the stalls. His house almost faces the west front of the church, and is a fine red-brick building of William the Third's time.

Here Dr. Haynes, already a mature man, took up his abode with his sister in the year 1810. The dignity had long been the object of his wishes, but his predecessor refused to depart until he had attained the age of ninety-two. About a week after he had held a modest festival in celebration of that ninety-second birthday, there came a morning, late in the year, when Dr. Haynes, hurrying cheerfully into his breakfast-room, rubbing his hands and humming a tune, was greeted, and checked in his genial flow of spirits, by the sight of his sister, seated, indeed, in her usual place behind the tea-urn, but bowed forward and sobbing unrestrainedly into her handkerchief. "What – what is the matter? What bad news?" he began. "Oh, Johnny, you've not heard? The poor dear archdeacon!" "The archdeacon, yes? What is it – ill, is he?" "No, no; they found him on the staircase this morning; it is so shocking." "Is it possible! Dear, dear, poor Pulteney! Had there been any seizure?" "They don't think so, and that is almost the worst thing about it. It seems to have been all the fault of that stupid maid of theirs, Jane." Dr. Haynes paused. "I don't quite understand, Letitia. How was the maid at fault?" "Why, as far as I can make out, there was a stair-rod missing, and she never mentioned it, and the poor archdeacon set his foot quite on the edge of the step – you know how slippery that oak is – and it seems he must have fallen almost the whole flight and broken his neck. It *is* so sad for poor Miss Pulteney. Of course, they will get rid of the girl at once. I never liked her." Miss Haynes's grief resumed its sway, but eventually relaxed so far as to permit of her taking some breakfast. Not so her brother, who, after standing in silence before the window for some minutes, left the room, and did not appear again that morning.

I need only add that the careless maid-servant was dismissed forthwith, but that the missing stair-rod was very shortly afterwards found *under* the stair-carpet – an additional proof, if any were needed, of extreme stupidity and carelessness on her part.

For a good many years Dr. Haynes had been marked out by his ability, which seems to have been really considerable, as the likely successor of Archdeacon Pulteney, and no disappointment was in store for him. He was duly installed, and entered with zeal upon the discharge of those functions which are appropriate to one in his position. A considerable space in his journals is occupied with exclamations upon the confusion in which Archdeacon Pulteney had left the business of his office and the documents appertaining to it. Dues upon Wringham and Barnswood have been uncollected for something like twelve years, and are largely irrecoverable; no visitation has been held for seven years; four chancels are almost past mending. The persons deputised by the archdeacon have been nearly as incapable as himself. It was almost a matter for thankfulness that this state of things had not been permitted to continue, and a letter from a friend confirms this view. '[Greek:] *ho katechôn*,' it says (in rather cruel allusion to the Second Epistle to the Thessalonians), 'is removed at last. My poor friend! Upon what a scene of confusion will you be entering! I give you my word that, on the last occasion of my crossing his threshold, there was no single paper that he could lay hands upon, no syllable of mine that he could hear, and no fact in connexion with my business that he could remember. But now, thanks to a negligent maid and a loose stair-carpet, there is some prospect that necessary business will be transacted without a complete loss alike of voice and temper.' This letter was tucked into a pocket in the cover of one of the diaries.

There can be no doubt of the new archdeacon's zeal and enthusiasm. 'Give me but time to reduce to some semblance of order the innumerable errors and complications with which I am confronted, and I shall gladly and sincerely join with the aged Israelite in the canticle which too many, I fear, pronounce but with their lips.' This reflection I find, not in a diary, but a letter; the doctor's friends seem to have returned his correspondence to his surviving sister. He does not confine himself, however, to reflections. His investigation of the rights and duties of his office are very searching and business-like, and there is a calculation in one place that a period of three years will just suffice to set the business of the Archdeaconry upon a proper footing. The estimate appears to have been an exact one. For just three years he is occupied in reforms; but I look in vain at the end of that time for the promised *Nunc dimittis*. He has now found a new sphere of activity. Hitherto his duties have precluded him from more than an occasional attendance at the Cathedral services. Now he begins to take an interest in the fabric and the music. Upon his struggles with the organist, an old gentleman who had been in office since 1786, I have no time to dwell; they were not attended with any marked success. More to the purpose is his sudden growth of enthusiasm for the Cathedral itself and its furniture. There is a draft of a letter to Sylvanus Urban (which I do not think was ever sent) describing the stalls in the choir. As I have said, these were of fairly late date – of about the year 1700, in fact.

*The archdeacon's stall, situated at the south-east end, west of the episcopal throne (now so worthily occupied by the truly excellent prelate who adorns the See of Barchester), is distinguished by some curious ornamentation. In addition to the arms of Dean West, by whose efforts the whole of the internal furniture of the choir was completed, the prayer-desk is terminated at the eastern extremity by three small but remarkable statuettes in the grotesque manner. One is an exquisitely modelled figure of a cat, whose crouching posture suggests with admirable spirit the suppleness, vigilance, and craft of the redoubted adversary of the genus Mus. Opposite to this is a figure seated upon a throne and invested with the attributes of royalty; but it is no earthly monarch whom the carver has sought to portray. His feet are studiously concealed by the long robe in which he is draped: but neither the crown nor the cap which he wears suffice to hide the prick-ears and curving horns which betray his Tartarean origin; and the hand which rests upon his knee is armed with talons of horrifying length and sharpness. Between these two figures stands a shape muffled in a long mantle. This might at first sight be mistaken for a monk or 'friar of orders gray', for the head is cowled and a knotted cord depends from somewhere about the waist. A slight inspection, however, will lead to a very different conclusion. The knotted cord is quickly seen to be a halter, held by a hand all but concealed within the draperies; while the sunken features and, horrid to relate, the rent flesh upon the cheek-bones, proclaim the King of Terrors. These figures are evidently the production of no unskilled chisel; and should it chance that any of your correspondents are able to throw light upon their origin and significance, my obligations to your valuable miscellany will be largely increased.*

There is more description in the paper, and, seeing that the woodwork in question has now disappeared, it has a considerable interest. A paragraph at the end is worth quoting:

*Some late researches among the Chapter accounts have shown me that the carving of the stalls was not, as was very usually reported, the work of Dutch artists, but was executed by a native of this city or district named Austin. The timber was procured from an oak copse in the vicinity, the property of the Dean and Chapter, known as Holywood. Upon a recent visit to the parish within whose boundaries it is situated, I learned from the aged and truly respectable incumbent that traditions still lingered amongst the inhabitants of the great size and age of the oaks employed to furnish the materials of the stately structure which has been, however imperfectly, described in the above lines. Of one in particular, which stood near the centre of the grove, it is remembered that it was known as the Hanging Oak. The propriety of that title is confirmed by the fact that a quantity of human bones was found in the soil about its roots, and that at certain times of the year it was the custom for those who wished to secure a successful issue to their affairs, whether of love or the ordinary business of life, to suspend from its boughs small images or puppets rudely fashioned of straw, twigs, or the like rustic materials.*

So much for the archdeacon's archaeological investigations. To return to his career as it is to be gathered from his diaries. Those of his first three years of hard and careful work show him throughout in high spirits, and, doubtless, during this time, that reputation for hospitality and urbanity which is mentioned in his obituary notice was well deserved. After that, as time goes on, I see a shadow coming over him – destined to develop into utter blackness – which I cannot but think must have been reflected in his outward demeanour. He commits a good deal of his fears and troubles to his diary; there was no other outlet for them. He was unmarried and his sister was not always with him. But I am much mistaken if he has told all that he might have told. A series of extracts shall be given:

*Aug. 30th 1816 – The days begin to draw in more perceptibly than ever. Now that the Archdeaconry papers are reduced to order, I must find some further employment for the evening hours of autumn and winter. It is a great blow that Letitia's health will not allow her to stay through these months. Why not go on with my Defence of Episcopacy? It may be useful.*

*Sept. 15. – Letitia has left me for Brighton.*

*Oct. 11. – Candles lit in the choir for the first time at evening prayers. It came as a shock: I find that I absolutely shrink from the dark season.*

*Nov. 17 – Much struck by the character of the carving on my desk: I do not know that I had ever carefully noticed it before. My attention was called to it by an accident. During the Magnificat I was, I regret to say, almost overcome with sleep. My hand was resting on the back of the carved figure of a cat which is the nearest to me of the three figures on the end of my stall. I was not aware of this, for I was not looking in that direction, until I was startled by what seemed a softness, a feeling as of rather rough and coarse fur, and a sudden movement, as if the creature were twisting round its head to bite me. I regained complete consciousness in an instant, and I have some idea that I must have uttered a suppressed exclamation, for I noticed that Mr. Treasurer turned his head quickly in my direction. The impression of the unpleasant feeling was so strong that I found myself rubbing my hand upon my surplice. This accident led me to examine the figures after prayers more carefully than I had done before, and I realised for the first time with what skill they are executed.*

*Dec. 6 – I do indeed miss Letitia's company. The evenings, after I have worked as long as I can at my Defence, are very trying. The house is too large for a lonely man, and visitors of any kind are too rare. I get an uncomfortable impression when going to my room that there is company of some kind. The fact is (I may as well formulate it to myself) that I hear voices. This, I am well aware, is a common symptom of incipient decay of the brain – and I believe that I should be less disquieted than I am if I had any suspicion that this was the cause. I have none — none whatever, nor is there anything in my family history to give colour to such an idea. Work, diligent work, and a punctual attention to the duties which fall to me is my best remedy, and I have little doubt that it will prove efficacious.*

*Jan. 1 — My trouble is, I must confess it, increasing upon me. Last night, upon my return after midnight from the Deanery, I lit my candle to go upstairs. I was nearly at the top when something whispered to me, "Let me wish you a happy New Year." I could not be mistaken: it spoke distinctly and with a peculiar emphasis. Had I dropped my candle, as I all but did, I tremble to think what the consequences must have been. As it was, I managed to get up the last flight, and was quickly in my room with the door locked, and experienced no other disturbance.*

*Jan. 15 — I had occasion to come downstairs last night to my workroom for my watch, which I had inadvertently left on my table when I went up to bed. I think I was at the top of the last flight when I had a sudden impression of a sharp whisper in my ear "Take care." I clutched the balusters and naturally looked round at once. Of course, there was nothing. After a moment I went on — it was no good turning back — but I had as nearly as possible fallen: a cat — a large one by the feel of it — slipped between my feet, but again, of course, I saw nothing. It may have been the kitchen cat, but I do not think it was.*

*Feb. 27 — A curious thing last night, which I should like to forget. Perhaps if I put it down here I may see it in its true proportion. I worked in the library from about 9 to 10. The hall and staircase seemed to be unusually full of what I can only call movement without sound: by this I mean that there seemed to be continuous going and coming, and that whenever I ceased writing to listen, or looked out into the hall, the stillness was absolutely unbroken. Nor, in going to my room at an earlier hour than usual — about half-past ten — was I conscious of anything that I could call a noise. It so happened that I had told John to come to my room for the letter to the bishop which I wished to have delivered early in the morning at the Palace. He was to sit up, therefore, and come for it when he heard me retire. This I had for the moment forgotten, though I had remembered to carry the letter with me to my room. But when, as I was winding up my watch, I heard a light tap at the door, and a low voice saying, "May I come in?" (which I most undoubtedly did hear), I recollected the fact, and took up the letter from my dressing-table, saying, "Certainly: come in." No one, however, answered my summons, and it was now that, as I strongly suspect, I committed an error: for I opened the door and held the letter out. There was certainly no one at that moment in the passage, but, in the instant of my standing there, the door at the end opened and John appeared carrying a candle. I asked him whether he had come to the door earlier; but am satisfied that he had not. I do not like the situation; but although my senses were very much on the alert, and though it was some time before I could sleep, I must allow that I perceived nothing further of an untoward character.*

With the return of spring, when his sister came to live with him for some months, Dr. Haynes's entries become more cheerful, and, indeed, no symptom of depression is discernible until the early part of September, when he was again left alone. And now, indeed, there is evidence that he was incommoded again, and that more pressingly. To this matter I will return in a moment, but I digress to put in a document which, rightly or wrongly, I believe to have a bearing on the thread of the story.

The account-books of Dr. Haynes, preserved along with his other papers, show, from a date but little later than that of his institution as archdeacon, a quarterly payment of £25 to J.L. Nothing could have been made of this, had it stood by itself. But I connect with it a very dirty and ill-written letter, which, like another that I have quoted, was in a pocket in the cover of a diary. Of date or postmark there is no vestige, and the decipherment was not easy. It appears to run:

*Dr Sr.*

*I have bin expctin to her off you theis last wicks, and not Haveing done so must supose you have not got mine witch was saying how me and my man had met in with bad times this season all seems to go cross with us on the farm and which way to look for the rent we have no knowledge of it this been the sad case with us if you would have the great [liberality probably,* but the exact spelling defies reproduction] *to send fourty pounds otherwise steps will have to be took which I should not wish. Has you was the Means of me losing my place with Dr. Pulteney I think it is only just what I am asking and you know best what I could say if I was Put to it but I do not wish anything of that unpleasant Nature being one that always wish to have everything Pleasant about me.*

*Your obedt Servt,*

*Jane Lee.*

About the time at which I suppose this letter to have been written there is, in fact, a payment of £40 to J.L.

We return to the diary:

*Oct. 22 – At evening prayers, during the Psalms, I had that same experience which I recollect from last year. I was resting my hand on one of the carved figures, as before (I usually avoid that of the cat now), and – I was going to have said – a change came over it, but that seems attributing too much importance to what must, after all, be due to some physical affection in myself: at any rate, the wood seemed to become chilly and soft as if made of wet linen. I can assign the moment at which I became sensible of this. The choir were singing the words (Set thou an ungodly man to be ruler over him and let Satan stand at his right hand.)*

*The whispering in my house was more persistent tonight. I seemed not to be rid of it in my room. I have not noticed this before. A nervous man, which I am not, and hope I am not becoming, would have been much annoyed, if not alarmed, by it. The cat was on the stairs tonight. I think it sits there always. There is no kitchen cat.*

*Nov. 15 – Here again I must note a matter I do not understand. I am much troubled in sleep. No definite image presented itself, but I was pursued by the very vivid impression that wet lips were whispering into my ear with great rapidity and emphasis for some time together. After this, I suppose, I fell asleep, but was awakened with a start by a feeling as if a hand were laid on my shoulder. To my intense alarm I found myself standing at the top of the lowest flight of the first staircase. The moon was shining brightly enough through the large window to let me see that there was a large cat on the second or third step. I can make no comment. I crept up to bed again, I do not know how. Yes, mine is a heavy burden.* [Then follows a line or two which has been scratched out. I fancy I read something like *'acted for the best'*.]

Not long after this it is evident to me that the archdeacon's firmness began to give way under the pressure of these phenomena. I omit as unnecessarily painful and distressing the ejaculations and prayers which, in the months of December and January, appear for the first time and become increasingly frequent. Throughout this time, however, he is obstinate in clinging to his post. Why he did not plead ill-health and take refuge at Bath or Brighton I cannot tell; my impression is that it would have done him no good; that he was a man who, if he had confessed himself beaten by the annoyances, would have succumbed at once, and that he was conscious of this. He did seek to palliate them by inviting visitors to his house. The result he has noted in this fashion:

*Jan. 7 – I have prevailed on my cousin Allen to give me a few days, and he is to occupy the chamber next to mine.*

*Jan. 8 – A still night. Allen slept well, but complained of the wind. My own experiences were as before: still whispering and whispering: what is it that he wants to say?*

*Jan. 9 – Allen thinks this a very noisy house. He thinks, too, that my cat is an unusually large and fine specimen, but very wild.*

*Jan. 10 – Allen and I in the library until 11. He left me twice to see what the maids were doing in the hall: returning the second time he told me he had seen one of them passing through the door at the end of the passage, and said if his wife were here she would soon get them into better order. I asked him what coloured dress the maid wore; he said grey or white. I supposed it would be so.*

*Jan. 11 – Allen left me today. I must be firm.*

These words, *I must be firm*, occur again and again on subsequent days; sometimes they are the only entry. In these cases they are in an unusually large hand, and dug into the paper in a way which must have broken the pen that wrote them.

Apparently the archdeacon's friends did not remark any change in his behaviour, and this gives me a high idea of his courage and determination. The diary tells us nothing more than I have indicated of the last days of his life. The end of it all must be told in the polished language of the obituary notice:

*The morning of the 26th of February was cold and tempestuous. At an early hour the servants had occasion to go into the front hall of the residence occupied by the lamented subject of these lines. What was their horror upon observing the form of their beloved and respected master lying upon the landing of the principal staircase in an attitude which inspired the gravest fears. Assistance was procured, and an universal consternation was experienced upon the discovery that he had been the object of a brutal and a murderous attack. The vertebral column was fractured in more than one place. This might have been the result of a fall: it appeared that the stair-carpet was loosened at one point. But, in addition to this, there were injuries inflicted upon the eyes, nose and mouth, as if by the agency of some savage animal, which, dreadful to relate, rendered those features unrecognisable. The vital spark was, it is needless to add, completely extinct, and had been so, upon the testimony of respectable medical authorities, for several hours. The author or authors of this mysterious outrage are alike buried in mystery, and the most active conjecture has hitherto failed to suggest a solution of the melancholy problem afforded by this appalling occurrence.*

The writer goes on to reflect upon the probability that the writings of Mr. Shelley, Lord Byron, and M. Voltaire may have been instrumental in bringing about the disaster, and concludes by hoping, somewhat vaguely, that this event may 'operate as an example to the rising generation'; but this portion of his remarks need not be quoted in full.

I had already formed the conclusion that Dr. Haynes was responsible for the death of Dr. Pulteney. But the incident connected with the carved figure of death upon the archdeacon's stall was a very perplexing feature. The conjecture that it had been cut out of the wood of the Hanging Oak was not difficult, but seemed impossible to substantiate. However, I paid a visit to Barchester, partly with the view of finding out whether there were any relics of the woodwork to be heard of. I was introduced by one of the canons to the curator of the local museum, who was, my friend said, more likely to be able to give me information on the point than anyone else. I told this gentleman of the description of certain carved figures and arms formerly on the stalls, and asked whether any had survived. He was able to show me the arms of Dean West and some other fragments. These, he said, had been got from an old resident, who had also once owned a figure – perhaps one of those which I was inquiring for. There was a very odd thing about that figure, he said. "The old man who had it told me that he picked it up in a woodyard, whence he had obtained the still extant pieces, and had taken it home for his children. On the way home he was fiddling about with it and it came in two in his hands, and a bit of paper dropped out. This he picked up and, just noticing that there was writing on it, put it into his pocket, and subsequently into a vase on his mantelpiece. I was at his house not very long ago, and happened to pick up the vase and turn it over to see whether there were any marks on it, and the paper fell into my hand. The old man, on my handing it to him, told me the story I have told you, and said I might keep the paper. It was crumpled and rather torn, so

I have mounted it on a card, which I have here. If you can tell me what it means I shall be very glad, and also, I may say, a good deal surprised."

He gave me the card. The paper was quite legibly inscribed in an old hand, and this is what was on it:

> *When I grew in the Wood*
> *I was water'd w'th Blood*
> *Now in the Church I stand*
> *Who that touches me with his Hand*
> *If a Bloody hand he bear*
> *I councell him to be ware*
> *Lest he be fetcht away*
> *Whether by night or day,*
> *But chiefly when the wind blows high*
> *In a night of February.*
> *This I drempt, 26 Febr. Anno 1699.*
>
> **John Austin**

"I suppose it is a charm or a spell: wouldn't you call it something of that kind?" said the curator.

"Yes," I said, "I suppose one might. What became of the figure in which it was concealed?"

"Oh, I forgot," said he. "The old man told me it was so ugly and frightened his children so much that he burnt it."

# THE TRACTATE MIDDOTH

Towards the end of an autumn afternoon an elderly man with a thin face and grey Piccadilly weepers pushed open the swing-door leading into the vestibule of a certain famous library, and addressing himself to an attendant, stated that he believed he was entitled to use the library, and inquired if he might take a book out. Yes, if he were on the list of those to whom that privilege was given. He produced his card – Mr. John Eldred – and, the register being consulted, a favourable answer was given. "Now, another point," said he. "It is a long time since I was here, and I do not know my way about your building; besides, it is near closing-time, and it is bad for me to hurry up and down stairs. I have here the title of the book I want: is there anyone at liberty who could go and find it for me?" After a moment's thought the doorkeeper beckoned to a young man who was passing. "Mr. Garrett," he said, "have you a minute to assist this gentleman?" "With pleasure," was Mr. Garrett's answer. The slip with the title was handed to him. "I think I can put my hand on this; it happens to be in the class I inspected last quarter, but I'll just look it up in the catalogue to make sure. I suppose it is that particular edition that you require, sir?" "Yes, if you please; that, and no other," said Mr. Eldred; "I am exceedingly obliged to you." "Don't mention it I beg, sir," said Mr. Garrett, and hurried off.

"I thought so," he said to himself, when his finger, travelling down the pages of the catalogue, stopped at a particular entry. "Talmud: Tractate Middoth, with the commentary of Nachmanides, Amsterdam, 1707. 11.3.34. Hebrew class, of course. Not a very difficult job this."

Mr. Eldred, accommodated with a chair in the vestibule, awaited anxiously the return of his messenger – and his disappointment at seeing an empty-handed Mr. Garrett running down the staircase was very evident. "I'm sorry to disappoint you, sir," said the young man, "but the book is out." "Oh dear!" said Mr. Eldred, "is that so? You are sure there can be no mistake?" "I don't think there is much chance of it, sir: but it's possible, if you like to wait a minute, that you might meet the very gentleman that's got it. He must be leaving the library soon, and I *think* I saw him take that particular book out of the shelf." "Indeed! You didn't recognise him, I suppose? Would it be one of the professors or one of the students?" "I don't think so: certainly not a professor. I should have known him; but the light isn't very good in that part of the library at this time of day, and I didn't see his face. I should have said he was a shortish old gentleman, perhaps a clergyman, in a cloak. If you could wait, I can easily find out whether he wants the book very particularly."

"No, no," said Mr. Eldred, "I won't – I can't wait now, thank you – no. I must be off. But I'll call again tomorrow if I may, and perhaps you could find out who has it."

"Certainly, sir, and I'll have the book ready for you if we—" But Mr. Eldred was already off, and hurrying more than one would have thought wholesome for him.

Garrett had a few moments to spare; and, thought he, "I'll go back to that case and see if I can find the old man. Most likely he could put off using the book for a few days. I dare say the other one doesn't want to keep it for long." So off with him to the Hebrew class. But when he got there it was unoccupied, and the volume marked 11.3.34 was in its place on the shelf. It was vexatious to Garrett's self-respect to have disappointed an inquirer with so little reason: and he would have liked, had it not been against library rules, to take the book down to the vestibule then and there, so that it might be ready for Mr. Eldred when he called. However, next morning he would be on the look out for him, and he begged the doorkeeper to send and let him know when the moment came. As a matter of fact, he was himself in the vestibule when Mr. Eldred arrived, very soon after the library opened, and when hardly anyone besides the staff were in the building.

"I'm very sorry," he said; "it's not often that I make such a stupid mistake, but I did feel sure that the old gentleman I saw took out that very book and kept it in his hand without opening it, just as people do, you know, sir, when they mean to take a book out of the library and not merely refer to it. But, however, I'll run up now at once and get it for you this time."

And here intervened a pause. Mr. Eldred paced the entry, read all the notices, consulted his watch, sat and gazed up the staircase, did all that a very impatient man could, until some twenty minutes had run out. At last he addressed himself to the doorkeeper and inquired if it was a very long way to that part of the library to which Mr. Garrett had gone.

"Well, I was thinking it was funny, sir: he's a quick man as a rule, but to be sure he might have been sent for by the libarian, but even so I think he'd have mentioned to him that you was waiting. I'll just speak him up on the toob and see." And to the tube he addressed himself. As he absorbed the reply to his question his face changed, and he made one or two supplementary inquiries which were shortly answered. Then he came forward to his counter and spoke in a lower tone. "I'm sorry to hear, sir, that something seems to have 'appened a little awkward. Mr. Garrett has been took poorly, it appears, and the libarian sent him 'ome in a cab the other way. Something of an attack, by what I can hear." "What, really? Do you mean that someone has injured him?" "No, sir, not violence 'ere, but, as I should judge, attacted with an attack, what you might term it, of illness. Not a strong constitootion, Mr. Garrett. But as to your book, sir, perhaps you might be able to find it for yourself. It's too bad you should be disappointed this way twice over—" "Er – well, but I'm so sorry that Mr. Garrett should have been taken ill in this way while he was obliging me. I think I must leave the book, and call and inquire after him. You can give me his address, I suppose." That was easily done: Mr. Garrett, it appeared, lodged in rooms not far from the station. "And, one other question. Did you happen to notice if an old gentleman, perhaps a clergyman, in a – yes – in a black cloak, left the library after I did yesterday. I think he may have been a – I think, that is, that he may be staying – or rather that I may have known him."

"Not in a black cloak, sir; no. There were only two gentlemen left later than what you done, sir, both of them youngish men. There was Mr. Carter took out a music-book and one of the prefessors with a couple o' novels. That's the lot, sir; and then I went off to me tea, and glad to get it. Thank you, sir, much obliged."

⋆　　⋆　　⋆

Mr. Eldred, still a prey to anxiety, betook himself in a cab to Mr. Garrett's address, but the young man was not yet in a condition to receive visitors. He was better, but his landlady considered that he must have had a severe shock. She thought most likely from what the doctor said that he would be able to see Mr. Eldred tomorrow. Mr. Eldred returned to his hotel at dusk and spent, I fear, but a dull evening.

On the next day he was able to see Mr. Garrett. When in health Mr. Garrett was a cheerful and pleasant-looking young man. Now he was a very white and shaky being, propped up in an arm-chair by the fire, and inclined to shiver and keep an eye on the door. If however, there were visitors whom he was not prepared to welcome, Mr. Eldred was not among them. "It really is I who owe you an apology, and I was despairing of being able to pay it, for I didn't know your address. But I am very glad you have called. I do dislike and regret giving all this trouble, but you know I could not have foreseen this – this attack which I had."

"Of course not; but now, I am something of a doctor. You'll excuse my asking; you have had, I am sure, good advice. Was it a fall you had?"

"No. I did fall on the floor – but not from any height. It was, really, a shock."

"You mean something startled you. Was it anything you thought you saw?"

"Not much *thinking* in the case, I'm afraid. Yes, it was something I saw. You remember when you called the first time at the library?"

"Yes, of course. Well, now, let me beg you not to try to describe it – it will not be good for you to recall it, I'm sure."

"But indeed it would be a relief to me to tell anyone like yourself: you might be able to explain it away. It was just when I was going into the class where your book is—"

"Indeed, Mr. Garrett, I insist; besides, my watch tells me I have but very little time left in which to get my things together and take the train. No – not another word – it would be more distressing to you than you imagine, perhaps. Now there is just one thing I want to say. I feel that I am really indirectly responsible for this illness of yours, and I think I ought to defray the expense which it has – eh?"

But this offer was quite distinctly declined. Mr. Eldred, not pressing it, left almost at once: not, however, before Mr. Garrett had insisted upon his taking a note of the class-mark of the Tractate Middoth, which, as he said, Mr. Eldred could at leisure get for himself. But Mr. Eldred did not reappear at the library.

★   ★   ★

William Garrett had another visitor that day in the person of a contemporary and colleague from the library, one George Earle. Earle had been one of those who found Garrett lying insensible on the floor just inside the 'class' or cubicle (opening upon the central alley of a spacious gallery) in which the Hebrew books were placed, and Earle had naturally been very anxious about his friend's condition. So as soon as library hours were over he appeared at the lodgings. "Well," he said (after other conversation), "I've no notion what it was that put you wrong, but I've got the idea that there's something wrong in the atmosphere of the library. I know this, that just before we found you I was coming along the gallery with Davis, and I said to him, "Did ever you know such a musty smell anywhere as there is about here? It can't be wholesome." Well now, if one goes on living a long time with a smell of that kind (I tell you it was worse than I ever knew it) it must get into the system and break out some time, don't you think?"

Garrett shook his head. "That's all very well about the smell – but it isn't always there, though I've noticed it the last day or two – a sort of unnaturally strong smell of dust. But no – that's not what did for me. It was something I *saw*. And I want to tell you about it. I went into that Hebrew class to get a book for a man that was inquiring for it down below. Now that same book I'd made a mistake about the day before. I'd been for it, for the same man, and made sure that I saw an old parson in a cloak taking it out. I told my man it was out: off he went, to call again next day. I went back to see if I could get it out of the parson: no parson there, and the book on the shelf. Well, yesterday, as I say, I went again. This time, if you please – ten o'clock in the morning, remember, and as much light as ever you get in those classes, and there was my parson again, back to me, looking at the books on the shelf I wanted. His hat was on the table, and he had a bald head. I waited a second or two looking at him rather particularly. I tell you, he had a very nasty bald head. It looked to me dry, and it looked dusty, and the streaks of hair across it were much less like hair than cobwebs. Well, I made a bit of a noise on purpose, coughed and moved my feet. He turned round and let me see his face – which I hadn't seen before. I tell you again, I'm not mistaken. Though, for one reason or another I didn't take in the lower part of his face, I did see the upper part; and it was perfectly dry, and the eyes were very deep-sunk; and over them, from the eyebrows to the cheek-bone, there were *cobwebs* – thick. Now that closed me up, as they say, and I can't tell you anything more."

★   ★   ★

What explanations were furnished by Earle of this phenomenon it does not very much concern us to inquire; at all events they did not convince Garrett that he had not seen what he had seen.

★   ★   ★

Before William Garrett returned to work at the library, the librarian insisted upon his taking a week's rest and change of air. Within a few days' time, therefore, he was at the station with his bag, looking for a desirable smoking compartment in which to travel to Burnstow-on-Sea, which he had not previously visited. One compartment and one only seemed to be suitable. But, just as he approached it, he saw, standing in front of the door, a figure so like one bound up with recent unpleasant associations that, with a sickening qualm, and hardly knowing what he did, he tore open the door of the next compartment and pulled himself into it as quickly as if death were at his heels. The train moved off, and he must have turned quite faint, for he was next conscious of a smelling-bottle being put to his nose. His physician was a nice-looking old lady, who, with her daughter, was the only passenger in the carriage.

But for this incident it is not very likely that he would have made any overtures to his fellow-travellers. As it was, thanks and inquiries and general conversation supervened inevitably; and Garrett found himself provided before the journey's end not only with a physician, but with a landlady: for Mrs. Simpson had apartments to let at Burnstow, which seemed in all ways suitable. The place was empty at that season, so that Garrett was thrown a good deal into the society of the mother and daughter. He found them very acceptable company. On the third evening of his stay he was on such terms with them as to be asked to spend the evening in their private sitting-room.

During their talk it transpired that Garrett's work lay in a library. "Ah, libraries are fine places," said Mrs. Simpson, putting down her work with a sigh; "but for all that, books have played me a sad turn, or rather *a* book has."

"Well, books give me my living, Mrs. Simpson, and I should be sorry to say a word against them: I don't like to hear that they have been bad for you."

"Perhaps Mr. Garrett could help us to solve our puzzle, mother," said Miss Simpson.

"I don't want to set Mr. Garrett off on a hunt that might waste a lifetime, my dear, nor yet to trouble him with our private affairs."

"But if you think it in the least likely that I could be of use, I do beg you to tell me what the puzzle is, Mrs. Simpson. If it is finding out anything about a book, you see, I am in rather a good position to do it."

"Yes, I do see that, but the worst of it is that we don't know the name of the book."

"Nor what it is about?"

"No, nor that either."

"Except that we don't think it's in English, mother – and that is not much of a clue."

"Well, Mr. Garrett," said Mrs. Simpson, who had not yet resumed her work, and was looking at the fire thoughtfully, "I shall tell you the story. You will please keep it to yourself, if you don't mind? Thank you. Now it is just this. I had an old uncle, a Dr. Rant. Perhaps you may have heard of him. Not that he was a distinguished man, but from the odd way he chose to be buried."

"I rather think I have seen the name in some guidebook."

"That would be it," said Miss Simpson. "He left directions – horrid old man! – that he was to be put, sitting at a table in his ordinary clothes, in a brick room that he'd had made underground in a field near his house. Of course the country people say he's been seen about there in his old black cloak."

"Well, dear, I don't know much about such things," Mrs. Simpson went on, "but anyhow he is dead, these twenty years and more. He was a clergyman, though I'm sure I can't imagine how he got to be one: but he did no duty for the last part of his life, which I think was a good thing; and he lived on his own property: a very nice estate not a great way from here. He had no wife or family; only one niece, who was myself, and one nephew, and he had no particular liking for either of us – nor for anyone else, as far as that goes. If anything, he liked my cousin better than he did me – for John was much more like him in his temper, and, I'm afraid I must say, his very mean sharp ways. It might have been different if I had not married; but I did, and that he very much resented. Very well: here he was with this estate and a good deal of money, as it turned out, of which he had the absolute disposal, and it was understood that we – my cousin and I – would share it equally at his death. In a certain winter, over twenty years back, as I said, he was taken ill, and I was sent for to nurse him. My husband was alive then, but the old man would not hear of *his* coming.

As I drove up to the house I saw my cousin John driving away from it in an open fly and looking, I noticed, in very good spirits. I went up and did what I could for my uncle, but I was very soon sure that this would be his last illness; and he was convinced of it too. During the day before he died he got me to sit by him all the time, and I could see there was something, and probably something unpleasant, that he was saving up to tell me, and putting it off as long as he felt he could afford the strength – I'm afraid purposely in order to keep me on the stretch. But, at last, out it came. 'Mary,' he said, – 'Mary, I've made my will in John's favour: he has everything, Mary.' Well, of course that came as a bitter shock to me, for we – my husband and I – were not rich people, and if he could have managed to live a little easier than he was obliged to do, I felt it might be the prolonging of his life. But I said little or nothing to my uncle, except that he had a right to do what he pleased: partly because I couldn't think of anything to say, and partly because I was sure there was more to come: and so there was. 'But, Mary,' he said, 'I'm not very fond of John, and I've made another will in *your* favour. *You* can have everything. Only you've got to find the will, you see: and I don't mean to tell you where it is.' Then he chuckled to himself, and I waited, for again I was sure he hadn't finished. 'That's a good girl,' he said after a time, – 'you wait, and I'll tell you as much as I told John. But just let me remind you, you can't go into court with what I'm saying to you, for *you* won't be able to produce any collateral evidence beyond your own word, and John's a man that can do a little hard swearing if necessary. Very well then, that's understood. Now, I had the fancy that I wouldn't write this will quite in the common way, so I wrote it in a book, Mary, a printed book. And there's several thousand books in this house. But there! you needn't trouble yourself with them, for it isn't one of them. It's in safe keeping elsewhere: in a place where John can go and find it any day, if he only knew, and you can't. A good will it is: properly signed and witnessed, but I don't think you'll find the witnesses in a hurry.'

"Still I said nothing: if I had moved at all I must have taken hold of the old wretch and shaken him. He lay there laughing to himself, and at last he said:

"'Well, well, you've taken it very quietly, and as I want to start you both on equal terms, and John has a bit of a purchase in being able to go where the book is, I'll tell you just two other things which I didn't tell him. The will's in English, but you won't know that if ever you see it. That's one thing, and another is that when I'm gone you'll find an envelope in my desk directed to you, and inside it something that would help you to find it, if only you have the wits to use it.'

"In a few hours from that he was gone, and though I made an appeal to John Eldred about it—"

"John Eldred? I beg your pardon, Mrs. Simpson – I think I've seen a Mr. John Eldred. What is he like to look at?"

"It must be ten years since I saw him: he would be a thin elderly man now, and unless he has shaved them off, he has that sort of whiskers which people used to call Dundreary or Piccadilly something."

"—weepers. Yes, that *is* the man."

"Where did you come across him, Mr. Garrett?"

"I don't know if I could tell you," said Garrett mendaciously, 'in some public place. But you hadn't finished."

"Really I had nothing much to add, only that John Eldred, of course, paid no attention whatever to my letters, and has enjoyed the estate ever since, while my daughter and I have had to take to the lodging-house business here, which I must say has not turned out by any means so unpleasant as I feared it might."

"But about the envelope."

"To be sure! Why, the puzzle turns on that. Give Mr. Garrett the paper out of my desk."

It was a small slip, with nothing whatever on it but five numerals, not divided or punctuated in any way: 11334.

Mr. Garrett pondered, but there was a light in his eye. Suddenly he 'made a face', and then asked, "Do you suppose that Mr. Eldred can have any more clue than you have to the title of the book?"

"I have sometimes thought he must," said Mrs. Simpson, "and in this way: that my uncle must have made the will not very long before he died (that, I think, he said himself), and got rid of the book immediately afterwards. But all his books were very carefully catalogued: and John has the catalogue: and John was most particular that no books whatever should be sold out of the house. And I'm told that he is always journeying about to booksellers and libraries; so I fancy that he must have found out just which books are missing from my uncle's library of those which are entered in the catalogue, and must be hunting for them."

"Just so, just so," said Mr. Garrett, and relapsed into thought.

★   ★   ★

No later than next day he received a letter which, as he told Mrs. Simpson with great regret, made it absolutely necessary for him to cut short his stay at Burnstow.

Sorry as he was to leave them (and they were at least as sorry to part with him), he had begun to feel that a crisis, all-important to Mrs. (and shall we add, Miss?) Simpson, was very possibly supervening.

In the train Garrett was uneasy and excited. He racked his brains to think whether the press mark of the book which Mr. Eldred had been inquiring after was one in any way corresponding to the numbers on Mrs. Simpson's little bit of paper. But he found to his dismay that the shock of the previous week had really so upset him that he could neither remember any vestige of the title or nature of the book, or even of the locality to which he had gone to seek it. And yet all other parts of library topography and work were clear as ever in his mind.

And another thing – he stamped with annoyance as he thought of it – he had at first hesitated, and then had forgotten, to ask Mrs. Simpson for the name of the place where Eldred lived. That, however, he could write about.

At least he had his clue in the figures on the paper. If they referred to a press mark in his library, they were only susceptible of a limited number of interpretations. They might be divided into 1.13.34, 11.33.4, or 11.3.34. He could try all these in the space of a few minutes, and if any one were missing he had every means of tracing it. He got very quickly to work, though a few minutes had to be spent in explaining his early return to his landlady and his colleagues. 1.13.34. was in place and contained no extraneous writing. As he drew near to Class 11 in the same gallery, its association struck him like a chill. But he *must* go on. After a cursory glance at 11.33.4 (which first confronted him, and was a perfectly new book) he ran his eye along the line of quartos which fills 11.3. The gap he feared was there: 34 was out. A moment was spent in making sure that it had not been misplaced, and then he was off to the vestibule.

"Has 11.3.34 gone out? Do you recollect noticing that number?"

"Notice the number? What do you take me for, Mr. Garrett? There, take and look over the tickets for yourself, if you've got a free day before you."

"Well then, has a Mr. Eldred called again? – the old gentleman who came the day I was taken ill. Come! you'd remember him."

"What do you suppose? Of course I recollect of him: no, he haven't been in again, not since you went off for your 'oliday. And yet I seem to – there now. Roberts'll know. Roberts, do you recollect of the name of Heldred?"

"Not arf," said Roberts. "You mean the man that sent a bob over the price for the parcel, and I wish they all did."

"Do you mean to say you've been sending books to Mr. Eldred? Come, do speak up! Have you?"

"Well now, Mr. Garrett, if a gentleman sends the ticket all wrote correct and the seckretry says this book may go and the box ready addressed sent with the note, and a sum of money sufficient to deefray the railway charges, what would be *your* action in the matter, Mr. Garrett, if I may take the liberty to ask such a question? Would you or would you not have taken the trouble to oblige, or would you have chucked the 'ole thing under the counter and—"

"You were perfectly right, of course, Hodgson – perfectly right: only, would you kindly oblige me by showing me the ticket Mr. Eldred sent, and letting me know his address?"

"To be sure, Mr. Garrett; so long as I'm not 'ectored about and informed that I don't know my duty, I'm willing to oblige in every way feasible to my power. There is the ticket on the file. J. Eldred, 11.3.34. Title of work: T-a-l-m – well, there, you can make what you like of it – not a novel, I should 'azard the guess. And here is Mr. Heldred's note applying for the book in question, which I see he terms it a track."

"Thanks, thanks: but the address? There's none on the note."

"Ah, indeed; well, now … stay now, Mr. Garrett, I 'ave it. Why, that note come inside of the parcel, which was directed very thoughtful to save all trouble, ready to be sent back with the book inside; and if I *have* made any mistake in this 'ole transaction, it lays just in the one point that I neglected to enter the address in my little book here what I keep. Not but what I dare say there was good reasons for me not entering of it: but there, I haven't the time, neither have you, I dare say, to go into 'em just now. And – no, Mr. Garrett, I do *not* carry it in my 'ed, else what would be the use of me keeping this little book here – just a ordinary common notebook, you see, which I make a practice of entering all such names and addresses in it as I see fit to do?"

"Admirable arrangement, to be sure – but – all right, thank you. When did the parcel go off?"

"Half-past ten, this morning."

"Oh, good; and it's just one now."

Garrett went upstairs in deep thought. How was he to get the address? A telegram to Mrs. Simpson: he might miss a train by waiting for the answer. Yes, there was one other way. She had said that Eldred lived on his uncle's estate. If this were so, he might find that place entered in the donation-book. That he could run through quickly, now that he knew the title of the book. The register was soon before him, and, knowing that the old man had died more than twenty years ago, he gave him a good margin, and turned back to 1870. There was but one entry possible. 1875, August 14th. *Talmud: Tractatus Middoth cum comm. R. Nachmanidae.* Amstelod. 1707. Given by J. Rant, D.D., of Bretfield Manor.

A gazetteer showed Bretfield to be three miles from a small station on the main line. Now to ask the doorkeeper whether he recollected if the name on the parcel had been anything like Bretfield.

"No, nothing like. It was, now you mention it, Mr. Garrett, either Bredfield or Britfield, but nothing like that other name what you coated."

So far well. Next, a time-table. A train could be got in twenty minutes – taking two hours over the journey. The only chance, but one not to be missed; and the train was taken.

If he had been fidgety on the journey up, he was almost distracted on the journey down. If he found Eldred, what could he say? That it had been discovered that the book was a rarity and must be recalled? An obvious untruth. Or that it was believed to contain important manuscript notes? Eldred would of course show him the book, from which the leaf would already have been removed. He might, perhaps, find traces of the removal – a torn edge of a fly-leaf probably – and who could disprove, what Eldred was certain to say, that he too had noticed and regretted the mutilation? Altogether the chase seemed very hopeless. The one chance was this. The book had left the library at 10:30: it might not have been put into the first possible train, at 11:20. Granted that, then he might be lucky enough to arrive simultaneously with it and patch up some story which would induce Eldred to give it up.

It was drawing towards evening when he got out upon the platform of his station, and, like most country stations, this one seemed unnaturally quiet. He waited about till the one or two passengers who got out with him had drifted off, and then inquired of the station-master whether Mr. Eldred was in the neighbourhood.

"Yes, and pretty near too, I believe. I fancy he means calling here for a parcel he expects. Called for it once today already, didn't he, Bob?" (to the porter).

"Yes, sir, he did; and appeared to think it was all along of me that it didn't come by the two o'clock. Anyhow, I've got it for him now," and the porter flourished a square parcel, which a glance assured Garrett contained all that was of any importance to him at that particular moment.

"Bretfield, sir? Yes – three miles just about. Short cut across these three fields brings it down by half a mile. There: there's Mr. Eldred's trap."

A dog-cart drove up with two men in it, of whom Garrett, gazing back as he crossed the little station yard, easily recognised one. The fact that Eldred was driving was slightly in his favour – for most likely he would not open the parcel in the presence of his servant. On the other hand, he would get home quickly, and unless Garrett were there within a very few minutes of his arrival, all would be over. He must hurry; and that he did. His short cut took him along one side of a triangle, while the cart had two sides to traverse; and it was delayed a little at the station, so that Garrett was in the third of the three fields when he heard the wheels fairly near. He had made the best progress possible, but the pace at which the cart was coming made him despair. At this rate it *must* reach home ten minutes before him, and ten minutes would more than suffice for the fulfilment of Mr. Eldred's project.

It was just at this time that the luck fairly turned. The evening was still, and sounds came clearly. Seldom has any sound given greater relief than that which he now heard: that of the cart pulling up. A few words were exchanged, and it drove on. Garrett, halting in the utmost anxiety, was able to see as it drove past the stile (near which he now stood) that it contained only the servant and not Eldred; further, he made out that Eldred was following on foot. From behind the tall hedge by the stile leading into the road he watched the thin wiry figure pass quickly by with the parcel beneath its arm, and feeling in its pockets. Just as he passed the stile something fell out of a pocket upon the grass, but with so little sound that Eldred was not conscious of it. In a moment more it was safe for Garrett to cross the stile into the road and pick up – a box of matches. Eldred went on, and, as he went, his arms made hasty movements, difficult to interpret in the shadow of the trees that overhung the road. But, as Garrett followed cautiously, he found at various points the key to them – a piece of string, and then the wrapper of the parcel – meant to be thrown over the hedge, but sticking in it.

Now Eldred was walking slower, and it could just be made out that he had opened the book and was turning over the leaves. He stopped, evidently troubled by the failing light. Garrett slipped into a gate-opening, but still watched. Eldred, hastily looking around, sat down on a felled tree-trunk by the roadside and held the open book up close to his eyes. Suddenly he laid it, still open, on his knee, and felt in all his pockets: clearly in vain, and clearly to his annoyance. "You would be glad of your matches now," thought Garrett. Then he took hold of a leaf, and was carefully tearing it out, when two things happened. First, something black seemed to drop upon the white leaf and run down it, and then as Eldred started and was turning to look behind him, a little dark form appeared to rise out of the shadow behind the tree-trunk and from it two arms enclosing a mass of blackness came before Eldred's face and covered his head and neck. His legs and arms were wildly flourished, but no sound came. Then, there was no more movement. Eldred was alone. He had fallen back into the grass behind the tree-trunk. The book was cast into the roadway. Garrett, his anger and suspicion gone for the moment at the sight of this horrid struggle, rushed up with loud cries of "Help!" and so too, to his enormous relief, did a labourer who had just emerged from a field opposite. Together they bent over and supported Eldred, but to no purpose. The conclusion that he was dead was inevitable. "Poor gentleman!" said Garrett to the labourer, when they had laid him down, "what happened to him, do you think?" "I wasn't two hundred yards away," said the man, "when I see Squire Eldred setting reading in his book, and to my thinking he was took with one of these fits – face seemed to go all over black." "Just so," said Garrett. "You didn't see anyone near him? It couldn't have been an assault?" "Not possible – no one couldn't have got away without you or me seeing them." "So I thought. Well, we must get some help, and the doctor and the policeman; and perhaps I had better give them this book."

It was obviously a case for an inquest, and obvious also that Garrett must stay at Bretfield and give his evidence. The medical inspection showed that, though some black dust was found on the face and in the mouth of the deceased, the cause of death was a shock to a weak heart, and not asphyxiation. The fateful book was produced, a respectable quarto printed wholly in Hebrew, and not of an aspect likely to excite even the most sensitive.

"You say, Mr. Garrett, that the deceased gentleman appeared at the moment before his attack to be tearing a leaf out of this book?"

"Yes; I think one of the fly-leaves."

"There is here a fly-leaf partially torn through. It has Hebrew writing on it. Will you kindly inspect it?"

"There are three names in English, sir, also, and a date. But I am sorry to say I cannot read Hebrew writing."

"Thank you. The names have the appearance of being signatures. They are John Rant, Walter Gibson, and James Frost, and the date is 20 July, 1875. Does anyone here know any of these names?"

The Rector, who was present, volunteered a statement that the uncle of the deceased, from whom he inherited, had been named Rant.

The book being handed to him, he shook a puzzled head. "This is not like any Hebrew I ever learnt."

"You are sure that it is Hebrew?"

"What? Yes – I suppose.... No – my dear sir, you are perfectly right – that is, your suggestion is exactly to the point. Of course – it is not Hebrew at all. It is English, and it is a will."

It did not take many minutes to show that here was indeed a will of Dr. John Rant, bequeathing the whole of the property lately held by John Eldred to Mrs. Mary Simpson. Clearly the discovery of such a document would amply justify Mr. Eldred's agitation. As to the partial tearing of the leaf, the coroner pointed out that no useful purpose could be attained by speculations whose correctness it would never be possible to establish.

$$\star \quad \star \quad \star$$

The Tractate Middoth was naturally taken in charge by the coroner for further investigation, and Mr. Garrett explained privately to him the history of it, and the position of events so far as he knew or guessed them.

He returned to his work next day, and on his walk to the station passed the scene of Mr. Eldred's catastrophe. He could hardly leave it without another look, though the recollection of what he had seen there made him shiver, even on that bright morning. He walked round, with some misgivings, behind the felled tree. Something dark that still lay there made him start back for a moment: but it hardly stirred. Looking closer, he saw that it was a thick black mass of cobwebs; and, as he stirred it gingerly with his stick, several large spiders ran out of it into the grass.

★　　★　　★

There is no great difficulty in imagining the steps by which William Garrett, from being an assistant in a great library, attained to his present position of prospective owner of Bretfield Manor, now in the occupation of his mother-in-law, Mrs. Mary Simpson.

# THE TREASURE OF
# ABBOT THOMAS

## CHAPTER I

*Verum usque in praesentem diem multa garriunt inter se Canonici de
abscondito quodam istius Abbatis Thomae thesauro, quem saepe, quanquam
adhuc incassum, quaesiverunt Steinfeldenses. Ipsum enim Thomam adhuc
florida in aetate existentem ingentem auri massam circa monasterium defodisse
perhibent; de quo multoties interrogatus ubi esset, cum risu respondere
solitus erat: "Job, Johannes, et Zacharias vel vobis vel posteris indicabunt";
idemque aliquando adiicere se inventuris minime invisurum. Inter alia
huius Abbatis opera, hoc memoria praecipue dignum iudico quod fenestram
magnam in orientali parte alae australis in ecclesia sua imaginibus optime in
vitro depictis impleverit: id quod et ipsius effigies et insignia ibidem posita
demonstrant. Domum quoque Abbatialem fere totam restauravit: puteo in
atrio ipsius effosso et lapidibus marmoreis pulchre caelatis exornato. Decessit
autem, morte aliquantulum subitanea perculsus, aetatis suae anno lxxiido,
incarnationis vero Dominiae mdxxixo.*

"**I suppose** I shall have to translate this," said the antiquary to himself,
as he finished copying the above lines from that rather rare and
exceedingly diffuse book, the *Sertum Steinfeldense Norbertinum.*
"Well, it may as well be done first as last," and accordingly the following
rendering was very quickly produced:

*An account of the Premonstratensian abbey of Steinfeld, in the Eiffel,
with lives of the Abbots, published at Cologne in 1712 by Christian*

*Albert Erhard, a resident in the district. The epithet Norbertinum is due
to the fact that St. Norbert was founder of the Premonstratensian Order.*

Up to the present day there is much gossip among the Canons
about a certain hidden treasure of this Abbot Thomas, for which
those of Steinfeld have often made search, though hitherto in vain.
The story is that Thomas, while yet in the vigour of life, concealed
a very large quantity of gold somewhere in the monastery. He was
often asked where it was, and always answered, with a laugh: "Job,
John, and Zechariah will tell either you or your successors." He
sometimes added that he should feel no grudge against those who
might find it. Among other works carried out by this Abbot I may
specially mention his filling the great window at the east end of the
south aisle of the church with figures admirably painted on glass, as
his effigy and arms in the window attest. He also restored almost
the whole of the Abbot's lodging, and dug a well in the court of it,
which he adorned with beautiful carvings in marble. He died rather
suddenly in the seventy-second year of his age, A.D. 1529.

The object which the antiquary had before him at the moment
was that of tracing the whereabouts of the painted windows of the
Abbey Church of Steinfeld. Shortly after the Revolution, a very
large quantity of painted glass made its way from the dissolved abbeys
of Germany and Belgium to this country, and may now be seen
adorning various of our parish churches, cathedrals, and private
chapels. Steinfeld Abbey was among the most considerable of these
involuntary contributors to our artistic possessions (I am quoting
the somewhat ponderous preamble of the book which the antiquary
wrote), and the greater part of the glass from that institution can
be identified without much difficulty by the help, either of the
numerous inscriptions in which the place is mentioned, or of the
subjects of the windows, in which several well-defined cycles or
narratives were represented.

The passage with which I began my story had set the antiquary
on the track of another identification. In a private chapel – no

matter where – he had seen three large figures, each occupying a whole light in a window, and evidently the work of one artist. Their style made it plain that that artist had been a German of the sixteenth century; but hitherto the more exact localising of them had been a puzzle. They represented – will you be surprised to hear it? – JOB PATRIARCHA, JOHANNES EVANGELISTA, ZACHARIAS PROPHETA, and each of them held a book or scroll, inscribed with a sentence from his writings. These, as a matter of course, the antiquary had noted, and had been struck by the curious way in which they differed from any text of the Vulgate that he had been able to examine. Thus the scroll in Job's hand was inscribed: *Auro est locus in quo absconditur* (for *conflatur*)[1]; on the book of John was: *Habent in vestimentis suis scripturam quam nemo novit*[2] (for in *vestimento scriptum*, the following words being taken from another verse); and Zacharias had: *Super lapidem unum septem oculi sunt*[3] (which alone of the three presents an unaltered text).

A sad perplexity it had been to our investigator to think why these three personages should have been placed together in one window. There was no bond of connexion between them, either historic, symbolic, or doctrinal, and he could only suppose that they must have formed part of a very large series of Prophets and Apostles, which might have filled, say, all the clerestory windows of some capacious church. But the passage from the *Sertum* had altered the situation by showing that the names of the actual personages represented in the glass now in Lord D—'s chapel had been constantly on the lips of Abbot Thomas von Eschenhausen of Steinfeld, and that this Abbot had put up a painted window, probably about the year 1520, in the south aisle of his abbey church. It was no very wild conjecture that the three figures might have formed part of Abbot Thomas's

---

1   'There is a place for gold where it is hidden.'

2   'They have on their raiment a writing which no man knoweth.'

3   'Upon one stone are seven eyes.'

offering; it was one which, moreover, could probably be confirmed or set aside by another careful examination of the glass. And, as Mr. Somerton was a man of leisure, he set out on pilgrimage to the private chapel with very little delay. His conjecture was confirmed to the full. Not only did the style and technique of the glass suit perfectly with the date and place required, but in another window of the chapel he found some glass, known to have been bought along with the figures, which contained the arms of Abbot Thomas von Eschenhausen.

At intervals during his researches Mr. Somerton had been haunted by the recollection of the gossip about the hidden treasure, and, as he thought the matter over, it became more and more obvious to him that if the Abbot meant anything by the enigmatical answer which he gave to his questioners, he must have meant that the secret was to be found somewhere in the window he had placed in the abbey church. It was undeniable, furthermore, that the first of the curiously-selected texts on the scrolls in the window might be taken to have a reference to hidden treasure.

Every feature, therefore, or mark which could possibly assist in elucidating the riddle which, he felt sure, the Abbot had set to posterity he noted with scrupulous care, and, returning to his Berkshire manor-house, consumed many a pint of the midnight oil over his tracings and sketches. After two or three weeks, a day came when Mr. Somerton announced to his man that he must pack his own and his master's things for a short journey abroad, whither for the moment we will not follow him.

# CHAPTER II

Mr. Gregory, the Rector of Parsbury, had strolled out before breakfast, it being a fine autumn morning, as far as the gate of his carriage-drive, with intent to meet the postman and sniff the cool air. Nor was he disappointed of either purpose. Before he had had time to answer more than ten or eleven of the miscellaneous questions propounded to him in the lightness of their hearts by his young offspring, who had accompanied him, the postman was seen approaching; and among the morning's budget was one letter bearing a foreign postmark and stamp (which became at once the objects of an eager competition among the youthful Gregorys), and was addressed in an uneducated, but plainly an English hand.

When the Rector opened it, and turned to the signature, he realised that it came from the confidential valet of his friend and squire, Mr. Somerton. Thus it ran:

> *HONOURED SIR,*
> *Has I am in a great anxiety about Master I write at is Wish to beg you Sir if you could be so good as Step over. Master Has add a Nastey Shock and keeps His Bedd. I never Have known Him like this but No wonder and Nothing will serve but you Sir. Master says would I mintion the Short Way Here is Drive to Cobblince and take a Trap. Hopeing I Have maid all Plain, but am much Confused in Myself what with Anxiatey and Weakfulness at Night. If I might be so Bold Sir it will be a Pleasure to see a Honnest Brish Face among all These Forig ones.*
> *I am Sir*
> *Your obedt Servt*
> *William Brown.*
> *P.S. – The Village for Town I will not Turm. It is name Steenfeld.*

The reader must be left to picture to himself in detail the surprise, confusion, and hurry of preparation into which the receipt of such a letter would be likely to plunge a quiet Berkshire parsonage in the year of grace 1859. It is enough for me to say that a train to town was caught in the course of the day, and that Mr. Gregory was able to secure a cabin in the Antwerp boat and a place in the Coblentz train. Nor was it difficult to manage the transit from that centre to Steinfeld.

I labour under a grave disadvantage as narrator of this story in that I have never visited Steinfeld myself, and that neither of the principal actors in the episode (from whom I derive my information) was able to give me anything but a vague and rather dismal idea of its appearance. I gather that it is a small place, with a large church despoiled of its ancient fittings; a number of rather ruinous great buildings, mostly of the seventeenth century, surround this church; for the abbey, in common with most of those on the Continent, was rebuilt in a luxurious fashion by its inhabitants at that period. It has not seemed to me worth while to lavish money on a visit to the place, for though it is probably far more attractive than either Mr. Somerton or Mr. Gregory thought it, there is evidently little, if anything, of first-rate interest to be seen – except, perhaps, one thing, which I should not care to see.

The inn where the English gentleman and his servant were lodged is, or was, the only 'possible' one in the village. Mr. Gregory was taken to it at once by his driver, and found Mr. Brown waiting at the door. Mr. Brown, a model when in his Berkshire home of the impassive whiskered race who are known as confidential valets, was now egregiously out of his element, in a light tweed suit, anxious, almost irritable, and plainly anything but master of the situation. His relief at the sight of the 'honest British face' of his Rector was unmeasured, but words to describe it were denied him. He could only say:

"Well, I ham pleased, I'm sure, sir, to see you. And so I'm sure, sir, will master."

"How *is* your master, Brown?" Mr. Gregory eagerly put in.

"I think he's better, sir, thank you; but he's had a dreadful time of it. I 'ope he's gettin' some sleep now, but—"

"What has been the matter – I couldn't make out from your letter? Was it an accident of any kind?"

"Well, sir, I 'ardly know whether I'd better speak about it. Master was very partickler he should be the one to tell you. But there's no bones broke – that's one thing I'm sure we ought to be thankful—"

"What does the doctor say?" asked Mr. Gregory.

They were by this time outside Mr. Somerton's bedroom door, and speaking in low tones. Mr. Gregory, who happened to be in front, was feeling for the handle, and chanced to run his fingers over the panels. Before Brown could answer, there was a terrible cry from within the room.

"In God's name, who is that?" were the first words they heard. "Brown, is it?"

"Yes, sir – me, sir, and Mr. Gregory," Brown hastened to answer, and there was an audible groan of relief in reply.

They entered the room, which was darkened against the afternoon sun, and Mr. Gregory saw, with a shock of pity, how drawn, how damp with drops of fear, was the usually calm face of his friend, who, sitting up in the curtained bed, stretched out a shaking hand to welcome him.

"Better for seeing you, my dear Gregory," was the reply to the Rector's first question, and it was palpably true.

After five minutes of conversation Mr. Somerton was more his own man, Brown afterwards reported, than he had been for days. He was able to eat a more than respectable dinner, and talked confidently of being fit to stand a journey to Coblentz within twenty-four hours.

"But there's one thing," he said, with a return of agitation which Mr. Gregory did not like to see, "which I must beg you to do for me, my dear Gregory. Don't," he went on, laying his hand on Gregory's to forestall any interruption – "don't ask me what it is, or why I want it done. I'm not up to explaining it yet; it would throw me back – undo all the good you have done me by coming. The only word I will say about it is that you run no risk whatever by doing it, and that Brown can and will show you tomorrow what it is. It's merely to put back – to keep – something – No; I can't speak of it yet. Do you mind calling Brown?"

"Well, Somerton," said Mr. Gregory, as he crossed the room to the door, "I won't ask for any explanations till you see fit to give them. And if this bit of business is as easy as you represent it to be, I will very gladly undertake it for you the first thing in the morning."

"Ah, I was sure you would, my dear Gregory; I was certain I could rely on you. I shall owe you more thanks than I can tell. Now, here is Brown. Brown, one word with you."

"Shall I go?" interjected Mr. Gregory.

"Not at all. Dear me, no. Brown, the first thing tomorrow morning – (you don't mind early hours, I know, Gregory) – you must take the Rector to – *there*, you know" (a nod from Brown, who looked grave and anxious), "and he and you will put that back. You needn't be in the least alarmed; it's *perfectly* safe in the daytime. You know what I mean. It lies on the step, you know, where – where we put it." (Brown swallowed dryly once or twice, and, failing to speak, bowed.) "And – yes, that's all. Only this one other word, my dear Gregory. If you *can* manage to keep from questioning Brown about this matter, I shall be still more bound to you. Tomorrow evening, at latest, if all goes well, I shall be able, I believe, to tell you the whole story from start to finish. And now I'll wish you goodnight. Brown will be with me – he sleeps here – and if I were you, I should lock my door. Yes, be particular to do that. They – they like it, the people here, and it's better. Goodnight, goodnight."

They parted upon this, and if Mr. Gregory woke once or twice in the small hours and fancied he heard a fumbling about the lower part of his locked door, it was, perhaps, no more than what a quiet man, suddenly plunged into a strange bed and the heart of a mystery, might reasonably expect. Certainly he thought, to the end of his days, that he had heard such a sound twice or three times between midnight and dawn.

He was up with the sun, and out in company with Brown soon after. Perplexing as was the service he had been asked to perform for Mr. Somerton, it was not a difficult or an alarming one, and within half an hour from his leaving the inn it was over. What it was I shall not as yet divulge.

Later in the morning Mr. Somerton, now almost himself again, was able to make a start from Steinfeld; and that same evening, whether at Coblentz or at some intermediate stage on the journey I am not certain, he settled down to the promised explanation. Brown was present, but how much of the matter was ever really made plain to his comprehension he would never say, and I am unable to conjecture.

# CHAPTER III

This was Mr. Somerton's story:

"You know roughly, both of you, that this expedition of mine was undertaken with the object of tracing something in connexion with some old painted glass in Lord D——'s private chapel. Well, the starting-point of the whole matter lies in this passage from an old printed book, to which I will ask your attention."

And at this point Mr. Somerton went carefully over some ground with which we are already familiar.

"On my second visit to the chapel," he went on, "my purpose was to take every note I could of figures, lettering, diamond-scratchings on the glass, and even apparently accidental markings. The first point which I tackled was that of the inscribed scrolls. I could not doubt that the first of these, that of Job – 'There is a place for the gold where it is hidden' – with its intentional alteration, must refer to the treasure; so I applied myself with some confidence to the next, that of St. John – 'They have on their vestures a writing which no man knoweth.' The natural question will have occurred to you: Was there an inscription on the robes of the figures? I could see none; each of the three had a broad black border to his mantle, which made a conspicuous and rather ugly feature in the window. I was nonplussed, I will own, and, but for a curious bit of luck, I think I should have left the search where the Canons of Steinfeld had left it before me. But it so happened that there was a good deal of dust on the surface of the glass, and Lord D——, happening to come in, noticed my blackened hands, and kindly insisted on sending for a Turk's head broom to clean down the window. There must, I suppose, have been a rough piece in the broom; anyhow, as it passed over the border of one of the mantles, I noticed that it left a long scratch, and that some yellow stain instantly showed up. I asked the man to stop his work for a moment, and ran up the ladder to examine the place. The yellow stain was there, sure enough, and what had come away was a thick black pigment, which had evidently been laid on with the brush after the glass had been burnt, and could therefore be easily scraped off without doing any harm. I scraped, accordingly, and you will hardly believe – no, I do you an injustice; you will have guessed already – that I found under this black pigment two or three clearly-formed capital letters in yellow stain on a clear ground. Of course, I could hardly contain my delight.

"I told Lord D— that I had detected an inscription which I thought might be very interesting, and begged to be allowed to uncover the whole of it. He made no difficulty about it whatever, told me to do exactly as I pleased, and then, having an engagement, was obliged – rather to my relief, I must say – to leave me. I set to work at once, and found the task a fairly easy one. The pigment, disintegrated, of course, by time, came off almost at a touch, and I don't think that it took me a couple of hours, all told, to clean the whole of the black borders in all three lights. Each of the figures had, as the inscription said, 'a writing on their vestures which nobody knew'.

"This discovery, of course, made it absolutely certain to my mind that I was on the right track. And, now, what was the inscription? While I was cleaning the glass I almost took pains not to read the lettering, saving up the treat until I had got the whole thing clear. And when that was done, my dear Gregory, I assure you I could almost have cried from sheer disappointment. What I read was only the most hopeless jumble of letters that was ever shaken up in a hat. Here it is:

Job. DREVICIOPEDMOOMSMVIVLISLCAVIBASBATAOVT
St. John. RDIIEAMRLESIPVSPODSEEIRSETTAAESGIAVNNR
Zechariah. DREVICIOPEDMOOMSMVIVLISLCAVIBA SBATAOVT

"Blank as I felt and must have looked for the first few minutes, my disappointment didn't last long. I realised almost at once that I was dealing with a cipher or cryptogram; and I reflected that it was likely to be of a pretty simple kind, considering its early date. So I copied the letters with the most anxious care. Another little point, I may tell you, turned up in the process which confirmed my belief in the cipher. After copying the letters on Job's robe I counted them, to make sure that I had them right. There were thirty-eight; and, just as I finished going through them, my eye fell on a scratching made with a sharp point on the edge of the border. It was simply the number xxxviii in Roman numerals. To cut the matter short, there was a similar note, as I may call it, in each of the other lights; and that made it plain to me that the glass-painter had had very strict orders from Abbot Thomas about the inscription, and had taken pains to get it correct.

"Well, after that discovery you may imagine how minutely I went over the whole surface of the glass in search of further light. Of course, I did not neglect the inscription on the scroll of Zechariah – 'Upon one stone are seven eyes', but I very quickly concluded that this must refer to some mark on a stone which could only be found *in situ*, where the treasure was concealed. To be short, I made all possible notes and sketches and tracings, and then came back to Parsbury to work out the cipher at leisure. Oh, the agonies I went through! I thought myself very clever at first, for I made sure that the key would be found in some of the old books on secret writing. The *Steganographia* of Joachim Trithemius, who was an earlier contemporary of Abbot Thomas, seemed particularly promising; so I got that and Selenius's *Cryptographia* and Bacon's *de Augmentis Scientiarum* and some more. But I could hit upon nothing. Then I tried the principle of the 'most frequent letter', taking first Latin and then German as a basis. That didn't help, either; whether it ought to have done so, I am not clear. And then I came back to the window itself, and read over my notes, hoping almost against hope that the Abbot might himself have somewhere supplied the key I wanted. I could make nothing out of the colour or pattern of the robes. There were no landscape backgrounds with subsidiary objects; there was nothing in the canopies. The only resource possible seemed to be in the attitudes of the figures. 'Job,' I read: 'scroll in left hand, forefinger of right hand extended upwards. John: holds inscribed book in left hand; with right hand blesses, with two fingers. Zechariah: scroll in left hand; right hand extended upwards, as Job, but with three fingers pointing up.' In other words, I reflected, Job has *one* finger extended, John has *two*, Zechariah has *three*. May not there be a numeral key concealed in that? My dear

Gregory," said Mr. Somerton, laying his hand on his friend's knee, "that *was* the key. I didn't get it to fit at first, but after two or three trials I saw what was meant. After the first letter of the inscription you skip *one* letter, after the next you skip *two*, and after that skip *three*. Now look at the result I got. I've underlined the letters which form words:

[D]R[E]VI[C]IOP[E]D[M]OO[M]SMV[I]V[L]IS[L]CAV[I]B[A]
SB[A]TAO[V]T
[R]DI[I]EAM[R]L[E]SI[P]VSP[O]D[S]EE[I]RSE[T]T[A]AE[S]
GIA[V]N[N]R
F[T]EEA[I]L[N]QD[P]VAI[V]M[T]LE[E]ATT[O]H[I]OO[N]
VMC[A]A[T].H.Q.E.

"Do you see it? '*Decem millia auri reposita sunt in puteo in at...*' (Ten thousand [pieces] of gold are laid up in a well in ...), followed by an incomplete word beginning *at*. So far so good. I tried the same plan with the remaining letters; but it wouldn't work, and I fancied that perhaps the placing of dots after the three last letters might indicate some difference of procedure. Then I thought to myself, 'Wasn't there some allusion to a well in the account of Abbot Thomas in that book the "Sertum"?' Yes, there was: he built a *puteus in atrio* (a well in the court). There, of course, was my word *atrio*. The next step was to copy out the remaining letters of the inscription, omitting those I had already used. That gave what you will see on this slip:

RVIIOPDOOSMVVISCAVB SBTAOTDIEAMLSIVSPDEERSETA
EGIANRFEEALQDVAIML EATTHOOVMCA.H.Q.E.

"Now, I knew what the three first letters I wanted were – namely, *rio* – to complete the word *atrio*; and, as you will see, these are all to be found in the first five letters. I was a little confused at first by the occurrence of two *i's*, but very soon I saw that every alternate letter must be taken in the remainder of the inscription. You can work it out for yourself; the result, continuing where the first 'round' left off, is this:

*'rio domus abbatialis de Steinfeld a me, Thoma, qui
posui custodem super ea. Gare à qui la touche'.*

"So the whole secret was out:

*'Ten thousand pieces of gold are laid up in the well in the court of the
Abbot's house of Steinfeld by me, Thomas, who have set a guardian over
them. Gare à qui la touche.'*

"The last words, I ought to say, are a device which Abbot Thomas
had adopted. I found it with his arms in another piece of glass at Lord
D—'s, and he drafted it bodily into his cipher, though it doesn't quite
fit in point of grammar.

"Well, what would any human being have been tempted to do,
my dear Gregory, in my place? Could he have helped setting off, as I
did, to Steinfeld, and tracing the secret literally to the fountain-head?
I don't believe he could. Anyhow, I couldn't, and, as I needn't tell
you, I found myself at Steinfeld as soon as the resources of civilisation
could put me there, and installed myself in the inn you saw. I must tell
you that I was not altogether free from forebodings – on one hand of
disappointment, on the other of danger. There was always the possibility
that Abbot Thomas's well might have been wholly obliterated, or else
that someone, ignorant of cryptograms, and guided only by luck, might
have stumbled on the treasure before me. And then" – there was a very
perceptible shaking of the voice here – 'I was not entirely easy, I need
not mind confessing, as to the meaning of the words about the guardian
of the treasure. But, if you don't mind, I'll say no more about that until
– until it becomes necessary.

"At the first possible opportunity Brown and I began exploring
the place. I had naturally represented myself as being interested in the
remains of the abbey, and we could not avoid paying a visit to the
church, impatient as I was to be elsewhere. Still, it did interest me to
see the windows where the glass had been, and especially that at the east
end of the south aisle. In the tracery lights of that I was startled to see

some fragments and coats-of-arms remaining – Abbot Thomas's shield was there, and a small figure with a scroll inscribed *Oculos habent, et non videbunt* (They have eyes, and shall not see), which, I take it, was a hit of the Abbot at his Canons.

"But, of course, the principal object was to find the Abbot's house. There is no prescribed place for this, so far as I know, in the plan of a monastery; you can't predict of it, as you can of the chapter-house, that it will be on the eastern side of the cloister, or, as of the dormitory, that it will communicate with a transept of the church. I felt that if I asked many questions I might awaken lingering memories of the treasure, and I thought it best to try first to discover it for myself. It was not a very long or difficult search. That three-sided court south-east of the church, with deserted piles of building round it, and grass-grown pavement, which you saw this morning, was the place. And glad enough I was to see that it was put to no use, and was neither very far from our inn nor overlooked by any inhabited building; there were only orchards and paddocks on the slopes east of the church. I can tell you that fine stone glowed wonderfully in the rather watery yellow sunset that we had on the Tuesday afternoon.

"Next, what about the well? There was not much doubt about that, as you can testify. It is really a very remarkable thing. That curb is, I think, of Italian marble, and the carving I thought must be Italian also. There were reliefs, you will perhaps remember, of Eliezer and Rebekah, and of Jacob opening the well for Rachel, and similar subjects; but, by way of disarming suspicion, I suppose, the Abbot had carefully abstained from any of his cynical and allusive inscriptions.

"I examined the whole structure with the keenest interest, of course – a square well-head with an opening in one side; an arch over it, with a wheel for the rope to pass over, evidently in very good condition still, for it had been used within sixty years, or perhaps even later, though not quite recently. Then there was the question of depth and access to the interior. I suppose the depth was about sixty to seventy feet; and as to the other point, it really seemed as if the Abbot had wished to lead searchers up to the very door of his treasure-house, for, as you tested for yourself, there were big blocks of stone bonded into the masonry, and leading down in a regular staircase round and round the inside of the well.

"It seemed almost too good to be true. I wondered if there was a trap – if the stones were so contrived as to tip over when a weight was placed on them; but I tried a good many with my own weight and with my stick, and all seemed, and actually were, perfectly firm. Of course, I resolved that Brown and I would make an experiment that very night.

"I was well prepared. Knowing the sort of place I should have to explore, I had brought a sufficiency of good rope and bands of webbing to surround my body, and cross-bars to hold to, as well as lanterns and candles and crowbars, all of which would go into a single carpet-bag and excite no suspicion. I satisfied myself that my rope would be long enough, and that the wheel for the bucket was in good working order, and then we went home to dinner.

"I had a little cautious conversation with the landlord, and made out that he would not be overmuch surprised if I went out for a stroll with my man about nine o'clock, to make (Heaven forgive me!) a sketch of the abbey by moonlight. I asked no questions about the well, and am not likely to do so now. I fancy I know as much about it as anyone in Steinfeld: at least" – with a strong shudder – "I don't want to know any more.

"Now we come to the crisis, and, though I hate to think of it, I feel sure, Gregory, that it will be better for me in all ways to recall it just as it happened. We started, Brown and I, at about nine with our bag, and attracted no attention; for we managed to slip out at the hinder end of the inn-yard into an alley which brought us quite to the edge of the village. In five minutes we were at the well, and for some little time we sat on the edge of the well-head to make sure that no one was stirring or spying on us. All we heard was some horses cropping grass out of sight farther down the eastern slope. We were perfectly unobserved, and had plenty of light from the gorgeous full moon to allow us to get the rope properly fitted over the wheel. Then I secured the band round my body beneath the arms. We attached the end of the rope very securely to a ring in the stonework. Brown took the lighted lantern and followed me; I had a crowbar. And so we began to descend cautiously, feeling every step before we set foot on it, and scanning the walls in search of any marked stone.

"Half aloud I counted the steps as we went down, and we got as far as the thirty-eighth before I noted anything at all irregular in the surface of the masonry. Even here there was no mark, and I began to feel very blank, and to wonder if the Abbot's cryptogram could possibly be an elaborate hoax. At the forty-ninth step the staircase ceased. It was with a very sinking heart that I began retracing my steps, and when I was back on the thirty-eighth – Brown, with the lantern, being a step or two above me – I scrutinised the little bit of irregularity in the stonework with all my might; but there was no vestige of a mark.

"Then it struck me that the texture of the surface looked just a little smoother than the rest, or, at least, in some way different. It might possibly be cement and not stone. I gave it a good blow with my iron bar. There was a decidedly hollow sound, though that might be the result of our being in a well. But there was more. A great flake of cement dropped on to my feet, and I saw marks on the stone underneath. I had tracked the Abbot down, my dear Gregory; even now I think of it with a certain pride. It took but a very few more taps to clear the whole of the cement away, and I saw a slab of stone about two feet square, upon which was engraven a cross. Disappointment again, but only for a moment. It was you, Brown, who reassured me by a casual remark. You said, if I remember right:

"'It's a funny cross: looks like a lot of eyes.'

"I snatched the lantern out of your hand, and saw with inexpressible pleasure that the cross *was* composed of seven eyes, four in a vertical line, three horizontal. The last of the scrolls in the window was explained in the way I had anticipated. Here was my 'stone with the seven eyes'. So far the Abbot's data had been exact, and, as I thought of this, the anxiety about the 'guardian' returned upon me with increased force. Still, I wasn't going to retreat now.

"Without giving myself time to think, I knocked away the cement all round the marked stone, and then gave it a prise on the right side with my crowbar. It moved at once, and I saw that it was but a thin light slab, such as I could easily lift out myself, and that it stopped the entrance to a cavity. I did lift it out unbroken, and set it on the step, for it might be very important to us to be able to replace it. Then I waited for several minutes on the step just above. I don't know why, but I think to see if any dreadful thing would rush out. Nothing happened. Next I lit a candle, and very cautiously I placed it inside the cavity, with some idea of seeing whether there were foul air, and of getting a glimpse of what was inside. There *was* some foulness of air which nearly extinguished the flame, but in no long time it burned quite steadily. The hole went some little way back, and also on the right and left of the entrance, and I could see some rounded light-coloured objects within which might be bags. There was no use in waiting. I faced the cavity, and looked in. There was nothing immediately in the front of the hole. I put my arm in and felt to the right, very gingerly….

"Just give me a glass of cognac, Brown. I'll go on in a moment, Gregory….

"Well, I felt to the right, and my fingers touched something curved, that felt – yes – more or less like leather; dampish it was, and evidently part of a heavy, full thing. There was nothing, I must say, to alarm one. I grew bolder, and putting both hands in as well as I could, I pulled it to me, and it came. It was heavy, but moved more easily than I had expected. As I pulled it towards the entrance, my left elbow knocked over and extinguished the candle. I got the thing fairly in front of the mouth and began drawing it out. Just then Brown gave a sharp ejaculation and ran quickly up the steps with the lantern. He will tell you why in a moment. Startled as I was, I looked round after him, and saw him stand for a minute at the top and then walk away a few yards. Then I heard him call softly, 'All right, sir', and went on pulling out the great bag, in complete darkness. It hung for an instant on the edge of the hole, then slipped forward on to my chest, and *put its arms round my neck*.

"My dear Gregory, I am telling you the exact truth. I believe I am now acquainted with the extremity of terror and repulsion which a man can endure without losing his mind. I can only just manage to tell you now the bare outline of the experience. I was conscious of a most horrible smell of mould, and of a cold kind of face pressed against my own, and moving slowly over it, and of several − I don't know how many − legs or arms or tentacles or something clinging to my body. I screamed out, Brown says, like a beast, and fell away backward from the step on which I stood, and the creature slipped downwards, I suppose, on to that same step. Providentially the band round me held firm. Brown did not lose his head, and was strong enough to pull me up to the top and get me over the edge quite promptly. How he managed it exactly I don't know, and I think he would find it hard to tell you. I believe he contrived to hide our implements in the deserted building nearby, and with very great difficulty he got me back to the inn. I was in no state to make explanations, and Brown knows no German; but next morning I told the people some tale of having had a bad fall in the abbey ruins, which, I suppose, they believed. And now, before I go further, I should just like you to hear what Brown's experiences during those few minutes were. Tell the Rector, Brown, what you told me."

"Well, sir," said Brown, speaking low and nervously, "it was just this way. Master was busy down in front of the 'ole, and I was 'olding the lantern and looking on, when I 'eard somethink drop in the water from the top, as I thought. So I looked up, and I see someone's 'ead lookin' over at us. I s'pose I must ha' said somethink, and I 'eld the light up and run up the steps, and my light shone right on the face. That was a bad un, sir, if ever I see one! A holdish man, and the face very much fell in, and larfin', as I thought. And I got up the steps as quick pretty nigh as I'm tellin' you, and when I was out on the ground there warn't a sign of any person. There 'adn't been the time for anyone to get away, let alone a hold chap, and I made sure he warn't crouching down by the well, nor nothink. Next thing I hear master cry out somethink 'orrible, and hall I see was him hanging out by the rope, and, as master says, 'owever I got him up I couldn't tell you."

"You hear that, Gregory?" said Mr. Somerton. "Now, does any explanation of that incident strike you?"

"The whole thing is so ghastly and abnormal that I must own it puts me quite off my balance; but the thought did occur to me that possibly the – well, the person who set the trap might have come to see the success of his plan."

"Just so, Gregory, just so. I can think of nothing else so – *likely*, I should say, if such a word had a place anywhere in my story. I think it must have been the Abbot.... Well, I haven't much more to tell you. I spent a miserable night, Brown sitting up with me. Next day I was no better; unable to get up; no doctor to be had; and, if one had been available, I doubt if he could have done much for me. I made Brown write off to you, and spent a second terrible night. And, Gregory, of this I am sure, and I think it affected me more than the first shock, for it lasted longer: there was someone or something on the watch outside my door the whole night. I almost fancy there were two. It wasn't only the faint noises I heard from time to time all through the dark hours, but there was the smell – the hideous smell of mould. Every rag I had had on me on that first evening I had stripped off and made Brown take it away. I believe he stuffed the things into the stove in his room; and yet the smell was there, as intense as it had been in the well; and, what is more, it came from outside the door. But with the first glimmer of dawn it faded out, and the sounds ceased, too; and that convinced me that the thing or things were creatures of darkness, and could not stand the daylight; and so I was sure that if anyone could put back the stone, it or they would be powerless until someone else took it away again. I had to wait until you came to get that done. Of course, I couldn't send Brown to do it by himself, and still less could I tell anyone who belonged to the place.

"Well, there is my story; and, if you don't believe it, I can't help it. But I think you do."

"Indeed," said Mr. Gregory, "I can find no alternative. I *must* believe it! I saw the well and the stone myself, and had a glimpse, I thought, of the bags or something else in the hole. And, to be plain with you, Somerton, I believe my door was watched last night, too."

"I dare say it was, Gregory; but, thank goodness, that is over. Have you, by the way, anything to tell about your visit to that dreadful place?"

"Very little," was the answer. "Brown and I managed easily enough to get the slab into its place, and he fixed it very firmly with the irons and wedges you had desired him to get, and we contrived to smear the surface with mud so that it looks just like the rest of the wall. One thing I did notice in the carving on the well-head, which I think must have escaped you. It was a horrid, grotesque shape – perhaps more like a toad than anything else, and there was a label by it inscribed with the two words, '*Depositum custodi*'."

# TWO DOCTORS

It is a very common thing, in my experience, to find papers shut up in old books; but one of the rarest things to come across any such that are at all interesting. Still it does happen, and one should never destroy them unlooked at. Now it was a practice of mine before the war occasionally to buy old ledgers of which the paper was good, and which possessed a good many blank leaves, and to extract these and use them for my own notes and writings. One such I purchased for a small sum in 1911. It was tightly clasped, and its boards were warped by having for years been obliged to embrace a number of extraneous sheets. Three-quarters of this inserted matter had lost all vestige of importance for any living human being: one bundle had not. That it belonged to a lawyer is certain, for it is endorsed: *The strangest case I have yet met*, and bears initials, and an address in Gray's Inn. It is only materials for a case, and consists of statements by possible witnesses. The man who would have been the defendant or prisoner seems never to have appeared. The *dossier* is not complete, but, such as it is, it furnishes a riddle in which the supernatural appears to play a part. You must see what you can make of it.

The following is the setting and the tale as I elicit it.

Dr. Abell was walking in his garden one afternoon waiting for his horse to be brought round that he might set out on his visits for the day. As the place was Islington, the month June, and the year 1718, we conceive the surroundings as being countrified and pleasant. To him entered his confidential servant, Luke Jennett, who had been with him twenty years.

"I said I wished to speak to him, and what I had to say might take some quarter of an hour. He accordingly bade me go into his study, which was a room opening on the terrace path where he was walking, and came in himself and sat down. I told him that, much against my will, I must look out for another place. He inquired what was my reason, in consideration I had been so long with him. I said if he would excuse me he would do me a great kindness, because (this appears to have been common form even in 1718) I was one that always liked to have everything pleasant about me. As well as I can remember, he said that was his case likewise, but he would wish to know why I should change my mind after so many years, and, says he, 'you know there can be no talk of a remembrance of you in my will if you leave my service now.' I said I had made my reckoning of that.

"'Then,' says he, 'you must have some complaint to make, and if I could I would willingly set it right.' And at that I told him, not seeing how I could keep it back, the matter of my former affidavit and of the bedstaff in the dispensing-room, and said that a house where such things happened was no place for me. At which he, looking very black upon me, said no more, but called me fool, and said he would pay what was owing me in the morning; and so, his horse being waiting, went out. So for that night I lodged with my sister's husband near Battle Bridge and came early next morning to my late master, who then made a great matter that I had not lain in his house and stopped a crown out of my wages owing.

"After that I took service here and there, not for long at a time, and saw no more of him till I came to be Dr. Quinn's man at Dodds Hall in Islington."

There is one very obscure part in this statement, namely, the reference to the former affidavit and the matter of the bedstaff. The former affidavit is not in the bundle of papers. It is to be feared that it was taken out to be read because of its special oddity, and not put back. Of what nature the story was may be guessed later, but as yet no clue has been put into our hands.

The Rector of Islington, Jonathan Pratt, is the next to step forward. He furnishes particulars of the standing and reputation of Dr. Abell and Dr. Quinn, both of whom lived and practised in his parish.

"It is not to be supposed," he says, "that a physician should be a regular attendant at morning and evening prayers, or at the Wednesday lectures, but within the measure of their ability I would say that both these persons fulfilled their obligations as loyal members of the Church of England. At the same time (as you desire my private mind) I must say, in the language of the schools, *distinguo*. Dr. A. was to me a source of perplexity, Dr. Q. to my eye a plain, honest believer, not inquiring over closely into points of belief, but squaring his practice to what lights he had. The other interested himself in questions to which Providence, as I hold, designs no answer to be given us in this state: he would ask me, for example, what place I believed those beings now to hold in the scheme of creation which by some are thought neither to have stood fast when the rebel angels fell, nor to have joined with them to the full pitch of their transgression.

"As was suitable, my first answer to him was a question, What warrant he had for supposing any such beings to exist? for that there was none in Scripture I took it he was aware. It appeared – for as I am on the subject, the whole tale may be given – that he grounded himself on such passages as that of the satyr which Jerome tells us conversed with Antony; but thought too that some parts of Scripture might be cited in support. 'And besides,' said he, 'you know 'tis the universal belief among those that spend their days and nights abroad, and I would add that if your calling took you so continuously as it does me about the country lanes by night, you might not be so surprised as I see you to be by my suggestion.' 'You are then of John Milton's mind,' I said, 'and hold that:

*'Millions of spiritual creatures walk the earth*
*Unseen, both when we wake and when we sleep.'*

"'I do not know,' he said, 'why Milton should take upon himself to say "unseen"; though to be sure he was blind when he wrote that. But for the rest, why, yes, I think he was in the right.' 'Well,' I said, 'though not so often as you, I am not seldom called abroad pretty late; but I have no mind of meeting a satyr in our Islington lanes in all the years I have been here; and if you have had the better luck, I am sure the Royal Society would be glad to know of it.'

"I am reminded of these trifling expressions because Dr. A. took them so ill, stamping out of the room in a huff with some such word as that these high and dry parsons had no eyes but for a prayerbook or a pint of wine.

"But this was not the only time that our conversation took a remarkable turn. There was an evening when he came in, at first seeming gay and in good spirits, but afterwards as he sat and smoked by the fire falling into a musing way; out of which to rouse him I said pleasantly that I supposed he had had no meetings of late with his odd friends. A question which did effectually arouse him, for he looked most wildly, and as if scared, upon me, and said, '*You* were never there? I did not see you. Who brought you?' And then in a more collected tone, 'What was this about a meeting? I believe I must have been in a doze.' To which I answered that I was thinking of fauns and centaurs in the dark lane, and not of a witches' Sabbath; but it seemed he took it differently.

"'Well,' said he, 'I can plead guilty to neither; but I find you very much more of a sceptic than becomes your cloth. If you care to know about the dark lane you might do worse than ask my housekeeper that lived at the other end of it when she was a child.' 'Yes,' said I, 'and the old women in the almshouse and the children in the kennel. If I were you, I would send to your brother Quinn for a bolus to clear your brain.' 'Damn Quinn,' says he; 'talk no more of him: he has embezzled four of my best patients this month; I believe it is that cursed man of his, Jennett, that used to be with me, his tongue is never still; it should be nailed to the pillory if he had his deserts.' This, I may say, was the only time of his showing me that he had any grudge against either Dr. Quinn or Jennett, and as was my business, I did my best to persuade him he was mistaken in them. Yet it could not be denied that some respectable families in the parish had given him the cold shoulder, and for no reason that they were willing to allege. The end was that he said he had not done so ill at Islington but that he could afford to live at ease elsewhere when he chose, and anyhow he bore Dr. Quinn no malice. I think

I now remember what observation of mine drew him into the train of thought which he next pursued. It was, I believe, my mentioning some juggling tricks which my brother in the East Indies had seen at the court of the Rajah of Mysore. 'A convenient thing enough,' said Dr. Abell to me, 'if by some arrangement a man could get the power of communicating motion and energy to inanimate objects.' 'As if the axe should move itself against him that lifts it; something of that kind?' 'Well, I don't know that that was in my mind so much; but if you could summon such a volume from your shelf or even order it to open at the right page.'

"He was sitting by the fire – it was a cold evening – and stretched out his hand that way, and just then the fire-irons, or at least the poker, fell over towards him with a great clatter, and I did not hear what else he said. But I told him that I could not easily conceive of an arrangement, as he called it, of such a kind that would not include as one of its conditions a heavier payment than any Christian would care to make; to which he assented. 'But,' he said, 'I have no doubt these bargains can be made very tempting, very persuasive. Still, you would not favour them, eh, Doctor? No, I suppose not.'

"This is as much as I know of Dr. Abell's mind, and the feeling between these men. Dr. Quinn, as I said, was a plain, honest creature, and a man to whom I would have gone – indeed I have before now gone to him for advice on matters of business. He was, however, every now and again, and particularly of late, not exempt from troublesome fancies. There was certainly a time when he was so much harassed by his dreams that he could not keep them to himself, but would tell them to his acquaintances and among them to me. I was at supper at his house, and he was not inclined to let me leave him at my usual time. 'If you go,' he said, 'there will be nothing for it but I must go to bed and dream of the chrysalis.' 'You might be worse off,' said I. 'I do not think it,' he said, and he shook himself like a man who is displeased with the complexion of his thoughts. 'I only meant,' said I, 'that a chrysalis is an innocent thing.' 'This one is not,' he said, 'and I do not care to think of it.'

"However, sooner than lose my company he was fain to tell me (for I pressed him) that this was a dream which had come to him several times of late, and even more than once in a night. It was to this effect, that he seemed to himself to wake under an extreme compulsion to rise and go out of doors. So he would dress himself and go down to his garden door. By the door there stood a spade which he must take, and go out into the garden, and at a particular place in the shrubbery somewhat clear and upon which the moon shone, for there was always in his dream a full moon, he would feel himself forced to dig. And after some time the spade would uncover something light-coloured, which he would perceive to be a stuff, linen or woollen, and this he must clear with his hands. It was always the same: of the size of a man and shaped like the chrysalis of a moth, with the folds showing a promise of an opening at one end.

"He could not describe how gladly he would have left all at this stage and run to the house, but he must not escape so easily. So with many groans, and knowing only too well what to expect, he parted these folds of stuff, or, as it sometimes seemed to be, membrane, and disclosed a head covered with a smooth pink skin, which breaking as the creature stirred, showed him his own face in a state of death. The telling of this so much disturbed him that I was forced out of mere compassion to sit with him the greater part of the night and talk with him upon indifferent subjects. He said that upon every recurrence of this dream he woke and found himself, as it were, fighting for his breath."

Another extract from Luke Jennett's long continuous statement comes in at this point.

"I never told tales of my master, Dr. Abell, to anybody in the neighbourhood. When I was in another service I remember to have spoken to my fellow-servants about the matter of the bedstaff, but I am sure I never said either I or he were the persons concerned, and it met with so little credit that I was affronted and thought best to keep it to myself. And when I came back to Islington and found Dr. Abell still there, who I was told had left the parish, I was clear that it behoved me to use great discretion, for indeed I was afraid of the man, and it is certain I was no party to spreading any ill report of him. My master, Dr. Quinn, was a very just, honest man, and no maker of mischief. I am sure he never stirred a finger nor said a word by way of inducement to a soul to make them leave going to Dr. Abell and come to him; nay, he would hardly be persuaded to attend them that came, until he was convinced that if he did not they would send into the town for a physician rather than do as they had hitherto done.

"I believe it may be proved that Dr. Abell came into my master's house more than once. We had a new chambermaid out of Hertfordshire, and she asked me who was the gentleman that was looking after the master, that is Dr. Quinn, when he was out, and seemed so disappointed that he was out. She said whoever he was he knew the way of the house well, running at once into the study and then into the dispensing-room, and last into the bed-chamber. I made her tell me what he was like, and what she said was suitable enough to Dr. Abell; but besides she told me she saw the same man at church and someone told her that was the Doctor.

"It was just after this that my master began to have his bad nights, and complained to me and other persons, and in particular what discomfort he suffered from his pillow and bedclothes. He said he must buy some to suit him, and should do his own marketing. And accordingly brought home a parcel which he said was of the right quality, but where he bought it we had then no knowledge, only they were marked in thread with a coronet and a bird. The women said they were of a sort not commonly met with and very fine, and my master said they were the comfortablest he ever used, and he slept now both soft and deep. Also the feather pillows were the best sorted and his head would sink into them as if they were a cloud: which I have myself remarked several times when I came to wake him of a morning, his face being almost hid by the pillow closing over it.

"I had never any communication with Dr. Abell after I came back to Islington, but one day when he passed me in the street and asked me whether I was not looking for another service, to which I answered I was very well suited where I was, but he said I was a tickle-minded fellow and he doubted not he should soon hear I was on the world again, which indeed proved true."

Dr. Pratt is next taken up where he left off.

"On the 16th I was called up out of my bed soon after it was light – that is about five – with a message that Dr. Quinn was dead or dying. Making my way to his house I found there was no doubt which was the truth. All the persons in the house except the one that let me in were already in his chamber and standing about his bed, but none touching him. He was stretched in the midst of the bed, on his back, without any disorder, and indeed had the appearance of one ready laid out for burial. His hands, I think, were even crossed on his breast. The only thing not usual was that nothing was to be seen of his face, the two ends of the pillow or bolster appearing to be closed quite over it. These I immediately pulled apart, at the same time rebuking those present, and especially the man, for not at once coming to the assistance of his master. He, however, only looked at me and shook his head, having evidently no more hope than myself that there was anything but a corpse before us.

"Indeed it was plain to anyone possessed of the least experience that he was not only dead, but had died of suffocation. Nor could it be conceived that his death was accidentally caused by the mere folding of the pillow over his face. How should he not, feeling the oppression, have lifted his hands to put it away? whereas not a fold of the sheet which was closely gathered about him, as I now observed, was disordered. The next thing was to procure a physician. I had bethought me of this on leaving my house, and sent on the messenger who had come to me to Dr. Abell; but I now heard that he was away from home, and the nearest surgeon was got, who however could tell no more, at least without opening the body, than we already knew.

"As to any person entering the room with evil purpose (which was the next point to be cleared), it was visible that the bolts of the door were burst from their stanchions, and the stanchions broken away from the door-post by main force; and there was a sufficient body of witness, the smith among them, to testify that this had been done but a few minutes before I came. The chamber being moreover at the top of the house, the window was neither easy of access nor did it show any sign of an exit made that way, either by marks upon the sill or footprints below upon soft mould."

The surgeon's evidence forms of course part of the report of the inquest, but since it has nothing but remarks upon the healthy state of the larger organs and the coagulation of blood in various parts of the body, it need not be reproduced. The verdict was 'Death by the visitation of God'.

Annexed to the other papers is one which I was at first inclined to suppose had made its way among them by mistake. Upon further consideration I think I can divine a reason for its presence.

It relates to the rifling of a mausoleum in Middlesex which stood in a park (now broken up), the property of a noble family which I will not name. The outrage was not that of an ordinary resurrection man. The object, it seemed likely, was theft. The account is blunt and terrible. I shall not quote it. A dealer in the North of London suffered heavy penalties as a receiver of stolen goods in connexion with the affair.

# A VIEW FROM A HILL

**H**ow pleasant it can be, alone in a first-class railway carriage, on the first day of a holiday that is to be fairly long, to dawdle through a bit of English country that is unfamiliar, stopping at every station. You have a map open on your knee, and you pick out the villages that lie to right and left by their church towers. You marvel at the complete stillness that attends your stoppage at the stations, broken only by a footstep crunching the gravel. Yet perhaps that is best experienced after sundown, and the traveller I have in mind was making his leisurely progress on a sunny afternoon in the latter half of June.

He was in the depths of the country. I need not particularise further than to say that if you divided the map of England into four quarters, he would have been found in the south-western of them.

He was a man of academic pursuits, and his term was just over. He was on his way to meet a new friend, older than himself. The two of them had met first on an official inquiry in town, had found that they had many tastes and habits in common, liked each other, and the result was an invitation from Squire Richards to Mr. Fanshawe which was now taking effect.

The journey ended about five o'clock. Fanshawe was told by a cheerful country porter that the car from the Hall had been up to the station and left a message that something had to be fetched from half a mile farther on, and would the gentleman please to wait a few minutes till it came back? "But I see," continued the porter, "as you've got your bysticle, and very like you'd find it pleasanter to ride up to the 'All yourself. Straight up the road 'ere, and then first turn to the left – it ain't above two mile – and I'll see as your things is put in the car for you. You'll excuse me mentioning it, only I thought it were a nice evening for a ride. Yes, sir, very seasonable weather for the haymakers: let me see, I have your bike ticket. Thank you, sir; much obliged: you can't miss your road, etc., etc."

The two miles to the Hall were just what was needed, after the day in the train, to dispel somnolence and impart a wish for tea. The Hall, when sighted, also promised just what was needed in the way of a quiet resting-place after days of sitting on committees and college-meetings. It was neither excitingly old nor depressingly new. Plastered walls, sash-windows, old trees, smooth lawns, were the features which Fanshawe noticed as he came up the drive. Squire Richards, a burly man of sixty odd, was awaiting him in the porch with evident pleasure.

"Tea first," he said, "or would you like a longer drink? No? All right, tea's ready in the garden. Come along, they'll put your machine away. I always have tea under the lime-tree by the stream on a day like this."

Nor could you ask for a better place. Midsummer afternoon, shade and scent of a vast lime-tree, cool, swirling water within five yards. It was long before either of them suggested a move. But about six, Mr. Richards sat up, knocked out his pipe, and said: "Look here, it's cool enough now to think of a stroll, if you're inclined? All right: then what I suggest is that we walk up the park and get on to the hill-side, where we can look over the country. We'll have a map, and I'll show you where things are; and you can go off on your machine, or we can take the car, according as you want exercise or not. If you're ready, we can start now and be back well before eight, taking it very easy."

"I'm ready. I should like my stick, though, and have you got any field-glasses? I lent mine to a man a week ago, and he's gone off Lord knows where and taken them with him."

Mr. Richards pondered. "Yes," he said, "I have, but they're not things I use myself, and I don't know whether the ones I have will suit you. They're old-fashioned, and about twice as heavy as they make 'em now. You're welcome to have them, but I won't carry them. By the way, what do you want to drink after dinner?"

Protestations that anything would do were overruled, and a satisfactory settlement was reached on the way to the front hall, where

Mr. Fanshawe found his stick, and Mr. Richards, after thoughtful pinching of his lower lip, resorted to a drawer in the hall-table, extracted a key, crossed to a cupboard in the panelling, opened it, took a box from the shelf, and put it on the table. "The glasses are in there," he said, "and there's some dodge of opening it, but I've forgotten what it is. You try." Mr. Fanshawe accordingly tried. There was no keyhole, and the box was solid, heavy and smooth: it seemed obvious that some part of it would have to be pressed before anything could happen. "The corners," said he to himself, "are the likely places; and infernally sharp corners they are too," he added, as he put his thumb in his mouth after exerting force on a lower corner.

"What's the matter?" said the Squire.

"Why, your disgusting Borgia box has scratched me, drat it," said Fanshawe. The Squire chuckled unfeelingly. "Well, you've got it open, anyway," he said.

"So I have! Well, I don't begrudge a drop of blood in a good cause, and here are the glasses. They *are* pretty heavy, as you said, but I think I'm equal to carrying them."

"Ready?" said the Squire. "Come on then; we go out by the garden."

So they did, and passed out into the park, which sloped decidedly upwards to the hill which, as Fanshawe had seen from the train, dominated the country. It was a spur of a larger range that lay behind. On the way, the Squire, who was great on earthworks, pointed out various spots where he detected or imagined traces of war-ditches and the like. "And here," he said, stopping on a more or less level plot with a ring of large trees, "is Baxter's Roman villa." "Baxter?" said Mr. Fanshawe.

"I forgot; you don't know about him. He was the old chap I got those glasses from. I believe he made them. He was an old watch-maker down in the village, a great antiquary. My father gave him leave to grub about where he liked; and when he made a find he used to lend him a man or two to help him with the digging. He got a surprising lot of things together, and when he died – I dare say it's ten or fifteen years ago – I bought the whole lot and gave them to the town museum. We'll run in one of these days, and look over them. The glasses came to me with the rest, but of course I kept them. If you look at them, you'll see they're more or less amateur work – the body of them; naturally the lenses weren't his making."

"Yes, I see they are just the sort of thing that a clever workman in a different line of business might turn out. But I don't see why he made them so heavy. And did Baxter actually find a Roman villa here?"

"Yes, there's a pavement turfed over, where we're standing: it was too rough and plain to be worth taking up, but of course there are drawings of it: and the small things and pottery that turned up were quite good of their kind. An ingenious chap, old Baxter: he seemed to have a quite out-of-the-way instinct for these things. He was invaluable to our archaeologists. He used to shut up his shop for days at a time, and wander off over the district, marking down places, where he scented anything, on the ordnance map; and he kept a book with fuller notes of the places. Since his death, a good many of them have been sampled, and there's always been something to justify him."

"What a good man!" said Mr. Fanshawe.

"Good?" said the Squire, pulling up brusquely.

"I meant useful to have about the place," said Mr. Fanshawe. "But was he a villain?"

"I don't know about that either," said the Squire; "but all I can say is, if he was good, he wasn't lucky. And he wasn't liked: I didn't like him," he added, after a moment.

"Oh?" said Fanshawe interrogatively.

"No, I didn't; but that's enough about Baxter: besides, this is the stiffest bit, and I don't want to talk and walk as well."

Indeed it was hot, climbing a slippery grass slope that evening. "I told you I should take you the short way," panted the Squire, "and I wish I hadn't. However, a bath won't do us any harm when we get back. Here we are, and there's the seat."

A small clump of old Scotch firs crowned the top of the hill; and, at the edge of it, commanding the cream of the view, was a wide and solid seat, on which the two disposed themselves, and wiped their brows, and regained breath.

"Now, then," said the Squire, as soon as he was in a condition to talk connectedly, "this is where your glasses come in. But you'd better take a general look round first. My word! I've never seen the view look better."

Writing as I am now with a winter wind flapping against dark windows and a rushing, tumbling sea within a hundred yards, I find it hard to summon up the feelings and words which will put my reader in possession of the June evening and the lovely English landscape of which the Squire was speaking.

Across a broad level plain they looked upon ranges of great hills, whose uplands – some green, some furred with woods – caught the light of a sun, westering but not yet low. And all the plain was fertile, though the river which traversed it was nowhere seen. There were copses, green wheat, hedges and pasture-land: the little compact white moving cloud marked the evening train. Then the eye picked out red farms and grey houses, and nearer home scattered cottages, and then the Hall, nestled under the hill. The smoke of chimneys was very blue and straight. There was a smell of hay in the air: there were wild roses on bushes hard by. It was the acme of summer.

After some minutes of silent contemplation, the Squire began to point out the leading features, the hills and valleys, and told where the towns and villages lay. "Now," he said, "with the glasses you'll be able to pick out Fulnaker Abbey. Take a line across that big green field, then over the wood beyond it, then over the farm on the knoll."

"Yes, yes," said Fanshawe. "I've got it. What a fine tower!"

"You must have got the wrong direction," said the Squire; "there's not much of a tower about there that I remember, unless it's Oldbourne Church that you've got hold of. And if you call that a fine tower, you're easily pleased."

"Well, I do call it a fine tower," said Fanshawe, the glasses still at his eyes, "whether it's Oldbourne or any other. And it must belong to a largish church; it looks to me like a central tower – four big pinnacles at the corners, and four smaller ones between. I must certainly go over there. How far is it?"

"Oldbourne's about nine miles, or less," said the Squire. "It's a long time since I've been there, but I don't remember thinking much of it. Now I'll show you another thing."

Fanshawe had lowered the glasses, and was still gazing in the Oldbourne direction. "No," he said, "I can't make out anything with the naked eye. What was it you were going to show me?"

"A good deal more to the left – it oughtn't to be difficult to find. Do you see a rather sudden knob of a hill with a thick wood on top of it? It's in a dead line with that single tree on the top of the big ridge."

"I do," said Fanshawe, "and I believe I could tell you without much difficulty what it's called."

"Could you now?" said the Squire. "Say on."

"Why, Gallows Hill," was the answer.

"How did you guess that?"

"Well, if you don't want it guessed, you shouldn't put up a dummy gibbet and a man hanging on it."

"What's that?" said the Squire abruptly. "There's nothing on that hill but wood."

"On the contrary," said Fanshawe, "there's a largish expanse of grass on the top and your dummy gibbet in the middle; and I thought there was something on it when I looked first. But I see there's nothing – or is there? I can't be sure."

"Nonsense, nonsense, Fanshawe, there's no such thing as a dummy gibbet, or any other sort, on that hill. And it's thick wood – a fairly young plantation. I was in it myself not a year ago. Hand me the glasses, though I don't suppose I can see anything." After a pause: "No, I thought not: they won't show a thing."

Meanwhile Fanshawe was scanning the hill – it might be only two or three miles away. "Well, it's very odd," he said, "it does look exactly like a wood without the glass." He took it again. "That *is* one of the oddest effects. The gibbet is perfectly plain, and the grass field, and there even seem to be people on it, and carts, or *a* cart, with men in it. And yet when I take the glass away, there's nothing. It must be something in the way this afternoon light falls: I shall come up earlier in the day when the sun's full on it."

"Did you say you saw people and a cart on that hill?" said the Squire incredulously. "What should they be doing there at this time of day, even if the trees have been felled? Do talk sense – look again."

"Well, I certainly thought I saw them. Yes, I should say there were a few, just clearing off. And now – by Jove, it does look like something hanging on the gibbet. But these glasses are so beastly heavy I can't hold them steady for long. Anyhow, you can take it from me there's no wood. And if you'll show me the road on the map, I'll go there tomorrow."

The Squire remained brooding for some little time. At last he rose and said, "Well, I suppose that will be the best way to settle it. And now we'd better be getting back. Bath and dinner is my idea." And on the way back he was not very communicative.

They returned through the garden, and went into the front hall to leave sticks, etc., in their due place. And here they found the aged butler Patten evidently in a state of some anxiety. "Beg pardon, Master Henry," he began at once, "but someone's been up to mischief here, I'm much afraid." He pointed to the open box which had contained the glasses.

"Nothing worse than that, Patten?" said the Squire. "Mayn't I take out my own glasses and lend them to a friend? Bought with my own money, you recollect? At old Baxter's sale, eh?"

Patten bowed, unconvinced. "Oh, very well, Master Henry, as long as you know who it was. Only I thought proper to name it, for I didn't think that box'd been off its shelf since you first put it there; and, if you'll excuse me, after what happened….". The voice was lowered, and the rest was not audible to Fanshawe. The Squire replied with a few words and a gruff laugh, and called on Fanshawe to come and be shown his room. And I do not think that anything else happened that night which bears on my story.

Except, perhaps, the sensation which invaded Fanshawe in the small hours that something had been let out which ought not to have been let out. It came into his dreams. He was walking in a garden which he seemed half to know, and stopped in front of a rockery made of old wrought stones, pieces of window tracery from a church, and even bits of figures. One of these moved his curiosity: it seemed to be a sculptured capital with scenes carved on it. He felt he must pull it out, and worked away, and, with an ease that surprised him, moved the stones that obscured it aside, and pulled out the block. As he did so, a tin label fell down by his feet with a little clatter. He picked it up and read on it: 'On no account move this stone. Yours sincerely, J. Patten.' As often happens in dreams, he felt that this injunction was of extreme importance; and with an anxiety that amounted to anguish he looked to see if the stone had really been shifted. Indeed it had; in fact, he could not see it anywhere. The removal had disclosed the mouth of a burrow, and he bent down to look into it. Something stirred in the blackness, and then, to his intense horror, a hand emerged – a clean right hand in a neat cuff and coatsleeve, just in the attitude of a hand that means to shake yours. He wondered whether it would not be rude to let it alone. But, as he looked at it, it began to grow hairy and dirty and thin, and also to change its pose and stretch out as if to take hold of his leg. At that he dropped all thought of politeness, decided to run, screamed and woke himself up.

This was the dream he remembered; but it seemed to him (as, again, it often does) that there had been others of the same import before, but not so insistent. He lay awake for some little time, fixing the details of the last dream in his mind, and wondering in particular what the figures had been which he had seen or half seen on the carved capital. Something quite incongruous, he felt sure; but that was the most he could recall.

Whether because of the dream, or because it was the first day of his holiday, he did not get up very early; nor did he at once plunge into the exploration of the country. He spent a morning, half lazy, half instructive, in looking over the volumes of the County Archaeological Society's transactions, in which were many contributions from Mr. Baxter on finds of flint implements, Roman sites, ruins of monastic establishments – in fact, most departments of archaeology. They were written in an odd, pompous, only half-educated style. If the man had

had more early schooling, thought Fanshawe, he would have been a very distinguished antiquary; or he might have been (he thus qualified his opinion a little later), but for a certain love of opposition and controversy, and, yes, a patronising tone as of one possessing superior knowledge, which left an unpleasant taste. He might have been a very respectable artist. There was an imaginary restoration and elevation of a priory church which was very well conceived. A fine pinnacled central tower was a conspicuous feature of this; it reminded Fanshawe of that which he had seen from the hill, and which the Squire had told him must be Oldbourne. But it was not Oldbourne; it was Fulnaker Priory. "Oh, well," he said to himself, "I suppose Oldbourne Church may have been built by Fulnaker monks, and Baxter has copied Oldbourne tower. Anything about it in the letterpress? Ah, I see it was published after his death – found among his papers."

After lunch the Squire asked Fanshawe what he meant to do.

"Well," said Fanshawe, "I think I shall go out on my bike about four as far as Oldbourne and back by Gallows Hill. That ought to be a round of about fifteen miles, oughtn't it?"

"About that," said the Squire, "and you'll pass Lambsfield and Wanstone, both of which are worth looking at. There's a little glass at Lambsfield and the stone at Wanstone."

"Good," said Fanshawe, "I'll get tea somewhere, and may I take the glasses? I'll strap them on my bike, on the carrier."

"Of course, if you like," said the Squire. "I really ought to have some better ones. If I go into the town today, I'll see if I can pick up some."

"Why should you trouble to do that if you can't use them yourself?" said Fanshawe.

"Oh, I don't know; one ought to have a decent pair; and – well, old Patten doesn't think those are fit to use."

"Is he a judge?"

"He's got some tale: I don't know: something about old Baxter. I've promised to let him tell me about it. It seems very much on his mind since last night."

"Why that? Did he have a nightmare like me?"

"He had something: he was looking an old man this morning, and he said he hadn't closed an eye."

"Well, let him save up his tale till I come back."

"Very well, I will if I can. Look here, are you going to be late? If you get a puncture eight miles off and have to walk home, what then? I don't trust these bicycles: I shall tell them to give us cold things to eat."

"I shan't mind that, whether I'm late or early. But I've got things to mend punctures with. And now I'm off."

★　　★　　★

It was just as well that the Squire had made that arrangement about a cold supper, Fanshawe thought, and not for the first time, as he wheeled his bicycle up the drive about nine o'clock. So also the Squire thought and said, several times, as he met him in the hall, rather pleased at the confirmation of his want of faith in bicycles than sympathetic with his hot, weary, thirsty, and indeed haggard, friend. In fact, the kindest thing he found to say was: "You'll want a long drink tonight? Cider-cup do? All right. Hear that, Patten? Cider-cup, iced, lots of it." Then to Fanshawe, "Don't be all night over your bath."

By half-past nine they were at dinner, and Fanshawe was reporting progress, if progress it might be called.

"I got to Lambsfield very smoothly, and saw the glass. It is very interesting stuff, but there's a lot of lettering I couldn't read."

"Not with glasses?" said the Squire.

"Those glasses of yours are no manner of use inside a church – or inside anywhere, I suppose, for that matter. But the only places I took 'em into were churches."

"H'm! Well, go on," said the Squire.

"However, I took some sort of a photograph of the window, and I dare say an enlargement would show what I want. Then Wanstone; I should think that stone was a very out-of-the-way thing, only I don't know about that class of antiquities. Has anybody opened the mound it stands on?"

"Baxter wanted to, but the farmer wouldn't let him."

"Oh, well, I should think it would be worth doing. Anyhow, the next thing was Fulnaker and Oldbourne. You know, it's very odd about that tower I saw from the hill. Oldbourne Church is nothing like it, and of course there's nothing over thirty feet high at Fulnaker, though you can see it had a central tower. I didn't tell you, did I? that Baxter's fancy drawing of Fulnaker shows a tower exactly like the one I saw."

"So you thought, I dare say," put in the Squire.

"No, it wasn't a case of thinking. The picture actually *reminded* me of what I'd seen, and I made sure it was Oldbourne, well before I looked at the title."

"Well, Baxter had a very fair idea of architecture. I dare say what's left made it easy for him to draw the right sort of tower."

"That may be it, of course, but I'm doubtful if even a professional could have got it so exactly right. There's absolutely nothing left at Fulnaker but the bases of the piers which supported it. However, that isn't the oddest thing."

"What about Gallows Hill?" said the Squire. "Here, Patten, listen to this. I told you what Mr. Fanshawe said he saw from the hill."

"Yes, Master Henry, you did; and I can't say I was so much surprised, considering."

"All right, all right. You keep that till afterwards. We want to hear what Mr. Fanshawe saw today. Go on, Fanshawe. You turned to come back by Ackford and Thorfield, I suppose?"

"Yes, and I looked into both the churches. Then I got to the turning which goes to the top of Gallows Hill; I saw that if I wheeled my machine over the field at the top of the hill I could join the home road on this side. It was about half-past six when I got to the top of the hill, and there was a gate on my right, where it ought to be, leading into the belt of plantation."

"You hear that, Patten? A belt, he says."

"So I thought it was – a belt. But it wasn't. You were quite right, and I was hopelessly wrong. I *cannot* understand it. The whole top is planted quite thick. Well, I went on into this wood, wheeling and dragging my bike, expecting every minute to come to a clearing, and then my misfortunes began. Thorns, I suppose; first I realised that the front tyre was slack, then the back. I couldn't stop to do more than try to find the punctures and mark them; but even that was hopeless. So I ploughed on, and the farther I went, the less I liked the place."

"Not much poaching in that cover, eh, Patten?" said the Squire.

"No, indeed, Master Henry: there's very few cares to go—"

"No, I know: never mind that now. Go on, Fanshawe."

"I don't blame anybody for not caring to go there. I know I had all the fancies one least likes: steps crackling over twigs behind me, indistinct people stepping behind trees in front of me, yes, and even a hand laid on my shoulder. I pulled up very sharp at that and looked round, but there really was no branch or bush that could have done it. Then, when I was just about at the middle of the plot, I was convinced that there was someone looking down on me from above – and not with any pleasant intent. I stopped again, or at least slackened my pace, to look up. And as I did, down I came, and barked my shins abominably on, what do you think? a block of stone with a big square hole in the top of it. And within a few paces there were two others just like it. The three were set in a triangle. Now, do you make out what they were put there for?"

"I think I can," said the Squire, who was now very grave and absorbed in the story. "Sit down, Patten."

It was time, for the old man was supporting himself by one hand, and leaning heavily on it. He dropped into a chair, and said in a very tremulous voice, "You didn't go between them stones, did you, sir?"

"I did *not*," said Fanshawe, emphatically. "I dare say I was an ass, but as soon as it dawned on me where I was, I just shouldered my machine and did my best to run. It seemed to me as if I was in an unholy evil sort of graveyard, and I was most profoundly thankful that it was one of the longest days and still sunlight. Well, I had a horrid run, even if it was only a few hundred yards. Everything caught on everything: handles and spokes and carrier and pedals – caught in them viciously, or I fancied so. I fell over at least five times. At last I saw the hedge, and I couldn't trouble to hunt for the gate."

"There *is* no gate on my side," the Squire interpolated.

"Just as well I didn't waste time, then. I dropped the machine over somehow and went into the road pretty near head-first; some branch or something got my ankle at the last moment. Anyhow, there I was out of the wood, and seldom more thankful or more generally sore. Then came the job of mending my punctures. I had a good outfit and I'm not at all bad at the business; but this was an absolutely hopeless case. It was seven when I got out of the wood, and I spent fifty minutes over one tyre. As fast as I found a hole and put on a patch, and blew it up, it went flat again. So I made up my mind to walk. That hill isn't three miles away, is it?"

"Not more across country, but nearer six by road."

"I thought it must be. I thought I couldn't have taken well over the hour over less than five miles, even leading a bike. Well, there's my story: where's yours and Patten's?"

"Mine? I've no story," said the Squire. "But you weren't very far out when you thought you were in a graveyard. There must be a good few of them up there, Patten, don't you think? They left 'em there when they fell to bits, I fancy."

Patten nodded, too much interested to speak. "Don't," said Fanshawe.

"Now then, Patten," said the Squire, "you've heard what sort of a time Mr. Fanshawe's been having. What you make of it? Anything to do with Mr. Baxter? Fill yourself a glass of port, and tell us."

"Ah, that done me good, Master Henry," said Patten, after absorbing what was before him. "If you really wish to know what were in my thoughts, my answer would be clear in the affirmative. Yes," he went on, warming to his work, "I should say as Mr. Fanshawe's experience of today were very largely doo to the person you named. And I think, Master Henry, as I have some title to speak, in view of me 'aving been many years on speaking terms with him, and swore in to be jury on the Coroner's inquest near this time ten years ago, you being then, if you carry your mind back, Master Henry, travelling abroad, and no one 'ere to represent the family."

"Inquest?" said Fanshawe. "An inquest on Mr. Baxter, was there?"

"Yes, sir, on – on that very person. The facts as led up to that occurrence was these. The deceased was, as you may have gathered, a very peculiar individual in 'is 'abits – in my idear, at least, but all must speak as they find. He lived very much to himself, without neither chick nor child, as the saying is. And how he passed away his time was what very few could orfer a guess at."

"He lived unknown, and few could know when Baxter ceased to be," said the Squire to his pipe.

"I beg pardon, Master Henry, I was just coming to that. But when I say how he passed away his time – to be sure we know 'ow intent he was in rummaging and ransacking out all the 'istry of the neighbourhood and the number of things he'd managed to collect together – well, it was spoke of for miles round as Baxter's Museum, and many a time when he might be in the mood, and I might have an hour to spare, have he showed me his pieces of pots and what not, going back by his account to the times of the ancient Romans. However, you know more about that than what I do, Master Henry: only what I was a-going to say was this, as know what he might and interesting as he might be in his talk, there was something about the man – well, for one thing, no one ever remember to see him in church nor yet chapel at service-time. And that made talk. Our rector he never come in the house but once. 'Never ask me what the man said'; that was all anybody could ever get out of *him*. Then how did he spend his nights, particularly about this season of the year? Time and again the labouring men'd meet him coming back as they went out to their work, and he'd pass 'em by without a word, looking, they says, like someone straight out of the asylum. They see the whites of his eyes all round. He'd have a fish-basket with him, that they noticed, and he always come the same road. And the talk got to be that he'd made himself some business, and that not the best kind – well, not so far from where you was at seven o'clock this evening, sir.

"Well, now, after such a night as that, Mr. Baxter he'd shut up the shop, and the old lady that did for him had orders not to come in; and knowing what she did about his language, she took care to obey them orders. But one day it so happened, about three o'clock in the afternoon, the house being shut up as I said, there come a most fearful to-do inside, and smoke out of the windows, and Baxter crying out seemingly in an agony. So the man as lived next door he run round to the back premises and burst the door in, and several others come too. Well, he tell me he never in all his life smelt such a fearful – well, odour, as what there was in that kitchen-place. It seem as if Baxter had been boiling something in a pot and overset it on his leg. There he laid on the floor, trying to keep back the cries, but it was more than he could manage, and when he seen the people come in – oh, he was in a nice condition: if his tongue warn't blistered worse than his leg it warn't his fault. Well, they picked him up, and got him into a chair, and run for the medical man, and one of 'em was going to pick up the pot, and Baxter, he screams out to let it alone. So he did, but he couldn't see as there was anything in the pot but a few old brown bones. Then they says 'Dr. Lawrence'll be here in a minute, Mr. Baxter; he'll soon put you to rights.' And then he was off again. He must be got up to his room, he couldn't have the doctor come in there and see all that mess – they must throw a cloth over it – anything – the tablecloth out of the parlour; well, so they did. But that must have been poisonous stuff in that pot, for it was pretty near on two months afore Baxter were about agin. Beg pardon, Master Henry, was you going to say something?"

"Yes, I was," said the Squire. "I wonder you haven't told me all this before. However, I was going to say I remember old Lawrence telling me he'd attended Baxter. He was a queer card, he said. Lawrence was up in the bedroom one day, and picked up a little mask covered with black velvet, and put it on in fun and went to look at himself in the glass. He hadn't time for a proper look, for old Baxter shouted out to him from the bed: 'Put it down, you fool! Do you want to look through a dead man's eyes?' and it startled him so that he did put it down, and then he asked Baxter what he meant. And Baxter insisted on him handing it over, and said the man he bought it from was dead, or some such nonsense. But Lawrence felt it as he handed it over, and he declared he was sure it was made out of the front of a skull. He bought a distilling apparatus at Baxter's sale, he told me, but he could never use it: it seemed to taint everything, however much he cleaned it. But go on, Patten."

"Yes, Master Henry, I'm nearly done now, and time, too, for I don't know what they'll think about me in the servants' 'all. Well, this business of the scalding was some few years before Mr. Baxter was took, and he got about again, and went on just as he'd used. And one of the last jobs he done was finishing up them actual glasses what you took out last night. You see he'd made the body of them some long time, and got the pieces of glass for them, but there was somethink wanted to finish 'em, whatever it was, I don't know, but I picked up the frame one day, and I says: 'Mr. Baxter, why don't you make a job of this?' And he says, 'Ah, when I've done that, you'll hear news, you will: there's going to be no such pair of glasses as mine when they're filled and sealed,' and there he stopped, and I says: 'Why, Mr. Baxter, you talk as if they was wine bottles: filled and sealed – why, where's the necessity for that?' 'Did I say filled and sealed?' he says. 'O, well, I was suiting my conversation to my company.' Well, then come round this time of year, and one fine evening, I was passing his shop on my way home, and he was standing on the step, very pleased with hisself, and he says: 'All right and tight now: my best bit of work's finished, and I'll be out with 'em tomorrow.' 'What, finished them glasses?' I says, 'might I have a look at them?' 'No, no,' he says, 'I've put 'em to bed for tonight, and when I do show 'em you, you'll have to pay for peepin', so I tell you.' And that, gentlemen, were the last words I heard that man say.

"That were the 17th of June, and just a week after, there was a funny thing happened, and it was doo to that as we brought in 'unsound mind' at the inquest, for barring that, no one as knew Baxter in business could anyways have laid that against him. But George Williams, as lived in the next house, and do now, he was woke up that same night with a stumbling and tumbling about in Mr. Baxter's premises, and he got out o' bed, and went to the front window on the street to see if there was any rough customers about. And it being a very light night, he could make sure as there was not. Then he stood and listened, and he hear Mr. Baxter coming down his front stair one step after another very slow, and he got the idear as it was like someone bein' pushed or pulled down and holdin' on to everythin' he could. Next thing he hear the street door come open, and out come Mr. Baxter into the street in his day-clothes, 'at and all, with his arms straight down by his sides, and talking to hisself, and shakin' his head from one side to the other, and walking in that peculiar way that he appeared to be going as it were against his own will. George Williams put up the window, and hear him say: 'O mercy, gentlemen!' and then he shut up sudden as if, he said, someone clapped his hand over his mouth, and Mr. Baxter threw his head back, and his hat fell off. And Williams see his face looking something pitiful, so as he couldn't keep from calling out to him: 'Why, Mr. Baxter, ain't you well?' and he was goin' to offer to fetch Dr. Lawrence to him, only he heard the answer: ''Tis best you mind your own business. Put in your head.' But whether it were Mr. Baxter said it so hoarse-like and faint, he never could be sure. Still there weren't no one but him in the street, and yet Williams was that upset by the way he spoke that he shrank back from the window and went and sat on the bed. And he heard Mr. Baxter's step go on and up the road, and after a minute or more he couldn't help but look out once more and he see him going along the same curious way as before. And one thing he recollected was that Mr. Baxter never stopped to pick up his 'at when it fell off, and yet there it was on his head. Well, Master Henry, that was the last anybody see of Mr. Baxter, leastways for a week or more. There was a lot of people said he was called off on business, or made off because he'd got into some scrape, but he was well known for miles round, and none of the railway-people nor the public-house people hadn't seen him; and then ponds was looked into and nothink found; and at last one evening Fakes the keeper come down from over the hill to the village, and he says he seen the Gallows Hill planting black with birds, and that were a funny thing, because he never see no sign of a creature there in his time. So they looked at each other a bit, and first one says: 'I'm game to go up,' and another says: 'So am I, if you are,' and half a dozen of 'em set out in the evening time, and took Dr. Lawrence with them, and you know, Master Henry, there he was between them three stones with his neck broke."

Useless to imagine the talk which this story set going. It is not remembered. But before Patten left them, he said to Fanshawe: "Excuse me, sir, but did I understand as you took out them glasses with you today? I thought you did; and might I ask, did you make use of them at all?"

"Yes. Only to look at something in a church."

"Oh, indeed, you took 'em into the church, did you, sir?"

"Yes, I did; it was Lambsfield church. By the way, I left them strapped on to my bicycle, I'm afraid, in the stable-yard."

"No matter for that, sir. I can bring them in the first thing tomorrow, and perhaps you'll be so good as to look at 'em then."

Accordingly, before breakfast, after a tranquil and well-earned sleep, Fanshawe took the glasses into the garden and directed them to a distant hill. He lowered them instantly, and looked at top and bottom, worked the screws, tried them again and yet again, shrugged his shoulders and replaced them on the hall-table.

"Patten," he said, "they're absolutely useless. I can't see a thing: it's as if someone had stuck a black wafer over the lens."

"Spoilt my glasses, have you?" said the Squire. "Thank you: the only ones I've got."

"You try them yourself," said Fanshawe, "I've done nothing to them."

So after breakfast the Squire took them out to the terrace and stood on the steps. After a few ineffectual attempts, "Lord, how heavy they are!" he said impatiently, and in the same instant dropped them on to the stones, and the lens splintered and the barrel cracked: a little pool of liquid formed on the stone slab. It was inky black, and the odour that rose from it is not to be described.

"Filled and sealed, eh?" said the Squire. "If I could bring myself to touch it, I dare say we should find the seal. So that's what came of his boiling and distilling, is it? Old Ghoul!"

"What in the world do you mean?"

"Don't you see, my good man? Remember what he said to the doctor about looking through dead men's eyes? Well, this was another way of it. But they didn't like having their bones boiled, I take it, and the end of it was they carried him off whither he would not. Well, I'll get a spade, and we'll bury this thing decently."

As they smoothed the turf over it, the Squire, handing the spade to Patten, who had been a reverential spectator, remarked to Fanshawe: "It's almost a pity you took that thing into the church: you might have seen more than you did. Baxter had them for a week, I make out, but I don't see that he did much in the time."

"I'm not sure," said Fanshawe, "there is that picture of Fulnaker Priory Church."

# A VIGNETTE

You are asked to think of the spacious garden of a country rectory, adjacent to a park of many acres, and separated therefrom by a belt of trees of some age which we knew as the Plantation. It is but about thirty or forty yards broad. A close gate of split oak leads to it from the path encircling the garden, and when you enter it from that side you put your hand through a square hole cut in it and lift the hook to pass along to the iron gate which admits to the park from the Plantation. It has further to be added that from some windows of the rectory, which stands on a somewhat lower level than the Plantation, parts of the path leading thereto, and the oak gate itself can be seen. Some of the trees, Scotch firs and others, which form a backing and a surrounding, are of considerable size, but there is nothing that diffuses a mysterious gloom or imparts a sinister flavour – nothing of melancholy or funereal associations. The place is well clad, and there are secret nooks and retreats among the bushes, but there is neither offensive bleakness nor oppressive darkness. It is, indeed, a matter for some surprise when one thinks it over, that any cause for misgivings of a nervous sort have attached itself to so normal and cheerful a spot, the more so, since neither our childish mind when we lived there nor the more inquisitive years that came later ever nosed out any legend or reminiscence of old or recent unhappy things.

Yet to me they came, even to me, leading an exceptionally happy wholesome existence, and guarded – not strictly but as carefully as was any way necessary – from uncanny fancies and fear. Not that such guarding avails to close up all gates. I should be puzzled to fix the date at which any sort of misgiving about the Plantation gate first visited me. Possibly it was in the years just before I went to school, possibly on one later summer afternoon of which I have a faint memory, when I was coming back after solitary roaming in the park, or, as I bethink me, from tea at the Hall: anyhow, alone, and fell in with one of the villagers also homeward bound just as I was about to turn off the road on to the track leading to the Plantation. We broke off our talk with "goodnights", and when I looked back at him after a minute or so I was just a little surprised to see him standing still and looking after me. But no remark passed, and on I went. By the time I was within the iron gate and outside the park, dusk had undoubtedly come on; but there was no lack yet of light, and I could not account to myself for the questionings which certainly did rise as to the presence of anyone else among the trees, questionings to which I could not very certainly say "No", nor, I was glad to feel, "Yes", because if there were anyone they could not well have any business there. To be sure, it is difficult, in anything like a grove, to be quite certain that nobody is making a screen out of a tree trunk and keeping it between you and him as he moves round it and you walk on. All I can say is that if such an one was there he was no neighbour or acquaintance of mine, and there was some indication about him of being cloaked or hooded. But I think I may have moved at a rather quicker pace than before, and have been particular about shutting the gate. I think, too, that after that evening something of what Hamlet calls a 'gain-giving' may have been present in my mind when I thought of the Plantation, I do seem to remember looking out of a window which gave in that direction, and questioning whether there was or was not any appearance of a moving form among the trees. If I did, and perhaps I did, hint a suspicion to the nurse the only answer to it will have been "the hidea of such a thing!" and an injunction to make haste and get into my bed.

Whether it was on that night or a later one that I seem to see myself again in the small hours gazing out of the window across moonlit grass and hoping I was mistaken in fancying any movement in that half-hidden corner of the garden, I cannot now be sure. But it was certainly within a short while that I began to be visited by dreams which I would much rather not have had – which, in fact, I came to dread acutely; and the point round which they centred was the Plantation gate.

As years go on it but seldom happens that a dream is disturbing. Awkward it may be, as when, while I am drying myself after a bath, I open the bedroom door and step out on to a populous railway platform and have to invent rapid and flimsy excuses for the deplorable deshabille. But such a vision is not alarming, though it may make one despair of ever holding up one's head again. But in the times of which I am thinking, it did happen, not often, but oftener than I liked, that the moment a dream set in I knew that it was going to turn out ill, and that there was nothing I could do to keep it on cheerful lines.

Ellis the gardener might be wholesomely employed with rake and spade as I watched at the window; other familiar figures might pass and repass on harmless errands; but I was not deceived. I could see that the time was coming when the gardener and the rest would be gathering up their properties and setting off on paths that led homeward or into some safe outer world, and the garden would be left – to itself, shall we say, or to denizens who did not desire quite ordinary company and were only waiting for the word 'all clear' to slip into their posts of vantage.

Now, too, was the moment near when the surroundings began to take on a threatening look; that the sunlight lost power and a quality of light replaced it which, though I did not know it at the time my memory years after told me was the lifeless pallor of an eclipse. The effect of all this was to intensify the foreboding that had begun to possess me, and to make me look anxiously about, dreading that in some quarter my fear would take a visible shape. I had not much doubt which way to look. Surely behind those bushes, among those trees, there was motion, yes, and surely – and more quickly than seemed possible – there was motion, not now among the trees, but on the very path towards the house. I was still at the window, and before I could adjust myself to the new fear there came the impression of a tread on the stairs and a hand on the door. That was as far as the dream got, at first; and for me it was far enough. I had no notion what would have been the next development, more than that it was bound to be horrifying.

That is enough in all conscience about the beginning of my dreams. A beginning it was only, for something like it came again and again; how often I can't tell, but often enough to give me an acute distaste for being left alone in that region of the garden. I came to fancy that I could see in the behaviour of the village people whose work took them that way an anxiety to be past a certain point, and moreover a welcoming of company as they approached that corner of the park. But on this it will not do to lay overmuch stress, for, as I have said, I could never glean any kind of story bound up with the place.

However, the strong probability that there had been one once I cannot deny.

I must not by the way give the impression that the whole of the Plantation was haunted ground. There were trees there most admirably devised for climbing and reading in; there was a wall, along the top of which you could walk for many hundred yards and reach a frequented road, passing farmyard and familiar houses; and once in the park, which had its own delights of wood and water, you were well out of range of anything suspicious – or, if that is too much to say, of anything that suggested the Plantation gate.

But I am reminded, as I look on these pages, that so far we have had only preamble, and that there is very little in the way of actual incident to come, and that the criticism attributed to the devil when he sheared the sow is like to be justified. What, after all, was the outcome of the dreams to which without saying a word about them I was liable during a good space of time? Well, it presents itself to me thus. One afternoon – the day being neither overcast nor threatening – I was at my window in the upper floor of the house. All the family were out. From some obscure shelf in a disused room I had worried out a book, not very recondite: it was, in fact, a bound volume of a magazine in which were contained parts of a novel. I know now what novel it was, but I did not then, and a sentence struck and arrested me. Someone was walking at dusk up a solitary lane by an old mansion in Ireland, and being a man of imagination he was suddenly forcibly impressed by what he calls 'the aerial image of the old house, with its peculiar malign, scared, and skulking aspect' peering out of the shade of its neglected old trees. The words were quite enough to set my own fancy on a bleak track. Inevitably I looked and looked with apprehension, to the Plantation gate. As was but right it was shut, and nobody was upon the path that led to it or from it. But as I said a while ago, there was in it a square hole giving access to the fastening; and through that hole, I could see – and it struck like a blow on the diaphragm – something white or partly white. Now this I could not bear, and with an access of something like courage – only it was more like desperation, like determining that I must know the worst – I did steal down and, quite uselessly, of course, taking cover behind bushes as I went, I made progress until I was within range of the gate and the hole. Things were, alas! worse than I had feared; through that hole a face was looking my way. It was not monstrous, not pale, fleshless, spectral. Malevolent I thought and think it was; at any rate the eyes were large and open and fixed. It was pink and, I thought, hot, and just above the eyes the border of a white linen drapery hung down from the brows.

There is something horrifying in the sight of a face looking at one out of a frame as this did; more particularly if its gaze is unmistakably fixed upon you. Nor does it make the matter any better if the expression gives no clue to what is to come next. I said just now that I took this face to be malevolent, and so I did, but not in regard of any positive dislike or fierceness which it expressed. It was, indeed, quite without emotion: I was only conscious that I could see the whites of the eyes all round the pupil, and that, we know, has a glamour of madness about it. The immovable face was enough for me. I fled, but at what I thought must be a safe distance inside my own precincts I could not but halt and look back. There was no white thing framed in the hole of the gate, but there was a draped form shambling away among the trees.

Do not press me with questions as to how I bore myself when it became necessary to face my family again. That I was upset by something I had seen must have been pretty clear, but I am very sure that I fought off all attempts to describe it. Why I make a lame effort to do it now I cannot very well explain: it undoubtedly has had some formidable power of clinging through many years to my imagination. I feel that even now I should be circumspect in passing that Plantation gate; and every now and again the query haunts me: Are there here and there sequestered places which some curious creatures still frequent, whom once on a time anybody could see and speak to as they went about on their daily occasions, whereas now only at rare intervals in a series of years does one cross their paths and become aware of them; and perhaps that is just as well for the peace of mind of simple people.

# WAILING WELL

In the year 19— there were two members of the Troop of Scouts attached to a famous school, named respectively Arthur Wilcox and Stanley Judkins. They were the same age, boarded in the same house, were in the same division, and naturally were members of the same patrol. They were so much alike in appearance as to cause anxiety and trouble, and even irritation, to the masters who came in contact with them. But oh how different were they in their inward man, or boy!

It was to Arthur Wilcox that the Head Master said, looking up with a smile as the boy entered chambers, "Why, Wilcox, there will be a deficit in the prize fund if you stay here much longer! Here, take this handsomely bound copy of the *Life and Works of Bishop Ken*, and with it my hearty congratulations to yourself and your excellent parents." It was Wilcox again, whom the Provost noticed as he passed through the playing fields, and, pausing for a moment, observed to the Vice-Provost, "That lad has a remarkable brow!" "Indeed, yes," said the Vice-Provost. "It denotes either genius or water on the brain."

As a Scout, Wilcox secured every badge and distinction for which he competed. The Cookery Badge, the Map-making Badge, the Life-saving Badge, the Badge for picking up bits of newspaper, the Badge for not slamming the door when leaving pupil-room, and many others. Of the Life-saving Badge I may have a word to say when we come to treat of Stanley Judkins.

You cannot be surprised to hear that Mr. Hope Jones added a special verse to each of his songs, in commendation of Arthur Wilcox, or that the Lower Master burst into tears when handing him the Good

Conduct Medal in its handsome claret-coloured case: the medal which had been unanimously voted to him by the whole of Third Form. Unanimously, did I say? I am wrong. There was one dissentient, Judkins *mi.*, who said that he had excellent reasons for acting as he did. He shared, it seems, a room with his major. You cannot, again, wonder that in after years Arthur Wilcox was the first, and so far the only boy, to become Captain of both the School and of the Oppidans, or that the strain of carrying out the duties of both positions, coupled with the ordinary work of the school, was so severe that a complete rest for six months, followed by a voyage round the world, was pronounced an absolute necessity by the family doctor.

It would be a pleasant task to trace the steps by which he attained the giddy eminence he now occupies; but for the moment enough of Arthur Wilcox. Time presses, and we must turn to a very different matter: the career of Stanley Judkins – Judkins *ma.*

Stanley Judkins, like Arthur Wilcox, attracted the attention of the authorities; but in quite another fashion. It was to him that the Lower Master said with no cheerful smile, "What, again, Judkins? A very little persistence in this course of conduct, my boy, and you will have cause to regret that you ever entered this academy. There, take that, and that, and think yourself very lucky you don't get that and that!" It was Judkins, again, whom the Provost had cause to notice as he passed through the playing fields, when a cricket ball struck him with considerable force on the ankle, and a voice from a short way off cried, "Thank you, cut-over!" "I think," said the Provost, pausing for a moment to rub his ankle, "that that boy had better fetch his cricket ball for himself!" "Indeed, yes," said the Vice-Provost, "and if he comes within reach, I will do my best to fetch him something else."

As a Scout, Stanley Judkins secured no badge save those which he was able to abstract from members of other patrols. In the cookery competition he was detected trying to introduce squibs into the Dutch oven of the next-door competitors. In the tailoring competition he succeeded in sewing two boys together very firmly, with disastrous effect when they tried to get up. For the Tidiness Badge he was disqualified, because, in the Midsummer schooltime, which chanced to be hot, he could not be dissuaded from sitting with his fingers in the ink: as he said, for coolness' sake. For one piece of paper which he picked up, he must have dropped at least six banana skins or orange peels. Aged women seeing him approaching would beg him with tears in their eyes not to carry their pails of water across the road. They knew too well what the result would inevitably be. But it was in the life-saving competition that Stanley Judkins's conduct was most blameable and had the most far-reaching effects. The practice, as you know, was to throw a selected lower boy, of suitable dimensions, fully dressed, with his hands and feet tied together, into the deepest part of Cuckoo Weir, and to time the Scout whose turn it was to rescue him. On every occasion when he was entered for this competition Stanley Judkins was seized, at the critical moment, with a severe fit of cramp, which caused him to roll on the ground and utter alarming cries. This naturally distracted the attention of those present from the boy in the water, and had it not been for the presence of Arthur Wilcox the death-roll would have been a heavy one. As it was, the Lower Master found it necessary to take a firm line and say that the competition must be discontinued. It was in vain that Mr. Beasley Robinson represented to him that in five competitions only four lower boys had actually succumbed. The Lower Master said that he would be the last to interfere in any way with the work of the Scouts; but that three of these boys had been valued members of his choir, and both he and Dr. Ley felt that the inconvenience caused by the losses outweighed the advantages of the competitions. Besides, the correspondence with the parents of these boys had become annoying, and even distressing: they were no longer satisfied with the printed form which he was in the habit of sending out, and more than one of them had actually visited Eton and taken up much of his valuable time with complaints. So the life-saving competition is now a thing of the past.

In short, Stanley Judkins was no credit to the Scouts, and there was talk on more than one occasion of informing him that his services were no longer required. This course was strongly advocated by Mr.

Lambart: but in the end milder counsels prevailed, and it was decided
to give him another chance.

\*     \*     \*

So it is that we find him at the beginning of the Midsummer Holidays
of 19— at the Scouts' camp in the beautiful district of W (or X) in
the county of D (or Y).

It was a lovely morning, and Stanley Judkins and one or two of
his friends – for he still had friends – lay basking on the top of the
down. Stanley was lying on his stomach with his chin propped on his
hands, staring into the distance.

"I wonder what that place is," he said.

"Which place?" said one of the others.

"That sort of clump in the middle of the field down there."

"Oh, ah! How should I know what it is?"

"What do you want to know for?" said another.

"I don't know: I like the look of it. What's it called? Nobody got
a map?" said Stanley. "Call yourselves Scouts!"

"Here's a map all right," said Wilfred Pipsqueak, ever resourceful,
"and there's the place marked on it. But it's inside the red ring. We
can't go there."

"Who cares about a red ring?" said Stanley. "But it's got no name
on your silly map."

"Well, you can ask this old chap what it's called if you're so keen
to find out." 'This old chap' was an old shepherd who had come up
and was standing behind them.

"Good morning, young gents," he said, "you've got a fine day for
your doin's, ain't you?"

"Yes, thank you," said Algernon de Montmorency, with native
politeness. "Can you tell us what that clump over there's called? And
what's that thing inside it?"

"Course I can tell you," said the shepherd. "That's Wailin' Well,
that is. But you ain't got no call to worry about that."

"Is it a well in there?" said Algernon. "Who uses it?"

The shepherd laughed. "Bless you," he said, "there ain't from a man to a sheep in these parts uses Wailin' Well, nor haven't done all the years I've lived here."

"Well, there'll be a record broken today, then," said Stanley Judkins, "because I shall go and get some water out of it for tea!"

"Sakes alive, young gentleman!" said the shepherd in a startled voice, "don't you get to talkin' that way! Why, ain't your masters give you notice not to go by there? They'd ought to have done."

"Yes, they have," said Wilfred Pipsqueak.

"Shut up, you ass!" said Stanley Judkins. "What's the matter with it? Isn't the water good? Anyhow, if it was boiled, it would be all right."

"I don't know as there's anything much wrong with the water," said the shepherd. "All I know is, my old dog wouldn't go through that field, let alone me or anyone else that's got a morsel of brains in their heads."

"More fool them," said Stanley Judkins, at once rudely and ungrammatically. "Who ever took any harm going there?" he added.

"Three women and a man," said the shepherd gravely. "Now just you listen to me. I know these 'ere parts and you don't, and I can tell you this much: for these ten years last past there ain't been a sheep fed in that field, nor a crop raised off of it – and it's good land, too. You can pretty well see from here what a state it's got into with brambles and suckers and trash of all kinds. You've got a glass, young gentleman," he said to Wilfred Pipsqueak, "you can tell with that anyway."

"Yes," said Wilfred, "but I see there's tracks in it. Someone must go through it sometimes."

"Tracks!" said the shepherd. "I believe you! Four tracks: three women and a man."

"What d'you mean, three women and a man?" said Stanley, turning over for the first time and looking at the shepherd (he had been talking with his back to him till this moment: he was an ill-mannered boy).

"Mean? Why, what I says: three women and a man."

"Who are they?" asked Algernon. "Why do they go there?"

"There's some p'r'aps could tell you who they *was*," said the shepherd, "but it was afore my time they come by their end. And why they goes there still is more than the children of men can tell: except I've heard they was all bad 'uns when they was alive."

"By George, what a rum thing!" Algernon and Wilfred muttered: but Stanley was scornful and bitter.

"Why, you don't mean they're deaders? What rot! You must be a lot of fools to believe that. Who's ever seen them, I'd like to know?"

"*I've* seen 'em, young gentleman!" said the shepherd, "seen 'em from near by on that bit of down: and my old dog, if he could speak, he'd tell you he've seen 'em, same time. About four o'clock of the day it was, much such a day as this. I see 'em, each one of 'em, come peerin' out of the bushes and stand up, and work their way slow by them tracks towards the trees in the middle where the well is."

"And what were they like? Do tell us!" said Algernon and Wilfred eagerly.

"Rags and bones, young gentlemen: all four of 'em: flutterin' rags and whity bones. It seemed to me as if I could hear 'em clackin' as they got along. Very slow they went, and lookin' from side to side."

"What were their faces like? Could you see?"

"They hadn't much to call faces," said the shepherd, "but I could seem to see as they had teeth."

"Lor'!" said Wilfred, "and what did they do when they got to the trees?"

"I can't tell you that, sir," said the shepherd. "I wasn't for stayin' in that place, and if I had been, I was bound to look to my old dog: he'd gone! Such a thing he never done before as leave me; but gone he had, and when I came up with him in the end, he was in that state he didn't know me, and was fit to fly at my throat. But I kep' talkin' to him, and after a bit he remembered my voice and came creepin' up like a child askin' pardon. I never want to see him like that again, nor yet no other dog."

The dog, who had come up and was making friends all round, looked up at his master, and expressed agreement with what he was saying very fully.

The boys pondered for some moments on what they had heard: after which Wilfred said: "And why's it called Wailing Well?"

"If you was round here at dusk of a winter's evening, you wouldn't want to ask why," was all the shepherd said.

"Well, I don't believe a word of it," said Stanley Judkins, "and I'll go there next chance I get: blowed if I don't!"

"Then you won't be ruled by me?" said the shepherd. "Nor yet by your masters as warned you off? Come now, young gentleman, you don't want for sense, I should say. What should I want tellin' you a pack of lies? It ain't sixpence to me anyone goin' in that field: but I wouldn't like to see a young chap snuffed out like in his prime."

"I expect it's a lot more than sixpence to you," said Stanley. "I expect you've got a whisky still or something in there, and want to keep other people away. Rot I call it. Come on back, you boys."

So they turned away. The two others said, "Good evening" and "Thank you" to the shepherd, but Stanley said nothing. The shepherd shrugged his shoulders and stood where he was, looking after them rather sadly.

On the way back to the camp there was great argument about it all, and Stanley was told as plainly as he could be told all the sorts of fools he would be if he went to the Wailing Well.

That evening, among other notices, Mr. Beasley Robinson asked if all maps had got the red ring marked on them. "Be particular," he said, "not to trespass inside it."

Several voices – among them the sulky one of Stanley Judkins – said, "Why not, sir?"

"Because not," said Mr. Beasley Robinson, "and if that isn't enough for you, I can't help it." He turned and spoke to Mr. Lambart in a low voice, and then said, "I'll tell you this much: we've been asked to warn Scouts off that field. It's very good of the people to let us camp here at all, and the least we can do is to oblige them – I'm sure you'll agree to that."

Everybody said, "Yes, sir!" except Stanley Judkins, who was heard to mutter, "Oblige them be blowed!"

★　　★　　★

Early in the afternoon of the next day, the following dialogue was heard. "Wilcox, is all your tent there?"

"No, sir, Judkins isn't!"

"That boy is *the* most infernal nuisance ever invented! Where do you suppose he is?"

"I haven't an idea, sir."

"Does anybody else know?"

"Sir, I shouldn't wonder if he'd gone to the Wailing Well."

"Who's that? Pipsqueak? What's the Wailing Well?"

"Sir, it's that place in the field by – well, sir, it's in a clump of trees in a rough field."

"D'you mean inside the red ring? Good heavens! What makes you think he's gone there?"

"Why, he was terribly keen to know about it yesterday, and we were talking to a shepherd man, and he told us a lot about it and advised us not to go there: but Judkins didn't believe him, and said he meant to go."

"Young ass!" said Mr. Hope Jones, "did he take anything with him?"

"Yes, I think he took some rope and a can. We did tell him he'd be a fool to go."

"Little brute! What the deuce does he mean by pinching stores like that! Well, come along, you three, we must see after him. Why can't people keep the simplest orders? What was it the man told you? No, don't wait, let's have it as we go along."

And off they started – Algernon and Wilfred talking rapidly and the other two listening with growing concern. At last they reached that spur of down over-looking the field of which the shepherd had spoken the day before. It commanded the place completely; the well inside the clump of bent and gnarled Scotch firs was plainly visible, and so were the four tracks winding about among the thorns and rough growth.

It was a wonderful day of shimmering heat. The sea looked like a floor of metal. There was no breath of wind. They were all exhausted when they got to the top, and flung themselves down on the hot grass.

"Nothing to be seen of him yet," said Mr. Hope Jones, "but we must stop here a bit. You're done up – not to speak of me. Keep a sharp look-out," he went on after a moment, "I thought I saw the bushes stir."

"Yes," said Wilcox, "so did I. Look ... no, that can't be him. It's somebody though, putting their head up, isn't it?"

"I thought it was, but I'm not sure."

Silence for a moment. Then:

"That's him, sure enough," said Wilcox, "getting over the hedge on the far side. Don't you see? With a shiny thing. That's the can you said he had."

"Yes, it's him, and he's making straight for the trees," said Wilfred.

At this moment Algernon, who had been staring with all his might, broke into a scream.

"What's that on the track? On all fours – O, it's the woman. O, don't let me look at her! Don't let it happen!" And he rolled over, clutching at the grass and trying to bury his head in it.

"Stop that!" said Mr. Hope Jones loudly – but it was no use. "Look here," he said, "I must go down there. You stop here, Wilfred, and look after that boy. Wilcox, you run as hard as you can to the camp and get some help."

They ran off, both of them. Wilfred was left alone with Algernon, and did his best to calm him, but indeed he was not much happier himself. From time to time he glanced down the hill and into the field. He saw Mr. Hope Jones drawing nearer at a swift pace, and then, to his great surprise, he saw him stop, look up and round about him, and turn quickly off at an angle! What could be the reason? He looked at the field, and there he saw a terrible figure – something in ragged black – with whitish patches breaking out of it: the head, perched on a long thin neck, half hidden by a shapeless sort of blackened sun-bonnet. The creature was waving thin arms in the direction of the rescuer who was approaching, as if to ward him off: and between the two figures the air seemed to shake and shimmer as he had never seen it: and as he looked, he began himself to feel something of a waviness and confusion in his brain, which made him guess what might be the effect on someone within closer range of the influence. He looked away hastily, to see Stanley Judkins making his way pretty quickly towards the clump, and in proper Scout fashion; evidently picking his steps with care to avoid treading on snapping sticks or being caught by arms of brambles. Evidently, though he saw nothing, he suspected some sort of ambush, and was trying to go noiselessly. Wilfred saw all that, and he saw more, too. With a sudden and dreadful sinking at the heart, he caught sight of someone among the trees, waiting: and again of someone – another of the hideous black figures – working slowly along the track from another side of the field, looking from side to side, as the shepherd had described it. Worst of all, he saw a fourth – unmistakably a man this time – rising out of the bushes a few yards behind the wretched Stanley, and painfully, as it seemed, crawling into the track. On all sides the miserable victim was cut off.

Wilfred was at his wits' end. He rushed at Algernon and shook him. "Get up," he said. "Yell! Yell as loud as you can. Oh, if we'd got a whistle!"

Algernon pulled himself together. "There's one," he said, "Wilcox's: he must have dropped it."

So one whistled, the other screamed. In the still air the sound carried. Stanley heard: he stopped: he turned round: and then indeed a cry was heard more piercing and dreadful than any that the boys on the hill could raise. It was too late. The crouched figure behind Stanley sprang at him and caught him about the waist. The dreadful one that was standing waving her arms waved them again, but in exultation. The one that was lurking among the trees shuffled forward, and she too stretched out her arms as if to clutch at something coming her way; and the other, farthest off, quickened her pace and came on, nodding gleefully. The boys took it all in in an instant of terrible silence, and hardly could they breathe as they watched the horrid struggle between the man and his victim. Stanley struck with his can, the only weapon he had. The rim of a broken black hat fell off the creature's head and showed a white skull with stains that might be wisps of hair. By this time one of the women had reached the pair, and was pulling at the rope that was coiled about Stanley's neck. Between them they overpowered him in a moment: the awful screaming ceased, and then the three passed within the circle of the clump of firs.

Yet for a moment it seemed as if rescue might come. Mr. Hope Jones, striding quickly along, suddenly stopped, turned, seemed to rub his eyes, and then started running *towards* the field. More: the boys glanced behind them, and saw not only a troop of figures from the camp coming over the top of the next down, but the shepherd running up the slope of their own hill. They beckoned, they shouted, they ran a few yards towards him and then back again. He mended his pace.

Once more the boys looked towards the field. There was nothing. Or, was there something among the trees? Why was there a mist about the trees? Mr. Hope Jones had scrambled over the hedge, and was plunging through the bushes.

The shepherd stood beside them, panting. They ran to him and clung to his arms. "They've got him! In the trees!" was as much as they could say, over and over again.

"What? Do you tell me he've gone in there after all I said to him yesterday? Poor young thing! Poor young thing!" He would have said more, but other voices broke in. The rescuers from the camp had arrived. A few hasty words, and all were dashing down the hill.

They had just entered the field when they met Mr. Hope Jones. Over his shoulder hung the corpse of Stanley Judkins. He had cut it from the branch to which he found it hanging, waving to and fro. There was not a drop of blood in the body.

On the following day Mr. Hope Jones sallied forth with an axe and with the expressed intention of cutting down every tree in the clump, and of burning every bush in the field. He returned with a nasty cut in his leg and a broken axe-helve. Not a spark of fire could he light, and on no single tree could he make the least impression.

I have heard that the present population of the Wailing Well field consists of three women, a man, and a boy.

The shock experienced by Algernon de Montmorency and Wilfred Pipsqueak was severe. Both of them left the camp at once; and the occurrence undoubtedly cast a gloom – if but a passing one – on those who remained. One of the first to recover his spirits was Judkins *mi.*

Such, gentlemen, is the story of the career of Stanley Judkins, and of a portion of the career of Arthur Wilcox. It has, I believe, never been told before. If it has a moral, that moral is, I trust, obvious: if it has none, I do not well know how to help it.

# A WARNING
# TO THE CURIOUS

The place on the east coast which the reader is asked to consider is Seaburgh. It is not very different now from what I remember it to have been when I was a child. Marshes intersected by dykes to the south, recalling the early chapters of *Great Expectations*; flat fields to the north, merging into heath; heath, fir woods, and, above all, gorse, inland. A long sea-front and a street: behind that a spacious church of flint, with a broad, solid western tower and a peal of six bells. How well I remember their sound on a hot Sunday in August, as our party went slowly up the white, dusty slope of road towards them, for the church stands at the top of a short, steep incline. They rang with a flat clacking sort of sound on those hot days, but when the air was softer they were mellower too. The railway ran down to its little terminus farther along the same road. There was a gay white windmill just before you came to the station, and another down near the shingle at the south end of the town, and yet others on higher ground to the north. There were cottages of bright red brick with slate roofs...but why do I encumber you with these commonplace details? The fact is that they come crowding to the point of the pencil when it begins to write of Seaburgh. I should like to be sure that I had allowed the right ones to get on to the paper. But I forgot. I have not quite done with the word-painting business yet.

Walk away from the sea and the town, pass the station, and turn up the road on the right. It is a sandy road, parallel with the railway, and if you follow it, it climbs to somewhat higher ground. On your left (you are now going northward) is heath, on your right (the side towards the sea) is a belt of old firs, wind-beaten, thick at the top, with the slope that old seaside trees have; seen on the skyline from the train they would tell you in an instant, if you did not know it, that you were approaching a windy coast. Well, at the top of my little hill, a line of these firs strikes out and runs towards the sea, for there is a ridge that goes that way; and the ridge ends in a rather well-defined mound commanding the level fields of rough grass, and a little knot of fir trees crowns it. And here you may sit on a hot spring day, very well content to look at blue sea, white windmills, red cottages, bright green grass, church tower, and distant martello tower on the south.

As I have said, I began to know Seaburgh as a child; but a gap of a good many years separates my early knowledge from that which is more recent. Still it keeps its place in my affections, and any tales of it that I pick up have an interest for me. One such tale is this: it came to me in a place very remote from Seaburgh, and quite accidentally, from a man whom I had been able to oblige – enough in his opinion to justify his making me his confidant to this extent.

★   ★   ★

I know all that country more or less (he said). I used to go to Seaburgh pretty regularly for golf in the spring. I generally put up at the 'Bear', with a friend – Henry Long it was, you knew him perhaps – ("Slightly," I said) and we used to take a sitting-room and be very happy there. Since he died I haven't cared to go there. And I don't know that I should anyhow after the particular thing that happened on our last visit.

It was in April, 19—, we were there, and by some chance we were almost the only people in the hotel. So the ordinary public rooms were practically empty, and we were the more surprised when, after dinner, our sitting-room door opened, and a young man put his head in. We were aware of this young man. He was rather a rabbity anaemic subject – light hair and light eyes – but not unpleasing. So when he said: "I beg your pardon, is this a private room?" we did not growl and say: "Yes, it is," but Long said, or I did – no matter which: "Please come in." "Oh, may I?" he said, and seemed relieved. Of course it was obvious that he wanted company; and as he was a reasonable kind of person –

not the sort to bestow his whole family history on you – we urged him to make himself at home. "I dare say you find the other rooms rather bleak," I said. Yes, he did: but it was really too good of us, and so on. That being got over, he made some pretence of reading a book. Long was playing Patience, I was writing. It became plain to me after a few minutes that this visitor of ours was in rather a state of fidgets or nerves, which communicated itself to me, and so I put away my writing and turned to at engaging him in talk.

After some remarks, which I forget, he became rather confidential. "You'll think it very odd of me" (this was the sort of way he began), "but the fact is I've had something of a shock." Well, I recommended a drink of some cheering kind, and we had it. The waiter coming in made an interruption (and I thought our young man seemed very jumpy when the door opened), but after a while he got back to his woes again. There was nobody he knew in the place, and he did happen to know who we both were (it turned out there was some common acquaintance in town), and really he did want a word of advice, if we didn't mind. Of course we both said: "By all means," or "Not at all," and Long put away his cards. And we settled down to hear what his difficulty was.

"It began," he said, "more than a week ago, when I bicycled over to Froston, only about five or six miles, to see the church; I'm very much interested, in architecture, and it's got one of those pretty porches with niches and shields. I took a photograph of it, and then an old man who was tidying up in the churchyard came and asked if I'd care to look into the church. I said yes, and he produced a key and let me in. There wasn't much inside, but I told him it was a nice little church, and he kept it very clean, 'but,' I said, 'the porch is the best part of it.' We were just outside the porch then, and he said, 'Ah, yes, that is a nice porch; and do you know, sir, what's the meanin' of that coat of arms there?'

"It was the one with the three crowns, and though I'm not much of a herald, I was able to say yes, I thought it was the old arms of the kingdom of East Anglia.

"'That's right, sir,' he said, 'and do you know the meanin' of them three crowns that's on it?'

"I said I'd no doubt it was known, but I couldn't recollect to have heard it myself.

"'Well, then,' he said, 'for all you're a scholard, I can tell you something you don't know. Them's the three 'oly crowns what was buried in the ground near by the coast to keep the Germans from landing – ah, I can see you don't believe that. But I tell you, if it hadn't have been for one of them 'oly crowns bein' there still, them Germans would a landed here time and again, they would. Landed with their ships, and killed man, woman and child in their beds. Now then, that's the truth what I'm telling you, that is; and if you don't believe me, you ast the rector. There he comes: you ast him, I says.'

"I looked round, and there was the rector, a nice-looking old man, coming up the path; and before I could begin assuring my old man, who was getting quite excited, that I didn't disbelieve him, the rector struck in, and said: 'What's all this about, John? Good day to you, sir. Have you been looking at our little church?'

"So then there was a little talk which allowed the old man to calm down, and then the rector asked him again what was the matter.

"'Oh,' he said, 'it warn't nothink, only I was telling this gentleman he'd ought to ast you about them 'oly crowns.'

"'Ah, yes, to be sure,' said the rector, 'that's a very curious matter, isn't it? But I don't know whether the gentleman is interested in our old stories, eh?'

"'Oh, he'll be interested fast enough,' says the old man, 'he'll put his confidence in what you tells him, sir; why, you known William Ager yourself, father and son too.'

"Then I put in a word to say how much I should like to hear all about it, and before many minutes I was walking up the village street with the rector, who had one or two words to say to parishioners, and then to the rectory, where he took me into his study. He had made out, on the way, that I really was capable of taking an intelligent interest in a piece of folklore, and not quite the ordinary tripper. So he was very willing to talk, and it is rather surprising to me that the particular legend he told me has not made its way into print before. His account of it was this: 'There has always been a belief in these parts in the three holy crowns. The old people say they were buried in different places near the coast to keep off the Danes or the French or the Germans. And they say that one of the three was dug up a long time ago, and another has disappeared by the encroaching of the sea, and one's still left doing its work, keeping off invaders. Well, now, if you have read the ordinary guides and histories of this county, you will remember perhaps that in 1687 a crown, which was said to be the crown of Redwald, King of the East Angles, was dug up at Rendlesham, and alas! alas! melted down before it was even properly described or drawn. Well, Rendlesham isn't on the coast, but it isn't so very far inland, and it's on a very important line of access. And I believe that is the crown which the people mean when they say that one has been dug up. Then on the south you don't want me to tell you where there was a Saxon royal palace which is now under the sea, eh? Well, there was the second crown, I take it. And up beyond these two, they say, lies the third.'

'"Do they say where it is?' of course I asked.

"He said, 'Yes, indeed, they do, but they don't tell,' and his manner did not encourage me to put the obvious question. Instead of that I waited a moment, and said: 'What did the old man mean when he said you knew William Ager, as if that had something to do with the crowns?'

"'To be sure,' he said, 'now that's another curious story. These Agers – it's a very old name in these parts, but I can't find that they were ever people of quality or big owners – these Agers say, or said, that their branch of the family were the guardians of the last crown. A certain old Nathaniel Ager was the first one I knew – I was born and brought up quite near here – and he, I believe, camped out at the place during the whole of the war of 1870. William, his son, did the same, I know, during the South African War. And young William, *his* son, who has only died fairly recently, took lodgings at the cottage nearest the spot, and I've no doubt hastened his end, for he was a consumptive, by exposure and night watching. And he was the last of that branch. It was a dreadful grief to him to think that he was the last, but he could do nothing, the only relations at all near to him were in the colonies.

I wrote letters for him to them imploring them to come over on business very important to the family, but there has been no answer. So the last of the holy crowns, if it's there, has no guardian now.'

"That was what the rector told me, and you can fancy how interesting I found it. The only thing I could think of when I left him was how to hit upon the spot where the crown was supposed to be. I wish I'd left it alone.

"But there was a sort of fate in it, for as I bicycled back past the churchyard wall my eye caught a fairly new gravestone, and on it was the name of William Ager. Of course I got off and read it. It said 'of this parish, died at Seaburgh, 19—, aged 28.' There it was, you see. A little judicious questioning in the right place, and I should at least find the cottage nearest the spot. Only I didn't quite know what was the right place to begin my questioning at. Again there was fate: it took me to the curiosity-shop down that way – you know – and I turned over some old books, and, if you please, one was a prayer-book of 1740 odd, in a rather handsome binding – I'll just go and get it, it's in my room."

He left us in a state of some surprise, but we had hardly time to exchange any remarks when he was back, panting, and handed us the book opened at the fly-leaf, on which was, in a straggly hand:

> *Nathaniel Ager is my name and England is my nation,*
> *Seaburgh is my dwelling-place and Christ is my Salvation,*
> *When I am dead and in my Grave, and all my bones are rotton,*
> *I hope the Lord will think on me when I am quite forgotton.*

This poem was dated 1754, and there were many more entries of Agers, Nathaniel, Frederick, William, and so on, ending with William, 19—.

"You see," he said, "anybody would call it the greatest bit of luck. I did, but I don't now. Of course I asked the shopman about William Ager, and of course he happened to remember that he lodged in a cottage in the North Field and died there. This was just chalking the road for me. I knew which the cottage must be: there is only one sizable one about there. The next thing was to scrape some sort of acquaintance with the people, and I took a walk that way at once. A dog did the business for me: he made at me so fiercely that they had to run out and beat him off, and then naturally begged my pardon, and we got into talk. I had only to bring up Ager's name, and pretend I knew, or thought I knew something of him, and then the woman said how sad it was him dying so young, and she was sure it came of him spending the night out of doors in the cold weather. Then I had to say: 'Did he go out on the sea at night?' and she said: 'Oh, no, it was on the hillock yonder with the trees on it.' And there I was.

"I know something about digging in these barrows: I've opened many of them in the down country. But that was with owner's leave, and in broad daylight and with men to help. I had to prospect very carefully here before I put a spade in: I couldn't trench across the mound, and with those old firs growing there I knew there would be awkward tree roots. Still the soil was very light and sandy and easy, and there was a rabbit hole or so that might be developed into a sort of tunnel. The going out and coming back at odd hours to the hotel was going to be the awkward part. When I made up my mind about the way to excavate I told the people that I was called away for a night, and I spent it out there. I made my tunnel: I won't bore you with the details of how I supported it and filled it in when I'd done, but the main thing is that I got the crown."

Naturally we both broke out into exclamations of surprise and interest. I for one had long known about the finding of the crown at Rendlesham and had often lamented its fate. No one has ever seen an Anglo-Saxon crown – at least no one had. But our man gazed at us with a rueful eye. "Yes," he said, "and the worst of it is I don't know how to put it back."

"Put it back?" we cried out. "Why, my dear sir, you've made one of the most exciting finds ever heard of in this country. Of course it ought to go to the Jewel House at the Tower. What's your difficulty? If you're thinking about the owner of the land, and treasure-trove, and all that, we can certainly help you through. Nobody's going to make a fuss about technicalities in a case of this kind."

Probably more was said, but all he did was to put his face in his hands, and mutter: "I don't know how to put it back."

At last Long said: "You'll forgive me, I hope, if I seem impertinent, but are you *quite* sure you've got it?" I was wanting to ask much the same question myself, for of course the story did seem a lunatic's dream when one thought over it. But I hadn't quite dared to say what might hurt the poor young man's feelings. However, he took it quite calmly – really, with the calm of despair, you might say. He sat up and said: "Oh, yes, there's no doubt of that: I have it here, in my room, locked up in my bag. You can come and look at it if you like: I won't offer to bring it here."

We were not likely to let the chance slip. We went with him; his room was only a few doors off. The boots was just collecting shoes in the passage: or so we thought: afterwards we were not sure. Our visitor – his name was Paxton – was in a worse state of shivers than before, and went hurriedly into the room, and beckoned us after him, turned on the light, and shut the door carefully. Then he unlocked his kit-bag, and produced a bundle of clean pocket-handkerchiefs in which something was wrapped, laid it on the bed, and undid it. I can now say I *have* seen an actual Anglo-Saxon crown. It was of silver – as the Rendlesham one is always said to have been – it was set with some gems, mostly antique intaglios and cameos, and was of rather plain, almost rough workmanship. In fact, it was like those you see on the coins and in the manuscripts. I found no reason to think it was later than the ninth century. I was intensely interested, of course, and I wanted to turn it over in my hands, but Paxton prevented me. "Don't *you* touch it," he said, "I'll do that." And with a sigh that was, I declare to you, dreadful to hear, he took it up and turned it about so that we could see every part of it. "Seen enough?" he said at last, and we nodded. He wrapped it up and locked it in his bag, and stood looking at us dumbly. "Come back to our room," Long said, "and tell us what the trouble is." He thanked us, and said: "Will you go first and see if – if the coast is clear?" That wasn't very intelligible, for our proceedings hadn't been, after all, very suspicious, and the hotel, as I said, was practically empty. However, we were beginning to have inklings of – we didn't know what, and anyhow nerves are infectious. So we did go, first peering out as we opened the door, and fancying (I found we both had the fancy) that a shadow, or more than a shadow – but it made no sound – passed from before us to one side as we came out into the passage. "It's all right," we whispered to Paxton – whispering seemed the proper tone – and we went, with him between us, back to our sitting-room. I was preparing, when we got there, to be ecstatic about the unique interest of what we had seen, but when I looked at Paxton I saw that would be terribly out of place, and I left it to him to begin.

"What *is* to be done?" was his opening. Long thought it right (as he explained to me afterwards) to be obtuse, and said: "Why not find out who the owner of the land is, and inform—" "Oh, no, no!" Paxton broke in impatiently, "I beg your pardon: you've been very kind, but don't you see it's *got* to go back, and I daren't be there at night, and daytime's impossible. Perhaps, though, you don't see: well, then, the truth is that I've never been alone since I touched it." I was beginning some fairly stupid comment, but Long caught my eye, and I stopped. Long said: "I think I do see, perhaps: but wouldn't it be – a relief – to tell us a little more clearly what the situation is?"

Then it all came out: Paxton looked over his shoulder and beckoned to us to come nearer to him, and began speaking in a low voice: we listened most intently, of course, and compared notes afterwards, and I wrote down our version, so I am confident I have what he told us almost word for word. He said: "It began when I was first prospecting, and put me off again and again. There was always somebody – a man – standing by one of the firs. This was in daylight, you know. He was never in front of me. I always saw him with the tail of my eye on the left or the right, and he was never there when I looked straight for him. I would lie down for quite a long time and take careful observations, and make sure there was no one, and then when I got up and began prospecting again, there he was. And he began to give me hints, besides; for wherever I put that prayer-book – short of locking it up, which I did at last – when I came back to my room it was always out on my table open at the fly-leaf where the names are, and one of my razors across it to keep it open. I'm sure he just can't open my bag, or something more would have happened. You see, he's light and weak, but all the same I daren't face him. Well, then, when I was making the tunnel, of course it was worse, and if I hadn't been so keen I should have dropped the whole thing and run. It was like someone scraping at my back all the time: I thought for a long time it was only soil dropping on me, but as I got nearer the – the crown, it was unmistakable. And when I actually laid it bare and got my fingers into the ring of it and pulled it out, there came a sort of cry behind me – oh, I can't tell you how desolate it was! And horribly threatening too. It spoilt all my pleasure in my find – cut it off that moment. And if I hadn't been the wretched fool I am, I should have put the thing back and left it. But I didn't. The rest of the time was just awful. I had hours to get through before I could decently come back to the hotel. First I spent time filling up my tunnel and covering my tracks, and all the while he was there trying to thwart me. Sometimes, you know, you see him, and sometimes you don't, just as he pleases, I think: he's there, but he has some power over your eyes. Well, I wasn't off the spot very long before sunrise, and then I had to get to the junction for Seaburgh, and take a train back. And though it was daylight fairly soon, I don't know if that made it much better. There were always hedges, or gorse-bushes, or park fences along the road – some sort of cover, I mean – and I was never easy for a second. And then when I began to meet people going to work, they always looked behind me very strangely: it might have been that they were surprised at seeing anyone so early; but I didn't think it was only that, and I don't now: they didn't look exactly at *me*. And the porter at the train was like that too. And the guard held open the door after I'd got into the carriage – just as he would if there was somebody else coming, you know. Oh, you may be very sure it isn't my fancy," he said with a dull sort of laugh. Then he went on: "And even if I do get it put back, he won't forgive me: I can tell that. And I was so happy a fortnight ago." He dropped into a chair, and I believe he began to cry.

We didn't know what to say, but we felt we must come to the rescue somehow, and so – it really seemed the only thing – we said if he was so set on putting the crown back in its place, we would help him. And

I must say that after what we had heard it did seem the right thing. If these horrid consequences had come on this poor man, might there not really be something in the original idea of the crown having some curious power bound up with it, to guard the coast? At least, that was my feeling, and I think it was Long's too. Our offer was very welcome to Paxton, anyhow. When could we do it? It was nearing half-past ten. Could we contrive to make a late walk plausible to the hotel people that very night? We looked out of the window: there was a brilliant full moon – the Paschal moon. Long undertook to tackle the boots and propitiate him. He was to say that we should not be much over the hour, and if we did find it so pleasant that we stopped out a bit longer we would see that he didn't lose by sitting up. Well, we were pretty regular customers of the hotel, and did not give much trouble, and were considered by the servants to be not under the mark in the way of tips; and so the boots *was* propitiated, and let us out on to the sea-front, and remained, as we heard later, looking after us. Paxton had a large coat over his arm, under which was the wrapped-up crown.

So we were off on this strange errand before we had time to think how very much out of the way it was. I have told this part quite shortly on purpose, for it really does represent the haste with which we settled our plan and took action. "The shortest way is up the hill and through the churchyard," Paxton said, as we stood a moment before the hotel looking up and down the front. There was nobody about – nobody at all. Seaburgh out of the season is an early, quiet place. "We can't go along the dyke by the cottage, because of the dog," Paxton also said, when I pointed to what I thought a shorter way along the front and across two fields. The reason he gave was good enough. We went up the road to the church, and turned in at the churchyard gate. I confess to having thought that there might be some lying there who might be conscious of our business: but if it was so, they were also conscious that one who was on their side, so to say, had us under surveillance, and we saw no sign of them. But under observation we felt we were, as I have never felt it at another time. Specially was it so when we passed out of the churchyard into a narrow path with close high hedges, through which we hurried as Christian did through that Valley; and so got out into open fields. Then along hedges, though I would sooner have been in the open, where I could see if anyone was visible behind me; over a gate or two, and then a swerve to the left, taking us up on to the ridge which ended in that mound.

As we neared it, Henry Long felt, and I felt too, that there were what I can only call dim presences waiting for us, as well as a far more actual one attending us. Of Paxton's agitation all this time I can give you no adequate picture: he breathed like a hunted beast, and we could not either of us look at his face. How he would manage when we got to the very place we had not troubled to think: he had seemed so sure that that would not be difficult. Nor was it. I never saw anything like the dash with which he flung himself at a particular spot in the side of the mound, and tore at it, so that in a very few minutes the greater part of his body was out of sight. We stood holding the coat and that bundle of handkerchiefs, and looking, very fearfully, I must admit, about us. There was nothing to be seen: a line of dark firs behind us made one skyline, more trees and the church tower half a mile off on the right, cottages and a windmill on the horizon on the left, calm sea dead in front, faint barking of a dog at a cottage on a gleaming dyke between us and it: full moon making that path we know across the sea: the eternal whisper of the Scotch firs just above us, and of the sea in front. Yet, in all this quiet, an acute, an acrid consciousness of a restrained hostility very near us, like a dog on a leash that might be let go at any moment.

Paxton pulled himself out of the hole, and stretched a hand back to us. "Give it to me," he whispered, "unwrapped." We pulled off the handkerchiefs, and he took the crown. The moonlight just fell on it as he snatched it. We had not ourselves touched that bit of metal, and I have thought since that it was just as well. In another moment Paxton was out of the hole again and busy shovelling back the soil with hands that were already bleeding. He would have none of our help, though. It was much the longest part of the job to get the place to look undisturbed: yet – I don't know how – he made a wonderful success of it. At last he was satisfied, and we turned back.

We were a couple of hundred yards from the hill when Long suddenly said to him: "I say, you've left your coat there. That won't do. See?" And I certainly did see it – the long dark overcoat lying where the tunnel had been. Paxton had not stopped, however: he only shook his head, and held up the coat on his arm. And when we joined him, he said, without any excitement, but as if nothing mattered any more: "That wasn't my coat." And, indeed, when we looked back again, that dark thing was not to be seen.

Well, we got out on to the road, and came rapidly back that way. It was well before twelve when we got in, trying to put a good face on it, and saying – Long and I – what a lovely night it was for a walk. The boots was on the look-out for us, and we made remarks like that for his edification as we entered the hotel. He gave another look up and down the sea-front before he locked the front door, and said: "You didn't meet many people about, I s'pose, sir?" "No, indeed, not a soul," I said; at which I remember Paxton looked oddly at me. "Only I thought I see someone turn up the station road after you gentlemen," said the boots. "Still, you was three together, and I don't suppose he meant mischief." I didn't know what to say; Long merely said "Goodnight," and we went off upstairs, promising to turn out all lights, and to go to bed in a few minutes.

Back in our room, we did our very best to make Paxton take a cheerful view. "There's the crown safe back," we said; "very likely you'd have done better not to touch it" (and he heavily assented to that), "but no real harm has been done, and we shall never give this away to anyone who would be so mad as to go near it. Besides, don't you feel better yourself? I don't mind confessing," I said, "that on the way there I was very much inclined to take your view about – well, about being followed; but going back, it wasn't at all the same thing, was it?" No, it wouldn't do: "*You've* nothing to trouble yourselves about," he said, "but I'm not forgiven. I've got to pay for that miserable sacrilege still. I know what you are going to say. The Church might help. Yes, but it's the body that has to suffer. It's true I'm not feeling that he's waiting outside for me just now. But—" Then he stopped. Then he turned to thanking us, and we put him off as soon as we could. And naturally we pressed him to use our sitting-room next day, and said we should be glad to go out with him. Or did he play golf, perhaps? Yes, he did, but he didn't think he should care about that tomorrow. Well, we recommended him to get up late and sit in our room in the morning while we were playing, and we would have a walk later in the day. He was very submissive and *piano* about it all: ready to do just what we thought best, but clearly quite certain in his own mind that what was coming could not be averted or palliated. You'll wonder why we didn't insist on accompanying him to his home and seeing him safe into the care of brothers or someone. The fact was he had nobody. He had had a flat in town, but lately he had made up his mind to settle for a time in Sweden, and he had dismantled his flat and shipped off his belongings, and was whiling away a fortnight or three weeks before he made a start. Anyhow, we didn't see what we could do better than sleep on it – or not sleep very much, as was my case – and see what we felt like tomorrow morning.

We felt very different, Long and I, on as beautiful an April morning as you could desire; and Paxton also looked very different when we saw him at breakfast. "The first approach to a decent night I seem ever to have had," was what he said. But he was going to do as we had settled: stay in probably all the morning, and come out with us later. We went to the links; we met some other men and played with them in the morning, and had lunch there rather early, so as not to be late back. All the same, the snares of death overtook him.

Whether it could have been prevented, I don't know. I think he would have been got at somehow, do what we might. Anyhow, this is what happened.

We went straight up to our room. Paxton was there, reading quite peaceably. "Ready to come out shortly?" said Long, "say in half an hour's time?" "Certainly," he said: and I said we would change first, and perhaps have baths, and call for him in half an hour. I had my bath first, and went and lay down on my bed, and slept for about ten minutes. We came out of our rooms at the same time, and went together to the sitting-room. Paxton wasn't there – only his book. Nor was he in his room, nor in the downstair rooms. We shouted for him. A servant came out and said: "Why, I thought you gentlemen was gone out already, and so did the other gentleman. He heard you a-calling from the path there, and run out in a hurry, and I looked out of the coffee-room window, but I didn't see you. 'Owever, he run off down the beach that way."

Without a word we ran that way too – it was the opposite direction to that of last night's expedition. It wasn't quite four o'clock, and the day was fair, though not so fair as it had been, so there was really no reason, you'd say, for anxiety: with people about, surely a man couldn't come to much harm.

But something in our look as we ran out must have struck the servant, for she came out on the steps, and pointed, and said, "Yes, that's the way he went." We ran on as far as the top of the shingle bank, and there pulled up. There was a choice of ways: past the houses on the sea-front, or along the sand at the bottom of the beach, which, the tide being now out, was fairly broad. Or of course we might keep along the shingle between these two tracks and have some view of both of them; only that was heavy going. We chose the sand, for that was the loneliest, and someone *might* come to harm there without being seen from the public path.

Long said he saw Paxton some distance ahead, running and waving his stick, as if he wanted to signal to people who were on ahead of him. I couldn't be sure: one of these sea-mists was coming up very quickly from the south. There was someone, that's all I could say. And there were tracks on the sand as of someone running who wore shoes; and there were other tracks made before those – for the shoes sometimes trod in them and interfered with them – of someone not in shoes. Oh, of course, it's only my word you've got to take for all this: Long's dead, we'd no time or means to make sketches or take casts, and the next tide washed everything away. All we could do was to notice these marks as we hurried on. But there they were over and over again, and we had no doubt whatever that what we saw was the track of a bare foot, and one that showed more bones than flesh.

The notion of Paxton running after – after anything like this, and supposing it to be the friends he was looking for, was very dreadful to us.

You can guess what we fancied: how the thing he was following might stop suddenly and turn round on him, and what sort of face it would show, half-seen at first in the mist – which all the while was getting thicker and thicker. And as I ran on wondering how the poor wretch could have been lured into mistaking that other thing for us, I remembered his saying, "He has some power over your eyes." And then I wondered what the end would be, for I had no hope now that the end could be averted, and – well, there is no need to tell all the dismal and horrid thoughts that flitted through my head as we ran on into the mist. It was uncanny, too, that the sun should still be bright in the sky and we could see nothing. We could only tell that we were now past the houses and had reached that gap there is between them and the old martello tower. When you are past the tower, you know, there is nothing but shingle for a long way – not a house, not a human creature, just that spit of land, or rather shingle, with the river on your right and the sea on your left.

But just before that, just by the martello tower, you remember there is the old battery, close to the sea. I believe there are only a few blocks of concrete left now: the rest has all been washed away, but at this time there was a lot more, though the place was a ruin. Well, when we got there, we clambered to the top as quick as we could to take breath and look over the shingle in front if by chance the mist would let us see anything. But a moment's rest we must have. We had run a mile at least. Nothing whatever was visible ahead of us, and we were just turning by common consent to get down and run hopelessly on, when we heard what I can only call a laugh: and if you can understand what I mean by a breathless, a lungless laugh, you have it: but I don't suppose you can. It came from below, and swerved away into the mist. That was enough. We bent over the wall. Paxton was there at the bottom.

You don't need to be told that he was dead. His tracks showed that he had run along the side of the battery, had turned sharp round the corner of it, and, small doubt of it, must have dashed straight into the open arms of someone who was waiting there. His mouth was full of sand and stones, and his teeth and jaws were broken to bits. I only glanced once at his face.

At the same moment, just as we were scrambling down from the battery to get to the body, we heard a shout, and saw a man running down the bank of the martello tower. He was the caretaker stationed there, and his keen old eyes had managed to descry through the mist that something was wrong. He had seen Paxton fall, and had seen us a moment after, running up – fortunate this, for otherwise we could hardly have escaped suspicion of being concerned in the dreadful business. Had he, we asked, caught sight of anybody attacking our friend? He could not be sure.

We sent him off for help, and stayed by the dead man till they came with the stretcher. It was then that we traced out how he had come, on the narrow fringe of sand under the battery wall. The rest was shingle, and it was hopelessly impossible to tell whither the other had gone.

What were we to say at the inquest? It was a duty, we felt, not to give up, there and then, the secret of the crown, to be published in every paper. I don't know how much you would have told; but what we did agree upon was this: to say that we had only made acquaintance with Paxton the day before, and that he had told us he was under some apprehension of danger at the hands of a man called William Ager. Also that we had seen some other tracks besides Paxton's when we followed him along the beach. But of course by that time everything was gone from the sands.

No one had any knowledge, fortunately, of any William Ager living in the district. The evidence of the man at the martello tower freed us from all suspicion. All that could be done was to return a verdict of wilful murder by some person or persons unknown.

Paxton was so totally without connections that all the inquiries that were subsequently made ended in a No Thoroughfare. And I have never been at Seaburgh, or even near it, since.

# SOMEONE TO BLAME

## A Short Story by Ramsey Campbell

"**F**rancis," Frankie's mother said as if she had a pain she was growing tired of. "What's so terribly important now?"

He'd done nothing he shouldn't have. He'd muted his phone before following his parents into the old Swedish church. He wasn't going to feel judged by the picture overhead, where a stern robed figure on a lit-up throne was sending devils to drag people off. His mother glanced at the text he'd just sent Chaz, who was on a beach in Greece: *going to see more old stuff.* "I'm sorry if you've found our trip so dull," she said, though not as if she meant it much. "It's necessary for our work."

"I don't know how we'd liven up proceedings for you," his father said, taking a key off a nail on the wall by the pulpit, which was crawling with babies and angels. "Let's see if this can."

Frankie thought his parents were behaving worse than him. They hadn't just driven into the grounds of the manor house without an invitation, they'd come up to the church when nobody answered at the house. Maybe the owners were out, unless they didn't care for visitors, but shouldn't his parents have waited for permission? They seemed to think working at the museum meant they could go any old place they liked, and all his mother said was "Where does that take us?"

"I'm hoping to the mausoleum," his father told Frankie as well and led the way out of the church.

As they made for the building attached to it Frankie heard a lid creak. It was a tree in the wood below the hill they'd had to climb.

The lake encircled by the pines stirred like a sheet concealing a restless sleeper, and the wind pointed treetops at the mausoleum. The piny scent the wind raised made Frankie imagine the mausoleum needed disinfecting, not least since the white paint on all eight sides was flaking off like diseased skin. His father poked the key into the door at the top of the slippery greenish steps, and Frankie's heart jerked, or the phone in his breast pocket did. Chaz had replied BRING SOME BACK TO SHOW, and Frankie was about to stow the phone when he saw a letter start to writhe. No, a small legless insect was squirming across the screen as if it had emerged from the I. When he tried to brush it off he found it was under the glass. He felt he'd let it in by consulting the phone, which he pocketed with dismayed haste. "We're admitted," his father said, and the door lumbered wide.

Sunlight slanting through thin windows gathered on a trinity of metal coffins in the middle of the domed stone room. Twin crucified Christs lay on two of the lids, but the full-length figure engraved on the third had done without a cross. Fragments of a rusty padlock were strewn on the floor beneath the coffin, and another padlock drooped on its crumbled hasp while a last one remained locked. Frankie's parents made for marble monuments on opposite sides of the room, but only the coffin with the locks struck him as even slightly interesting. Scenes were engraved on its sides, and the image closest to the unopened padlock showed a man fleeing between trees with a hooded figure at his back, reaching a long stick or else a scrawny limb that lacked a hand out of its voluminous sleeve. Frankie would have liked to see more of the figure, and almost said so aloud. The other scenes were boring, and he looked at his phone instead. He couldn't see the insect, but would the phone work now? Perhaps it could be useful, proving he wasn't just a burden his parents had to bring with them. He activated the camera and framed the chase through the wood.

He didn't mean to use the flash. When it went off, the hooded figure appeared to start forward as if it had taken on substance, and Frankie heard movement close to him. It must have been his parents, because it came from more than one place. Surely only a shadow had shaken the padlock, but as he took hold to test it his father pulled him away. "We mustn't touch anything, Francis."

Frankie let go too late. His enforced lurch had snapped the rusty hasp. The lock clattered on the stone floor, rousing an echo that resembled shrill malicious laughter. "Now what have you done?" his mother complained.

"He made me."

"He has a name, if you don't mind."

Frankie could have fancied they were talking about the occupant of the coffin, since she'd prompted him to say "Dad's not a name."

"You know perfectly well what I mean, and you know we never use a flash in a church."

He was tempted to point out they weren't in one any longer, but said "I was only trying to help. I thought you could put the photo in the museum."

"Thanks for the intention, old fellow," his father said. "We've finished curating the show."

"Then why did we have to go all the places we went? Why did we come up here?"

"We can never learn too much about the past. Your mother saw the church and we had time to take a look."

"If you and your phone want to be useful you could see what you can find out about this place." When Frankie made to wake the phone by showing it his face, his mother said "Wait until we're in the car. I think we'd best leave before anyone does any more damage."

Frankie thought this should include his father. His mother locked the mausoleum and returned to the church to hang up the key. The acoustic made the clank of metal against stone sound louder than Frankie thought it should, and hard to locate. That was the case with the creak of a tree as they trotted downhill, urged faster by the slope. Once they were in the woods he heard no noises of that kind, even when wind ruffled the lake. The wide-brimmed hat he glimpsed somebody wearing among the trees must have been a slab of fungus sticking out at head height from a scaly trunk, next to a bush like a figure crouched to sprint and stretching out a leafless branch. Swarming shadows rendered all this indistinct, and when Frankie glanced back he couldn't even see where the shapes had been.

Though there was still no sign of life at the house, he felt they were being watched. While his father drove out of the grounds and up the wooded highway fast enough to suggest they were making an escape, Frankie consulted the map on his phone. He had to expand the image almost to the limit before the house appeared, tagged with a name. He thought he'd revived the insect, but the black mark that sped onto the sketch of a highway had to be a momentary flaw in the image – indeed, a pair of flaws. Fingering the name brought him a historical paragraph he began to read aloud. "Della who's that again?" his father said with a laugh.

"Let me see," Frankie's mother said and expelled a breath that blurred the screen. "It's duh la Gardie," she said, lifting the last syllable like a small startled cry or a bid to enliven the name.

Frankie had planned to make a related name he'd seen into a joke – Count Magnets or, since he supposed the seventeenth-century character had been somewhere in the mausoleum, Count Maggots – but it would be taken as just one more of his mistakes, and he shoved the phone into his pocket. "Don't sulk, Francis," his mother said, which ensured he did.

In half an hour they were at the airport. Once they reached the lounge, having returned the hired car, they had to wait several times as long. Why should Frankie be afraid this would let somebody come to find them? If anyone discovered the breakage in the mausoleum and could trace the number of the car, they might have time to search the airport before the family boarded the plane. Whenever Frankie glanced away from the departure monitor he felt compelled to look for people who might be hunting a miscreant. More than once he thought somebody new had come in, but could never locate them.

At last the monitor sent the family out of the lounge. Since their seats were at the front of the plane, they were among the first to board. Frankie had the window seat and saw their luggage being loaded. Had a strap come loose from the suitcase under his? The restless elongated item wasn't visible when a baggage handler slung Frankie's case into the hold. Frankie thought it might have fallen under the truck, but the tarmac was bare once the vehicle departed.

Eventually the plane did, no more swiftly than a hearse. The take-off transformed moisture on the window into unreadable messages in Morse before the plane rose above an elaborately rumpled quilt of cloud spread as wide as the sky. Frankie played games on his muted phone until he tired of killing monsters – their silence made them furtive, prone to appear with even less warning than usual – and then he dozed. His father's looming face wakened him, and Frankie turned to him, only to find himself turning to the window. He must have dreamed the face, and now he saw the shadow of the plane coasting across a white expanse. An irregularity in the cloudscape made it look as if a shape had dodged under the silhouette like an insect retreating beneath a stone. Frankie might have told his parents or at any rate spoken to them, but they were asleep.

As soon as the plane landed he switched on his phone. Photos Chaz had sent were waiting to be seen – girls of about their age in bikinis with practically empty cups. Frankie didn't need the frustration, and told himself he didn't need the beach. He would rather have stayed with Aunt Tanya while his parents were in Europe; she made more of him than they ever did. He replied with the photograph he'd taken in the mausoleum, prompting the response *LIKE YOU SAID OLD STUFF*. His father caught sight of the message and said "I should let it lie now" as if the boys were slighting someone who would know.

When the dogged circling of luggage on the carousel produced Frankie's case at last, it was partly unzipped. Had he seen a sleeve sprawling out of it while it waited to be loaded on the plane? His mother insisted on checking the contents, exposing Frankie's crumpled underwear to the public eye, until she was satisfied that nothing had been stolen. No wonder he felt watched, and too many people heard her say "Bed as soon as we're home. Important day tomorrow."

It would be for his parents – the grand reopening of their floor of the museum. In bed Frankie tried to follow up the information to which the map had led him, since the paragraph had said the count with the padlocked coffin had been into witchcraft. The paragraph had vanished, and there was nothing else about the man. Could his descendants have erased any information that had been online? Frankie was still searching when his mother came to turn his bedroom light off. "You try and get some sleep," she said as if something might prevent him, and a pair of sentences he'd happened upon lingered with him in the dark. "Mischief is the way evil toys with the world. Its presence can corrupt the very fabric of existence."

He seemed hardly to have slept when his mother wakened him. "We'll be off as soon as you're ready. We want to have a final check."

He suspected mostly she did, or perhaps only. If she was hiding nervousness, she was often like that on the first day of an exhibition. As soon as he and his father finished the breakfast she insisted they mustn't waste, she drove them to the museum through several warning lights and at least one red while his father visibly refrained from commenting. A banner for the exhibition was strung between a pair of massive columns outside the lofty doors of the museum. The title – *Discoveries and Disasters* – made Frankie feel as if one might lead to the other.

The guard at his oak desk in the marble lobby bade them all good morning and glanced behind them. The museum wasn't open to the public yet, and nobody had followed them in, but for a stupid moment Frankie thought the security arch was about to raise its alarm. The boxy metal lift that carried them to the top floor always felt intrusively modern, and today it seemed sluggish, as if it was bearing more weight than Frankie could see. "Let's get that oiled," his father said when the door slid open, emitting a squeal like the rusty hinges of a lid.

For several weeks the top floor would feature the century the Swedish mausoleum dated from. Frankie's parents went into their office while his father phoned an attendant to deal with the squeak. When would they decide Frankie was old enough to leave at home? He could only trail after them as they examined the exhibits. His mother turned back to give the King James Bible in its glass case a second scrutiny. "Did we leave it open there, Martin?"

"We must have. Nobody else would have touched it, would they?"

Frankie had deciphered just one phrase of the thick print – 𝖂𝖔𝖊 𝖚𝖓𝖙𝖔 𝖙𝖍𝖊𝖊 𝕮𝖍𝖔𝖗𝖆𝖟𝖎𝖓 – when his father said "No need to tag along with us, Francis. Have a wander on your own and see what comes to you."

Presumably this required Frankie to produce observations, and he went in search of something worthy of remark. The mezzotint of the Great Fire of London represented both a discovery – the invention of that printing method – and a disaster. Who were the two figures prancing in front of the blazing cathedral? When he stooped towards the display case he couldn't find them. They must have been reflected from the painting of Solomon's judgment, where a cloaked figure flourishing an outsize key lurked in the lower left-hand corner of the canvas. Before Frankie could examine the painting, the lift opened with an effortful squeal, and its occupant stretched forth a glistening tendril, the extended spout of an oil can. As the attendant set about oiling the door Frankie approached the canvas, only to find he couldn't locate any of the figures he thought he'd seen. "Stupid," he muttered, which failed to help.

The old books on display didn't inspire him. The *Pilgrim's Progress* featured somebody troubled by hobgoblins and evil spirits, while Milton declared "Incorporeal spirits to smallest forms reduc'd their shapes immense, and were at large." Both items discomposed his mother when she came to them, so that his father needed to say "That has to be how you left them, Carol." Frankie went to look at the disasters – a crowd of withered figures illustrating a Russian famine, a huddle of victims shrivelled by an eruption of Vesuvius, a deckful of colonists starving on the stranded *Mayflower* – but he could have done without the notion that each image hid at least one extra grisly shape he was unable to identify. He was glad when lunchtime brought his roaming to an end, and gladder that his parents didn't ask for comments on the exhibition.

They ate in the museum café, where Frankie's mother frowned at the ice cream his father let him have. "Finish that before we go upstairs," she said, because she disapproved of eating anywhere else in the museum.

As soon as they returned to the top floor she began prowling around the display, and halted in front of the Bible. "That isn't the same page."

𝔚𝔬𝔢 𝔳𝔫𝔱𝔬 𝔱𝔥𝔢𝔢 ℭ𝔥𝔬𝔯𝔞𝔷𝔦𝔫. "It is, mum."

"I really think it must be, Carol."

"It was Mark before, and now it's Luke." When his father looked as unconvinced as Frankie felt she said "Someone seems to think it's amusing to confuse us. Come down to the desk."

Though the guard in the lobby had seen nothing, she insisted on watching the playback. The viewpoint flipped from camera to camera but showed only Frankie and his parents scurrying about like performers in a comedy speeded up for extra fun, a spectacle unnecessarily reminiscent of panic. Soon the monitor reverted to viewing the top floor as it was now. The changing angles put Frankie in mind of pages turning, and he thought he glimpsed an indistinct shape dodging between them. "Who's that?" he blurted.

"What are you talking about, Francis?" his mother complained.

He peered at the screen hard enough to make his eyes sting, and was nearly sure he saw intrusive movement vanish in the instant the monitor picked up a different vantage. "That," he said. "Them."

His mother shook her head as if her nerves had twitched it. "Don't just talk for the sake of talking."

"We can do without any mischief just now," his father said. "If you want to be useful you can keep an eye on our floor for us."

Frankie saw no need for the offer of redemption, and staying alone on the top floor didn't appeal to him. "Can't you?"

"We've already plenty to do," his mother said. "Do try to be a little more helpful."

Whatever the plenty consisted of, it kept his parents in their office, murmuring together between outbursts of clattering that reminded Frankie of the padlock in the mausoleum even though he knew he was hearing them type. He sat on the bench closest to the office, a position that gave him a view of the room all the way to the lift. He might have wished the door hadn't been oiled, since he couldn't tell whether it kept creeping open unless he glanced up from his phone, which uttered a celebratory note every time Chaz sent another picture of the beach girls until Frankie's mother called to him to silence it. Once Frankie thought the attendant had returned, but the fleeting sight of a tendril must have been a symptom of a need for sleep. As the afternoon wore on the symptoms multiplied, so that he couldn't concentrate on any game for making sure there were no intruders even quieter than you were meant to be in a museum. He was forcing himself not to look by the time the lift released a squeal suggestive of hinges loath to stay oiled. It came from a café trolley delivering the first instalment of the buffet for the private view, but Frankie's mother darted out of the office as though she'd heard a trespasser. "Don't forget you're to take the tickets," she told Frankie. "See everyone has been invited."

The return of the shrill trolley brought his father out. "You know better than that, Francis," he said. "Don't play hide and seek in here."

"I wasn't and I'm not."

His father swung around as if Frankie had tricked him. "I thought you were over there."

"That's the waiters from the café."

"Not them," his father said and surveyed the room before tramping back into the office.

The first guests emerged from the lift the last trolley vacated. Frankie's parents greeted every arrival while he collected invitations, and soon his hands were full. One woman said she'd forgotten her ticket, and Frankie tried to bar her until his mother let her in. How was he supposed to know who had been invited if they had nothing to show him? At least he needn't feel required to look out for intruders any more, though as the room grew noisily crowded he thought some of the guests weren't behaving too well. Quite a few planted plastic tumblers of wine or paper plates on the display cases, and when he was able to load a plate he made sure his mother saw he wouldn't rest it anywhere to prompt her disapproval, but she frowned at the muted noise he couldn't avoid making with a straw in his drink of orange juice. Didn't her job let her tell off any of the guests? Perhaps it wasn't rude to leave your hat on, however wide it was, but Frankie knew you weren't allowed to keep your hood up in the museum. The wrongdoer seemed to be wielding a flexible cane as well, which might be a concession disability gave you, though Frankie thought his mother would have feared it could cause damage. Had these people removed their headgear? When he glanced about for a proper look he couldn't find either of them.

The guests started to disperse once the drinks ran out, and while the last of them departed Frankie helped the café staff to clear away used plates and crumpled tumblers. "I think that went quite well," his mother said and joined his father in thanking him. Frankie felt relieved the day had ended like this, but they were nearly at the lift when his father halted, emitting a breath fierce enough for a horse. "What the devil's someone done?"

He was glaring at the glass case containing the Bible. Somebody had left the imprint of a hand on the glass, a mark that could have been composed of reddish earth or rust or dried blood, unless it was a stain left by some item from the buffet. Either the hand had described an odd gesture or it possessed fewer fingers than a hand should have. Frankie's father tried to rub away the imprint, but it wasn't on the outside of the case. "I'd like to know who played that trick," he declared. "I'd like to see them play another."

He gave Frankie's mother a look that must have been apologising for his previous disbelief, and then his gaze strayed past her. There was movement at the far end of the supposedly deserted room, behind a display case crowded with seventeenth-century costumes modelled by headless mannequins dangling the stumps of their wrists. Had a mannequin lost its balance? Frankie wanted to believe that was the source of the restless shuffling as his father stalked across the room.

"Stay there," Frankie's mother told him and crossed the room as his father vanished behind the display case. There was silence for a moment, and then Frankie heard a cry so piercing that he thought it had to be his mother. It was accompanied and swiftly overwhelmed by another sound. Had an unnoticed guest lingered to finish their drink? The noise reminded Frankie of using the straw in his, though the substance involved sounded a good deal less liquid. He tried to think his father had cried out simply with surprise, and his mother was about to confront a noisy drinker as she dashed past the display case.

He saw her stagger backwards against the wall and jerk her hands towards her face. He thought she was shaking her head in disapproval until it began to move so fast that her fingers missed her eyes every time she tried to poke at them. All the same, she caught sight of Frankie as he forced himself to cross the room. "Go. Go. Go," she said as if this was the only word she had left, and her voice grew shriller until he obeyed. He'd stumbled into the lift and jabbed the ground-floor button before he thought to phone Aunt Tanya, the only person he could bring to mind who might help in any way. He was so desperate for an answer that at first he didn't wonder if the lift was ever going to move – if it had trapped him with the guilt he was afraid to feel while whatever it might attract came to find him.

# ABOUT THE AUTHORS

**M.R. JAMES** (1862–1936), whose works are regarded as being at the forefront of the ghost story genre, was born in Kent, England. James dispensed with the traditional, predictable techniques of ghost story construction, instead using realistic contemporary settings for his works. He was also a British medieval scholar, so his stories tended to incorporate antiquarian elements. His stories often reflect his childhood in Suffolk and his talented acting career, which both seem to have assisted in the build-up of tension and horror in his works.

**RAMSEY CAMPBELL** has been given more awards than any other writer in the field, including the **Grand Master Award of the World Horror Convention**, the **Lifetime Achievement Award of the Horror Writers Association**, the **Living Legend Award of the International Horror Guild**, and the **World Fantasy Lifetime Achievement Award**. Among his many novels are *The Hungry Moon*, *The Influence*, *The Wise Friend*, *Thirteen Days by Sunset Beach*, *Think Yourself Lucky*, *Somebody's Voice*, *Fellstones* and *The Lonely Lands*. His trilogy *The Three Births of Daoloth* further develops the cosmic horrors he invented in his first published book, *The Inhabitant of the Lake*. The Spanish film *La influencia* was based on his novel *The Influence*.

# SOURCES

**After Dark in the Playing Fields**
Originally Published in
*College Days*, 1924

**Canon Alberic's Scrap-book**
Originally Published in
*National Review*, 1895

**Count Magnus**
Originally Published in
*Ghost Stories of an Antiquary*, 1904

**The Diary of Mr. Poynter**
Originally Published in
*A Thin Ghost and Others*, 1919

**An Episode of Cathedral History**
Originally Published in
*Cambridge Review*, 1914

**The Haunted Dolls' House**
Originally Published in
*Empire Review*, 1923

**Lost Hearts**
Originally Published in
*Pall Mall Magazine*, 1895

**The Malice of Inanimate Objects**
Originally Published in
*The Masquerade*, 1933

**Rats**
Originally Published in
*At Random*, 1929

**The Rose Garden**
Originally Published in *More Ghost
Stories of an Antiquary*, 1911

**A School Story**
Originally Published in *More Ghost
Stories of an Antiquary*, 1911

**The Stalls of
Barchester Cathedral**
Originally Published in
*Contemporary Review*, 1910

# SOURCES

**The Tractate Middoth**
Originally Published in *More Ghost
Stories of an Antiquary*, 1911

**The Treasure of
Abbot Thomas**
Originally Published in
*Ghost Stories of an Antiquary*, 1904

**Two Doctors**
Originally Published in
*A Thin Ghost and Others*, 1919

**A View from a Hill**
Originally Published in
*London Mercury*, 1925

**A Vignette**
Originally Published in
*London Mercury*, 1936

**Wailing Well**
Originally Published in
*The Mill House Press*, 1928

**A Warning to the Curious**
Originally Published in
*London Mercury*, August 1925

**Someone to Blame,
by Ramsey Campbell**
© 2022 Ramsey Campbell,
Originally Published in
*Classic Monsters Unleashed*, edited by
James Aquilone, 2022

# FLAME TREE FICTION

A wide range of new and classic fiction, from myth to modern stories, with tales from the distant past to the far future. Flame Tree Fiction includes the trade fiction imprint, **Flame Tree Press**, featuring tales from both award-winning authors and original voices, along with short story anthologies, mythology and folklore collections and classic works in the **Beyond & Within, Collector's Editions, Collectable Classics, Gothic Fantasy** and **Epic Tales** series.

## OTHER TITLES

### SPECIAL RAMSEY CAMPBELL EDITIONS
*The Incubations: The New Novel*
*The Invocations: H.P. Lovecraft Short Stories*

### GOTHIC FANTASY COLLECTIONS
*Lovecraft Short Stories* • *Lovecraft Mythos New & Classic Collection*
*M.R. James Ghost Stories* • *Algernon Blackwood Horror Stories*

## OTHER TITLES BY RAMSEY CAMPBELL

*Ancient Images* • *Fellstones* • *Somebody's Voice* • *The Hungry Moon*
*The Influence* • *The Lonely Lands* • *The Nameless* • *The Wise Friend*
*Think Yourself Lucky* • *Thirteen Days by Sunset Beach*

***The Three Births of Daoloth* trilogy**
*The Searching Dead* • *Born to the Dark* • *The Way of the Worm*

Available at all good bookstores, and online
at flametreepublishing.com